I0667123

SPIRITS

Of

The Sodus Bay Shakers

Pat McGrath Avery

Copyright © 2019 Pat McGrath Avery

All rights reserved. No part of this book may be reproduced or transmitted in any form or by any means, electronic or mechanical, including photocopying, or within any commercial information retrieval and storage system, without permission in writing from the author.

Cover Design and Book Layout Design by Joyce Faulkner

Library of Congress Control Number: 2019937732

ISBN: 978-1-943267-63-7 paperback

ISBN: 978-1-943267-64-4 ebook

Cover Model John R.R. Faulkner

Photography by Pat McGrath Avery

Printed in the United States.

Red Engine Press

What People Are Saying...

Do you believe in ghosts? Perhaps not, but before you decide, come visit Cracker Box Palace. Get to know the 19th-century Shakers who established a farm community seeking salvation through joy and simplicity. Visit the new owners and their shelter for suffering animals and their gentle—although sometimes wounded—caretakers. Meet a little dog with a highly-developed sixth sense. And about those ghosts? Pat McGrath Avery may make a believer out of you.

Carolyn Schriber–multi-award-winning author of *Henrietta's Legacy* and many other historical novels.

* * *

In Spirits of Sodus Bay Shakers, Pat McGrath Avery weaves a tale of mystery and intrigue. She takes us on a journey back to the curious culture of the Shaker community in early 19th century America. As the story unfolds it weaves a thread into the present, where those whisked along on the journey must deal with both worlds. Spirits of Sodus Bay Shakers will keep you turning the pages. Highly recommended.

Joe Campolo Jr–award winning author of *Three Wars*

* * *

Some say the tragedies of the past never really go away. An excellent blend of history and suspense!

Bob Doerr–award winning author of *Greed Can Kill*

* * *

The Spirits of the Sodus Bay Shakers is a captivating telling of the Shaker culture and land from the 1830s. It is a work of fiction but its historical content is unmistakable. The book clearly describes the struggles believers face in maintaining dedication to beliefs that are difficult to live by. The author combines the history with a parallel tale of life at Cracker Box Palace Farm Animal Haven, the current owners of the land.

Though the book contains a lot of historical information, it is a fast-paced, enjoyable read.

Evelyn Staatz–Librarian (Retired), Metropolitan Community Colleges, Kansas City, MO.

*** ***

A well-written story that weaves together shattered souls from a Shaker community from centuries ago with fractured characters living in today's difficult world. Using historical facts as a backdrop, Avery has written a beautifully haunting novel that will keep readers up long after their bedtime...while keeping an extra light or two burning.

Janie DeVos–Author of the Glory Land Series

*** ***

Take romance, unrequited love, history, helping abused and abandoned farm animals, add one or two ghosts and you really got something. Pat has written a story combining these features with a mystery. Spirits of the Sodus Bay Shakers takes you on an adventure with the workers of Cracker Box Palace Animal Rescue, their challenges helping animals and coping with personal and sometime dangerous issues.

Griff Mangan–Co-owner of Paragraphs of Padre Blvd and former co-owner of Alasa Farms

For Griff ...

for the adventure and challenge

and for the introduction to Horace and Mary Ann

For Cheri ...

for the love and care you give to animals in need

For Everett...

for making the journey with me

RESIDENT OF CRACKER BOX PALACE

Blue skies softened by billowing clouds above

Trees laden with ripening fruit reach the shores

Of Sodus Bay, teeming with fish.

God's gift to New York

And the Shaker community.

Horace

1 8 3 0

Upon his first visit to the Shaker Tract.

***

The location was ideal. The land was heavily timbered with
stands of maple, beech, ash, bass, white wood, chestnut, red and
white oak and hemlock... The property fronted on Sodus Bay
and was traversed by two streams called Second Creek and Third
Creek. It had a good location for a wharf.

Shaker description of Alasa Farms

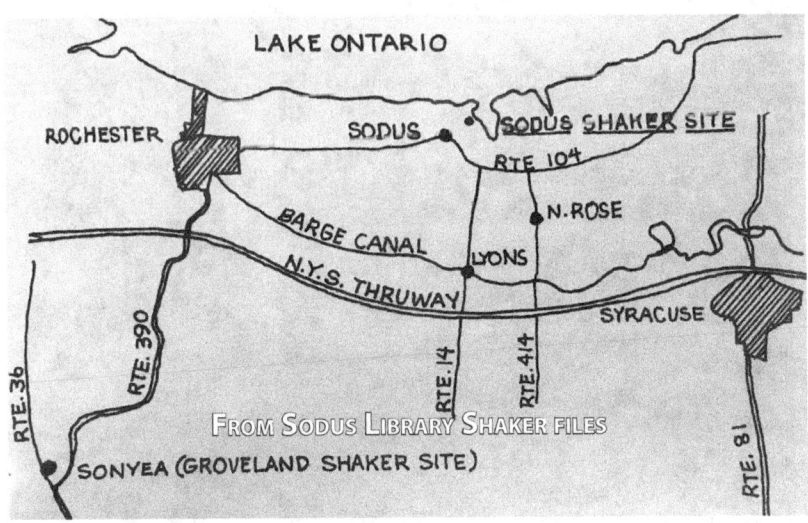

BOARDING HOUSE
ALASA'S OFFICE
MAIN HOUSE

PADDOCK AREA
ARENA

GRAINERY
POOL HOUSE & POOL

TENANT HOUSES
GARDEN & RAIL

STORMY'S PASTURE
CREAMERY & ICE HOUSE
(RESTROOM AREA)

U-PICK ORCHARD
MEMORIAL GARDEN

COW BARN
NATURE TRAIL
COMPOST FACILITY
TRAILS & CAMPING

FARM DIRECTORY

CHAPTER ONE

1833

So much is plain beyond dispute, That flesh is the forbidden fruit;
And those who may be so inclin'd, May propagate the human kind:
But, crossing the dividing line, Between the human and Divine,
Of flesh and sense we must beware, For Faith and Spirit govern here.

E. W., 1835, from Simple Wisdom by Kathleen Mahoney

DOCTOR JAMES MONTGOMERY STEPPED OUT of his buggy, pulled his coat collar tighter against the cold New York wind, and reached for his medical bag. He feared he wouldn't have the necessary tools to solve tonight's problems. It was hard enough to get called out in the middle of a wintry night without the almost certainty of a failed attempt to save a life.

He flexed his arthritic fingers, hoping to limber them up for the task at hand. He had been warned the call might come and he even considered refusing to assist at this notorious birthing.

Mary Ann. He remembered when he met her at a Shakers picnic. Full of youthful life and enthusiasm, that's what first struck him. No wonder she caught the eye of a man she couldn't, or wouldn't, refuse. She had never once revealed his name and he had to give her credit for that.

"If it had been me, I'd have taken him down with me," James muttered. Instead, she had been kicked out of the church community, shunned and shamed, while the father of the soon-to-be-born child suffered no consequences. James had learned long ago that life wasn't fair.

He didn't understand the Shakers dancing, but he admired their commitment to their ideals. However, that commitment sometimes

1

led them to harsh judgment. That rigid adherence to faith in the face of human failings was what brought him here tonight.

God, he was tired. Working day and night to heal broken bodies took its toll. He had always loved his work and grateful patients frequently paid with home-cooked meals and fresh produce. Since his Martha had passed on, he had appreciated every kindness even more. But dealing with broken hearts was far beyond his expertise. He had found no way to cure damages to the spirit. He shook away his morose thoughts as he approached the old boarding house.

A thin middle-aged woman answered his knock. "Good evening, Audrey," he shook the frost from his hat and handed it to her. She gave him a slight nod as she waited for his coat, scarf and gloves. She hung them on the hall tree and led him to Mary Ann's room. The dim lighting did little to hide the poverty of the old boardinghouse. A torn strip of wallpaper scraped against his valise. Cooking odors mixed with dust and grime assaulted his nostrils.

James frowned but concentrated on his purpose. The doctor in him needed answers. "How long has she been in labor?"

"Two days. We think the baby is turned sideways. There was nothing we could do."

"Why did you wait so long to call me?"

"You know Margaret births most little ones on her own. We hoped this one would turn. She tried to turn it. When we lost hope, we called you."

"I'll see what I can do. Do you have freshly boiled water?"

"It's on the fire, but I fear it's hopeless. The girl is almost gone already."

Doc Montgomery fought for the energy he would need in the next hours. "Let's see what we can do."

As he opened the door to her room, Mary Ann's moaning turned to a ragged scream.

Margaret turned toward the door. "Thank God you're here, Doc. I don't know what else to do. The poor little thing won't come. It's turned and I ..." Her shoulders slumped.

"You've done your best, Margaret. Let's see the patient." He set his bag on the single chair and opened it, talking as he did.

"Mary Ann, I'm here to help. I know you've been having pain way too long. Margaret says your baby is turned. I am going to examine you but I need your help."

Mary Ann's weak nod was her only response. He looked at her sweat-soaked hair and clothing, her red face and her protruding belly distended sideways. Tonight she was a far cry from the energetic young girl he had first met. He fought off the depression that swept through him.

"Please, God, help me." As he reached into her birth canal and felt the baby's body, he felt more like cursing God than pleading with Him. He knew there was nothing to do but use the instruments to try to force the baby into the birth canal. "Give her some whiskey," he instructed Margaret.

"I gave her a drink earlier. Will it stop the labor?"

"For heaven's sake, no, woman. Give it to her now. I have to try to take the baby and we need to soothe her as much as possible. Give her a good-sized shot, get another one ready and help me. Audrey, where is the fresh hot water? Get it for me and then hold her head and talk to her as I work." The older woman nodded but he wondered if he'd soon have another patient on his hands.

Audrey hustled back in the room with a black pot filled with water. He picked up his forceps and inserted them into Mary Ann's body. She screamed as he dug around her womb for some part of the baby's body. "Give her another shot and don't let her watch!" he ordered.

* * *

James Montgomery took the offered draught of whiskey, gave some final instructions and stepped out into the cold. God, it had been an awful night. He had done everything he could but he feared neither mother nor baby had any hope of surviving the night. Maybe it was for the best. They would have no place to go, but he had dedicated his life to saving people. He had read that new pain medications might soon be available, but it was too late to save Mary Ann from the most horrendous birthing he had ever witnessed. God rest her soul. No young woman, no matter what her sin, deserved that kind of torture.

* * *

Mary Ann relished the light and free feeling. Instead of pain, warmth flooded her being. A sense of peace replaced the fear and loneliness. Where was she? Where was her baby? She sat up. On the horizon, she saw a bright light. Was someone beckoning for her? She couldn't see clearly but she wanted to follow the light. She looked around. Where was her baby? She had to find it.

She looked down at her belly that no longer provided a home for her child. She'd lost her home and it had too. She remembered the excruciating pain, the sharp twisting and tearing apart of her body, the unbearable pain of whatever instrument the doctor had used. But most of all, she remembered the shake of his head when the baby didn't cry. Why hadn't she grabbed it? She would have slapped its little bottom until it cried. She knew her child would have cried for her.

"Why am I calling my baby an 'it'?" Why didn't the doctor or Margaret tell her if she had a boy or a girl? She hoped it was a boy, so he would never have to endure the shame and loneliness she knew while she carried him? On the other hand, what if he turned out to be like his father? No, she wouldn't let that happen. If it was a girl, she would teach her to be strong, to never let a man take advantage of her. Whichever, she would love it more than life itself. Nothing would ever separate them.

She strained to hear an infant's cry but silence was the only response.

"No, God, no! I'm sorry. I didn't mean to sin but he wouldn't stop when I begged him to," Mary Ann felt the despair returning. Was she cursed forever? Was God sending her to hell? "My wickedness killed my baby," she sobbed. The light in the distance receded. Where was she?

She needed to reach the light and beg for forgiveness. She walked toward the light but it never seemed to get any closer. Maybe God was testing her. Maybe if she could reach the light, He would let her baby live. Maybe ...

* * *

"Poor thing," Margaret said to Audrey as she pulled the sheet over Mary Ann's head. She lingered for a last look at the peace that had erased the pain on Mary Ann's still pretty face. The sweat had dried and her dark hair curled around her cheeks. "God rest your soul, little one. All your pain is gone forever." Mary Ann would never see the care on Margaret's face.

"Such a sweet soul." Millie had come in after Doc Montgomery left. Tears fell as she watched the sheet cover Mary Ann. Maybe it was for the best. The poor girl was in God's hands now.

"Them that sin must pay," Audrey muttered as she picked up the bloody rags around the bed.

CHAPTER TWO

Horace

You will not be punished for your anger, you will be punished by your anger
Buddha

I died in 1840 but peace has escaped me since 1833. My name is Horace and although the Shakers dismissed me as one who "got deranged and left," they remained clueless to the true story.

As for me, I've carried a rage that consumes me to this day. Sometimes it spills over into violent or destructive behavior. I freely admit to that because I will never be incarcerated for my actions. For the law cannot capture or prosecute a spirit that wanders the earth unseen and unheard.

How did it all start? With a friendship that turned into bitter enmity. With the Shaker religious fervor, or the lack thereof. With my best friend, Eaton.

We grew up in Lyons, a town that flourished after the building of the Erie Canal. Both of our families had prospered with the influx of people. But we were young and restless, and even with its growth, the town wasn't big enough to keep us. We worked loading the barges that traveled the canal, and in our free time, we'd ride to Rochester or Syracuse. Both were alive with activity and growth. We were saving our money to move, but hadn't decided to which city.

Then in 1830, Eaton and I traveled from Lyons to attend a Shaker service in Sodus. As we listened to their teachings and observed the frenzied dancing of their faith, I felt the call of the Lord. Eaton didn't, but he would be converted a few weeks later.

I told Elder John that I wanted to join. He questioned my intentions and beliefs. I told him I was raised an Episcopalian but I had never felt as close to God as I did at the Shaker service. He brought me to the Shaker community and told me I would live in the Main House. I would receive training until I was ready to be "united" with the true believers. To accept their faith, I would have to confess my sins to an elder, agree to a vow of celibacy, accept pacifism and adopt the communal lifestyle. I would give up all my worldly belongings, which to tell the truth weren't many, and from that day forward own nothing for myself alone. I would also work for the common good and learn simplicity in my personal and work life. Cleanliness and order ranked high on the Shaker list of virtues and I would strive to acquire both habits in my daily life.

At first, the many rules irritated me, but as time went by, I found that they encouraged their belief in simplicity. I had grown up in a world where the little things didn't matter, but the Shakers had a set of rules and manners that all believers followed. I never quite understood why we always started an activity with either the right hand or foot. We would line up for our meetings, men by one door and women another. Inside, we sat in different sections but we all joined together in our worship dancing.

I found none of this particularly difficult. Maybe if I were married, or had fallen for a woman, I would have thought differently about celibacy, but some of my married friends seemed willing to live out their lives as brother and sister. Many of us joined, and many of us found the beliefs too difficult to live by. Some left, or as the Shakers termed it, "turned off," and went back into the World.

One was kicked out, and another deserved to be.

I was gone when the Shakers sold the farm in 1836, but I came back in time to join in the move to Groveland. The elders agreed on what they termed my continuing mental instability. But I'm fine until I am reminded of Eaton. Then the rage returns.

Present Day - **April**

The greatness of a nation and its moral progress can be judged by the way its animals are treated.

Gandhi

"DAMN THE MAN TO HELL," Wayne County Sheriff Briggs struggled to tamp down his anger. "Call Cracker Box Palace. Get Cheri Roloson. Tell her we have a down horse with severe injuries."

"I should have stopped him," the man took off his cap and brushed his cold fingers through his sparse gray hair. Guilt blurred the sharp angles of his wind-tanned face. "I guess I knew, ... no, I did know that sooner or later, he'd take his anger out on one of his animals. I should have called you."

"Little you can do before the fact." Briggs stomped his feet and blew on his hands. A New York winter tested a healthy animal, let alone one with severe injuries. Thank God it wasn't cold enough to freeze the horse's open wounds. "He'll pay, you can count on it. No man in his right mind would beat a horse like this." Briggs looked at the blood oozing from the deep cuts running from the horse's front to rear flanks.

"Don't know if a horse can cry, but old Diamond here has grief in her eyes." The man watched the vet examine the horse. "Will she make it, Doc?"

"Lots of blood loss, deep wounds and a broken heart. Hard to say. There's always the danger of infection, but the worst damage is probably to her spirit. Some horses never recover. She's young, so there's hope." Jed Remmer filled a syringe and injected it into the horse's hip. He took a bottle and strips of gauze from his bag. He wet the strips with the liquid and gently placed it on one of the wounds. Briggs and the man watched as he repeated the procedure again and again.

"Did you call Cheri?" Briggs knew the man hadn't but couldn't blame him for being glued to the scene in front of them. "Sorry, I didn't get your name."

"Johnson. Sam Johnson. I live next farm over. I'll call Cheri now." He pulled his phone out of his jeans' pocket and looked up Cracker Box Palace.

"Have her call me. We need to move this horse to the clinic. We'll probably send her to Cornell." Jed looked at the white diamond that ran from between her ears to the top of her eyes. "Diamond, huh? Guess she's perfectly named."

By the time Cheri had rounded up the equipment and staff needed to move the horse, Jed had finished all he could do on site. Now, the moving of the animal fell to Cheri and Wayne County's Large Animal Rescue Team. The sheriff left, but soon called back to notify him they had apprehended the owner. Drunk and belligerent, he had resisted arrest, giving Briggs a small satisfaction to force him to the ground, cuff him and haul him into the county jail.

"I'm ready to sedate her," Doc told Cheri. "We'll need to do a vertical move. Lift her up and haul her."

"Okay, we'll get her blindfolded and bring in the sling." Cheri smiled as she noticed her team of volunteers already had the webbed sling, ropes, pole and other equipment unloaded. She walked over to them as they each put on their gloves and helmet. "Let's get Diamond in the trailer."

As Sam watched a car drive up and stop, a couple of young guys jumped out with their cell phones in hand. "Let's get on opposite sides," one motioned to the other.

"Man, this is going to make an awesome video for YouTube."

"What are you doing?" Doc looked up to see the camera focused on him.

"Making a movie, man. It'll be sweet." The photographer moved closer.

"Stay back and out of the way. Don't like you being here. If you do anything to disrupt the process or annoy this horse, you're out of here. Understood?"

"No worry, man. I got that recorded." He called to his friend and replayed the video, "We're good to go."

Like Doc, Sam wanted to chase the young fools away, but he focused instead on Cheri and her team. They worked well together. "Not their first rodeo," he mumbled to no one in particular.

"No, it isn't," Cheri called over her shoulder. "My guess is she weighs over a thousand pounds. We have our work cut out for us. Doesn't help that the ground is snow-packed."

Once the forklift was unloaded and the sling guided under the horse's shoulder and hip, they lifted her enough to maneuver the sling under the full length of her body. Then the slow and tedious process of moving her captivated those watching. Team members padded the trailer with blankets and hay. Cheri held Diamond's head and others watched out for her legs. Many hands guided her to an easy landing. Simultaneous sighs of relief filled the cold air when she was settled.

"I've called Cornell. They will be expecting us. I'll follow you." Doc had decided to forego a stop at the clinic. He deemed Diamond's condition too serious for a halfway measure. He said a silent prayer that she would make the long trip to Cornell. Seventy-five miles in her condition carried more risk than he wanted to think about. He wondered if it would have been kinder to just put her down.

Sam watched until the horse was out of sight. He said a silent prayer she'd survive and then slipped away, reached for his phone and made a call.

Diamond slept through the entire venture. She awoke and fear overtook the pain.

FARMHOUSE

CHAPTER THREE

1833-1834

Every time you get angry, you poison your own system.
Alfred A. Montapert

I spent days fighting my rage. Eaton and I had grown up together, joined the Shakers together and worked side-by-side in the fields. We had played marbles, shared jokes about girls and raced our horses and buggies. After we became united with the Shakers and gave up girls, we had turned to smoking pipes and brewing cider. Adapting to communal living had been easy but the evangelistic worship had presented a challenge until the Holy Spirit acted through us.

Everything had changed with Mary Ann. The three of us had become friends but through the months, I watched the friendship change. It started with the way Eaton looked at Mary Ann. At first, she seemed not to notice but then awareness crept in. I soon became a third party. Eaton and Mary Ann concentrated more and more on each other. Eaton hadn't shared the point in time when their passion flamed and crossed the Shaker boundaries. I walked across the field toward Eaton, growing angrier with every step.

"How can you stand here and let Mary Ann take all the blame?" I demanded.

"What can I do?"

"What can you do? You can be a man and stand by her side."

"You think I should get turned off, too? How did I

know she'd get with child?"

"I can't believe Mary Ann would willingly go against our religion."

"Well, she did and she made me fall too."

I turned away to keep from punching my friend's face. My anger spiked another notch when I heard Eaton mumble, "Besides, what difference does it make?"

"The difference is that she was kicked out of her church and home, lost her friends and has nowhere to go."

In the Shaker religion, women shared equality with men. "That's a joke." My sarcasm reached no human ear. I headed back to the barn and spent the rest of the day sawing timber. We had not started making furniture but I longed for the day we did. I loved the tables and chairs the original group had brought from New Lebanon. I ran my hand along a piece of cherry that would finish the banister in the new dwelling house. I appreciated the simplicity of the Shaker design. It was easier to make but more importantly, it looked so clean and elegant. Farmers didn't ordinarily think in terms of elegant, but Shaker furniture was in demand. For now, I was content to work on finishing the new place. This banister would serve us well over the years. I had been told it was unusual for us to build a dwelling with only one staircase. We would all use it, the women to go to their retiring rooms on the second floor and men to the third.

At dinner that night, I thought again of Mary Ann. I had no idea where she would spend her confinement but I felt guilty for not publicly standing up for her. I certainly hadn't proven to be a good friend, and Eaton was a coward. Our broken friendship was beyond mending.

Weeks went by and Mary Ann's name was never spoken. I wondered if she had food and shelter. Maybe someone took her in. I knew little of the surrounding area but there were villages and farms in all directions. I prayed that she found kind-hearted people somewhere. Eaton continually fed my anger with his nonchalance. He never showed remorse or concern. In fact, he never again mentioned Mary Ann.

I began questioning my faith. How can a God permit a church to kick out a woman at her most vulnerable time?

Was God really that vindictive? If there's equality, why do only certain people pay for their sins while others go free? I wanted to live by God's rules but sometimes I found it difficult to determine the difference between His and man's laws.

***

Mary Ann had walked away with her only piece of luggage, filled with everything she owned in the world. She supposed she should be thankful for Ruth, the oldest woman in the village, who showed her only kindness. When she had joined the Shakers, she had given up ownership of everything in her possession. The fact she left with more than the clothes she wore was due to Ruth, who had found an old valise and packed some undergarments, an extra dress, a modesty cape, an apron and a bonnet. She had also found the warmest coat in the communal closet and placed it over her shoulders. Mary Ann would never forget the empathy in Ruth's eyes.

"Thank you so much." She tugged on the coat and hugged it to her body. "I don't know where to go."

"Head into Sodus or Sodus Point. Visit the church people and ask for help. There's an old boarding house in Sodus Point. Try it if the churches don't help you. It has a questionable reputation but you'll be all right if you stick to yourself. You'll be in confinement so no one will expect you to do anything else."

"What do I tell people?"

"The truth, child. People in villages know us, and the word will get around anyway. Don't try to lie your way out of it. You're not alone anymore. You carry a child and you have a responsibility to bring that child into the world. Pray to God, keep faith in Him and He will see you through this."

"I'm so frightened."

"As you should be. It's not easy and I disagreed with the decision to make you leave. But it's been made and there's nothing you can do but look forward."

"I will try. I've always admired your level-headedness. I need some of that right now and I know that's what you're trying to give me. Thank you."

"May God bless you and the child you carry. I will try to find you and check on you but don't depend on me. You have to build a new life. I'm sorry you have this responsibility alone but maybe you are better off this way. The man who abandoned you is a coward. Unfortunately, the outside world will blame you and call your child a bastard. But you must stay strong and do what is right. I'm giving you some money I had hidden for an emergency. I know I can count on you to not tattle." Ruth grinned.

They hugged and Mary Ann walked off the farm. She thanked God that it was a cool, dry day. It had rained all day yesterday when she'd been expelled from the community. Thank God they gave her until today to make plans. She figured she had almost ten long miles to get to Sodus Point. She planned to follow Ruth's advice and visit the churches first. Surely some person of God would take pity on her. She walked for over an hour before the queasiness hit her. She stopped and looked around. She saw a fallen tree and leaned against the trunk. At least she had passed the morning sickness time. She had tried to so hard to hide it but women know. Several of the women asked if she was with child and she had denied it. Finally someone had turned her in to an elder. It didn't matter because her condition was fast becoming obvious.

She heard the bell in the tower chiming, as it called the Shakers in for breakfast. She hadn't realized how far away it could be heard, or maybe she hadn't walked as far as she imagined.

Mary Ann thought of Eaton. She had met him and Horace at the same time. They had joined the community just a few weeks after she had arrived. Their friendly banter with each other had drawn her to them. They enjoyed life and she enjoyed them. Horace was quieter and more reserved. When she thought of the worship dances, she thought of Eaton though. He became a graceful, uninhibited follower. He made her feel the love of the Lord. Afterwards, they would sing and smoke their pipes before going their separate ways.

It had happened during the cold of winter. They couldn't work in the fields, but the animals still needed to be fed and cared for. Mary Ann should have been indoors with the women. She had grown tired of weaving and wanted to check on Luke and the rest of the goats. She had named several of them and loved the way they constantly asked for attention. She would bundle up and slip out of the house every day to check on her brood. She found Eaton finishing up his chores in the barn. He joined her in petting the goats. One nudged her hard enough she tumbled into the hay. What a mistake!

Eaton plopped down beside her and they laughed at the goats' antics. The animals pushed into them, each wanting her share of attention. Eaton enjoyed the time too. He had been filled with enthusiasm. When Mary Ann realized how long they had stayed in the barn, she started to get up. Eaton pulled her back down. She laughed but when she looked into his eyes, he had changed. She recognized the look and made a joke about it.

"I need to hold you." He had pulled her into his arms. She felt the warmth of his body and her nerves tingled. His lips touched her hair and she shivered with anticipation. This couldn't be wrong, could it? His lips slowly moved down her forehead. He kissed the tip of her nose and then drew her into a gentle kiss. Mary Ann had never experienced such intense emotion. She threw all her feelings into her return kiss. The kiss deepened. When it ended, he still held her in his arms. She felt at peace and anxious at the same time. She snuggled even closer and marveled at the feelings coursing through her body. He kissed her again, this time with more passion. She felt a sudden desire to please him. "You are wonderful," she whispered.

Eaton untied her bonnet and pushed it off. He ran his fingers through her hair, sending pleasure through every nerve ending. He slid to the ground, taking her with him. She found herself on her back with his body covering hers.

"You are beautiful and I want to make you mine."

Mary Ann wanted nothing more than to be his. Maybe they'd spend lots of evenings kissing like this. She felt his hand slide up her bare leg.

"No." She tried to pull down her dress and her petticoat.

"It's all right," Eaton whispered. "I'm not going to hurt you."

She couldn't think with his hot hand caressing her thigh. She knew this was wrong, but maybe it would be all right for a minute or two. She wanted time enough to memorize the wonderful sensations that were flooding her. She whimpered as his hand moved up to her hip.

"I think we should go back," she managed to whisper. She didn't want to, but a tendril of fear was taking hold.

Eaton didn't seem to hear her and she felt him tugging on her undergarments. "Stop. This is wrong."

He continued to stroke her and panic arose. "We have to stop." Was he deaf? He didn't answer but his hand became more demanding and he kissed her with a new roughness.

Mary Ann felt the tears on her cheek. What could she do? She tried to push him back but he was too strong. His body completely covered her. "Please, please stop."

The more she fought against him, the more determined he became. "You want this too," he growled in her ear.

"No. Please God, no."

***

Mary Ann had stopped again to rest in a pasture for a few minutes when she heard a horse and buggy. She looked up at the sun and realized she had been walking for at least a couple of hours.

She shook off the memories of that horrible night and hoped some-one would help her. She picked up her valise and hurried back to the road.

An older man stopped his horse beside her. "Do you need a ride?"

"I'm going to Sodus Point. How far do I have to go?"

"It's still a fair piece down the road. Come on. I'll take you there." He stepped out of the buggy and took her valise. Unsure what to do, Mary Ann took the easy way. "Thank you." He loaded her luggage and held out his hand to assist her into the buggy. She took his hand and thanked him again.

"What has you walking all the way to Sodus Point by yourself?"

"I'm looking for a place to live." She remembered Ruth's advice and decided to answer truthfully.

"You're one of the Shakers, aren't you?"

"Can you tell by my clothes?"

"Yes," he smiled. "My name is Silas and I live on a farm close to Sodus Point. Do you know where you're going once you get there?"

"Yes. Not really. I mean, I have to find a place to stay. My friend Ruth told me to find some church people."

"Are you looking for a place to live or just stay a few days?"

"To live. I might as well tell you. I've sinned and the elders asked me to leave."

"We're all sinners, missy. What have you done that's so terrible?"

"I am with child."

He could barely hear her but the pain in her voice was loud and clear. He'd met some of the Shakers at the market but they kept to themselves. He never imagined they'd turn one of their own out on the streets. This poor girl needed help.

"I know the lady who runs the boarding house. Why don't I take you there and introduce you? Maybe she will have an open room. She serves decent food and works hard to keep good folks as board-ers. The third floor is for women so you won't be alone."

"I appreciate it." Mary Ann prayed that there would be room for her. Maybe Ruth was right. Maybe she could build a new life. They rode in silence the rest of the way. She had only been to Sodus Point a few times and she didn't know her way around the town. When they rode along the bay, she forgot her troubles and let the view soothe her. The shimmering blue water calmed the anguish within her. She brushed a strand of caramel-colored hair back under her bonnet. By the time they reached the inn, she felt renewed and ready.

"Here we are. The lady's name in Millie. Come and I'll intro-duce you."

"You've already helped me so much and I don't know your surname."

"Bretton, Silas Bretton. My wife and I live on a nearby farm." He unloaded her valise, walked her to the door and knocked.

A stout, middle-aged woman answered the door. "Why, Silas, what have we here?"

"This young lady needs a home and I thought of you."

"I have a room," she answered and studied Mary Ann. "Are you carryin'?"

"Yes, ma'am."

"Are you a Shaker?"

"I was."

"Millie, meet Mary Ann. The Shakers turned her out and she needs a place to stay. I think she'll do fine with you." Silas turned to Mary Ann, "Do you have money?"

"A little."

"Tell you what, Millie. I'll bring you another bushel of apples and apricots. I might even throw in some grapes if you take her in."

"You're a kind-hearted man, Silas. Guess I can do no less. Okay, miss. Come with me."

***

Mary Ann spent the next months at the boarding house. Millie often brought her meals to her and stayed to visit. Mary Ann appreciated her kindness and her company.

"You'll have a hard time of it, that's for sure. But keep your faith, dear. You're a child of God and so is the baby in your womb. Never forget that, even when people shame you. I hope you find a man who will take care of you."

"I'll be all right once the baby is here. I can work. I'm a decent seamstress and I'm strong. I can work in a house or in the fields." Mary Ann hoped she could stay at the boarding house but she didn't ask. Millie had already done so much for her.

"Child, you're a single woman with a baby. A fallen woman. A sinner. That's the way the world will see you. I know as a Shaker you had rights that other women don't have. It's different out here in the world."

Mary Ann knew Millie spoke the truth. She couldn't count her many nightmares about people shunning her child. Once again, she hoped for a boy. Life would be easier for him.

"Don't fret, child. You can stay here as long as you need to. You've already helped me with the sewing and mending. We'll find other duties for you once this is over."

The days and minutes dragged as the discomfort increased. Her feet swelled and her back hurt after she spent a couple of hours bending over her mending. Stretching her back brought momentary relief but that always caused discomfort in her belly. She sat in a Shaker chair that Millie had purchased. Mary Ann loved the chair but missed hanging it on the wall after she was finished. She looked around the room and knew that the community wouldn't approve of the clutter. She made the bed everyday, dusted the wardrobe and small chest daily, and kept her personal items picked up. But the small room still appeared cluttered.

She prayed as she sewed. Mary Ann accepted that she wasn't a Shaker anymore but she couldn't believe God had forsaken her, too. He knew she didn't really mean to sin. No, that wasn't fair. She had loved Eaton's touch. No one had ever told her that a man's hands could hold so much power over her body. The body that had betrayed her. Her sin started when she returned his first kiss. Then the sinning grew deeper and deeper. It was all her fault.

She missed the vitality of the Shaker community. She loved the new meetinghouse but would never see the inside of the completed dwelling house. She tried to imagine how the work was progressing. The house would have three stories, nine bedrooms and plenty of room for worship. Some days she resented that most of all. She'd never realize the dream. She had been there as the community expanded into packaging flower and vegetable seeds. Word of their products, especially their cheeses and butter, spread and business grew month after month. She pictured Eaton enjoying the fruits of their labor. Resentment became the seed that grew in her heart.

Life grew more difficult when Millie hired Audrey to help with the housework. Audrey was a strict Christian and Mary Ann felt her scorn. She often heard her mumble under her breath about sinners. Whenever Audrey stood tall and straightened her apron, Mary Ann knew the judgment would start. "I hope you're reading that day and night." Audrey would point to the Bible and harrumph as she left the room.

"Your time is near," Audrey announced one day. "Pray that God has mercy on your soul. He punishes sinners, you know. The Good Book tells us we will pay for our sins. I fear you will have great pain when he delivers you of your child."

"Ouch!" Mary Ann pricked her finger. She stared at the needle and fabric in her hands. Fear raced through her at the thought of unknown pain. What if Audrey was right? Would God punish her? Please God, don't punish the baby. I'm the sinner, not him. She had taken to calling the baby 'him' because she wanted it to be so.

"Did you hear me?"

"Yes, ma'am." What else could she say? She wanted to tell Audrey to leave her alone but didn't dare. After all, Audrey was the good Christian and she was the sinner. Eaton's face popped into her mind. Did he ever feel guilt for the sin they had committed? Did God forgive him? How did a man feel? Could he simply forget his actions and go on about his life? She couldn't. The life inside of her continually reminded her of her sin.

* * *

Melancholy became the blanket that Mary Ann draped around her shoulders, far heavier than the modesty cape she wore. Still months to go. Winter would be upon them before her baby was born. Cooler mornings had already arrived with the coming of September. She had missed the summer flowers and walks in the forest. Now she would miss the leaves turning into a palette of beautiful colors. She often thought that God was a great artist, that He created beauty in nature and renewed it every season by painting the earth in brilliant hues. Of course, she had never read that in the Bible or heard anyone else express it. In her eyes, the Shaker God was a strict disciplinarian, always watching for His people to cross that imaginary line into sin. That was the God that frightened her now. Was her sin too great for forgiveness? Was God vindictive? Would He take out his displeasure on her child? If only she could go outside and walk in the woods, she knew she could feel the kindness of her artistic God.

A knock broke into her thoughts. "Come in."

Audrey entered with a breakfast tray. She placed it on the table and turned to leave the room. Despite the constant disapproval Mary Ann saw on her face, she needed to hear a human voice.

"Thank you. Is the weather as nice as it looks from my window?"

Audrey nodded.

"Please talk to me. I ... I need to know what is happening outside this room."

"The world goes on and I have work to do. Some of us don't have time for idle chatter." Audrey opened the door and shut it behind her.

Mary Ann was alone again, but then, she'd been alone while Audrey was in her room. She wished Millie had brought her tray. Her kind words always brightened the room and warmed Mary Ann's heart. Lord, she needed kindness. She had mistaken Eaton's attention for kindness. She thought of Horace. Funny, she had almost forgotten about him. He had always been kind but quiet. Even when they were together, it had been easy to forget him. Eaton had been the center of attention. He decided what they should do and the topic of their conversations. She and Horace followed along. In the weeks before she was turned off, she avoided both of them. She never wanted to see Eaton again. No, that was a lie. Part of her ached to feel his hands on her body again, but he was part of her big sin. She had been so filled with shame that she avoided Horace, too. She didn't want to see the disdain on his face.

She picked up her needle and thread and began sewing on the apron Millie had requested. Everyday she had to stop more often to stretch her back and adjust her position. The baby weighed as heavy on her body as on her mind. She sewed and stretched her way through the morning.

"Good afternoon." Millie bustled into the room without knocking. "I've brought you some fresh bread and cheese. We picked more tomatoes this morning, so you'll have a vegetable too. In a couple of weeks, Silas will be bringing us new apples, too."

Mary Ann stood to stretch. "Thank you, Millie. I'm so grateful for everything you do for me. I don't think I could get through this without you."

"We can get through whatever God gives us, child. That's what makes us strong women. I've grown to care about you, but you could survive on your own. Never forget that."

"I don't know but I would try. Ruth was the strongest woman I knew in the community. She had the courage to help me even after the elders had their say. You are like her. You both have courage and heart. I hope I can be like that for my child."

"Don't you worry, child. You will be. Now let's talk about fun times. This morning I decided you needed more milk every day. Since you've done well with goat's milk, I saved more for you."

"Thank you. I like it."

"Me, too. Did I ever tell you about my favorite goat?"

"No, I didn't know you have them."

"Not now, but when my Arthur was alive, we always kept goats. We had this one old billy goat. I named him Samuel because he was a strong one. He would butt anything in sight. One time, Arthur was walking the fence line and Samuel came up behind him and butted him hard. Arthur landed on the ground in the middle of a cow patty. He was madder than an old wet hen at that goat."

Mary Ann laughed with Millie. "I wish I could have seen that. I had a pet goat named Luke. He was only two years old when I was turned off. You know Shakers can't own anything personally, so he was the farm's goat, but he followed me everywhere. He became my special friend. He knew how I was feeling and when I was too busy to play. Sometimes, he would let me pet him for as long as I wanted. We weren't supposed to waste time, so those times were rare."

"I'm glad you had him. Pets know when we need them. They can be our best friends."

"It's funny now that I think about it. Millie, he wasn't there that night I needed him, but he seemed to follow me everywhere the last few weeks. Do you suppose he knew?"

"Of course, he did. He knew you needed him."

"And I did. I told him everything. He was the only one I could admit my sin to, and he didn't condemn me. I wish he were here now. I get so lonely in this room."

"I know you do, and I'm sorry you have to stay inside, but it's necessary until your confinement is over. I think you should still talk to Luke when you need to. As I said, animals have a special sense. Now you eat your lunch, child. You need the nourishment for the baby."

Mary Ann finished her lunch after Millie left. Her thoughts turned to Luke. She remembered the day after the big sin, as she still thought of it. She had finished her weaving for the day and Eldress Lucy gave her permission to go for a walk. Luke came running when she left the house. She had petted him and told him she was going to the woods. He followed along, playfully butting her hand for another petting session. Finally, when she could no longer hold back the tears, she sank to her knees and hugged Luke. He stood still, giving her time to cry. The more she cried, the harder it was to stop. Still Luke stayed. When she finally lifted her head and dried her eyes, she saw the sympathy in his. Maybe he didn't understand her words but he knew her heart. She poured the story out, told him about her fall from grace and her guilt. Luke listened to every word and never condemned her actions. Mary Ann even admitted how wonderful it had felt in the beginning, before ....

"Luke, I know you're not here, but you were the only Shaker who didn't turn away. You'll always be my special friend. I wish you could hear me, but I guess even if you could, you wouldn't understand my words."

Mary Ann went to the window. Behind the shed, the trees lined what she thought was the bay shoreline. She could see the brilliant blue of the water, but not the shoreline. Color was starting to transform the trees. Soon the leaves would fall, and she would have a different view of the bay. She'd never been outside of New York, but she was sure it was the most beautiful spot on earth.

"Luke, if it's okay with you, I will tell you about my life here. All I do everyday is sew and mend. It's not hard work but my back and my eyes get tired. Millie is kind and never pushes me to work faster. Audrey is another matter. She disapproves of me. I think she disapproves of the fact I was a Shaker as much as that I'm a fallen woman. She says she's a Christian, but I have yet to see anything Christ-like in her."

She pictured walking in the woods with Luke trailing behind her. She once decided she should count the leaves he stopped to eat, but forgot about it halfway through the trail. She thought of the love in his yellow slitted eyes. Today she would tell him of loneliness. And fear. The fear of birthing a child, being a responsible adult, finding a way to provide for herself and the baby, and most of all, the fear of being alone forever.

By the time Audrey brought her dinner tray, Mary Ann realized that talking to Luke had made the hours pass much faster. It would be an easy habit to foster.

* * *

Eaton wrestled with his own demons but they had little to do with Mary Ann. She had served as a reminder of what he gave up when he united with the Shakers. Religion was one thing, but the feel of a woman's body was another. Mary Ann had not been the first and he didn't intend for her to be the last. He had felt momentary remorse when he realized how upset she really was. She had been willing enough in the beginning. Didn't girls know you can't yell 'stop' in the middle of the game?

It hadn't taken long for him to realize that he couldn't live by the Shakers' rules. However, he had no idea of what he wanted to do or where he would go. Over the ensuing weeks, he never saw Mary Ann alone. He suspected she was avoiding him. It was a clear message there would be no replay.

Spring planting began and every man on the farm worked from dawn to dusk. Nighttime brought worship services. There was little time to think and plan for the future. The weeks went by and the fields flourished. He occasionally thought about the future, but it would have to wait until fall.

Then the big scandal came to light. Mary Ann was with child and had been turned off. She would have to leave the community. He stayed in the background at the public announcement. His conscience told him he should talk to her, but what would he say? They had enjoyed a roll in the hay. He knew she had enjoyed it too. She had said no, but she didn't really mean it. So it ended their friendship but there would always be more girls. No, he could say nothing that would make it any better.

The work remained constant in the months after she left. The one thing that changed was his friendship with Horace. Who would have ever thought he could act so high and mighty? After all, what he and Mary Ann did was what nature intended. Nevertheless, Horace judged him. They'd had words and now they avoided each other. Either Horace would come down off his high horse or he'd lose a friend. They'd had fun but he could find other friends.

As fall arrived, Eaton made plans to leave. He would be turned off the rolls of the faithful, but he could no longer abide by the stringent rules. He'd been celibate again after Mary Ann, but he needed a woman's companionship. He might have left with Mary Ann if she had acted differently toward him. Her loss.

* * *

After Mary Ann's disgrace, I lived in constant agitation. My rage at Eaton grew in proportion to my concern for her. I made trips to Sodus and Alton, to no avail. Mary Ann seemed to have disappeared. I even went to Lyons and found no answers. I finally faced the possibility that she may have traveled on the Erie Canal either west to Rochester or east to Syracuse. Maybe in a city, her condition would be less scandalous.

Then, strangely enough, in the late fall, that crazy billy goat started following me around. I remembered how Mary Ann had been so crazy about him, named him Luke. She even talked to him.

"I tell him all my secrets," she had joked. Eaton had laughed, but I suspected that was true.

"Well, Luke, will you listen to my secrets too?" I asked the goat one evening. Luke tilted his head and focused those ridiculous side-slitted eyes on me. "Never mind, this is crazy."

I walked away from the goat. Luke didn't give up and continued to follow me around the farm. In early October, Eaton left without saying goodbye to anyone. He apparently had told one of the elders who had not tried to stop him.

"Thank God he's gone," I confided in Luke. "I'm not sure how much longer I could contain myself. I want him to pay for his sins."

Luke tilted his head and listened.

"She's paying for both of them. No one seems to care that it took two people. I wish you could tell me where to find her." I found comfort in Luke but my rage had festered too long and gone too deep. I knew I could never forgive Eaton. Although I was beginning to accept the fact I would never find Mary Ann, I knew I'd never stop trying. I felt that God have given me the responsibility to right the wrong that she had suffered.

"Brother Horace, I sense a lack of joy in your dancing tonight," Elder Joseph pulled me aside one evening after our service. "Is something bothering you? I've noticed you are keeping to yourself more than usual."

"Nothing. I'm fine. I've been working through something in my mind, that's all."

"Pray, Brother, pray more and ask God's help."

"Thank you. I will." I bid Elder Joseph good night and made a quick exit.

* * *

I thought about my efforts. I had finished unloading the seeds and vegetables at the Sodus, Alton and Sodus Point markets. The wagon had been overflowing that day so Elder John had asked me to help with his rounds. I rode my horse and followed the wagon. Normally, I was prohibited from going out into the World, so I eagerly anticipated the opportunity. For weeks, I had hoped for the excuse to leave the farm and search for Mary Ann.

Our last stop late in the afternoon was in Sodus Point. When I finished unloading the flower seeds and honey, I asked Elder John if I could ride back on my own. He agreed. I surveyed the village, taking in a couple of big houses, and a few old buildings. I continued along the lake, looking for a church. Mary Ann would probably have done the same. Along the shore, I saw the loads of rock that had been dumped. Our community had brought in several wagons full of rocks. We received one dollar for every load. They dumped the rocks near the new breakwater that would be built between the lake and the bay. I looked back at the lighthouse. Only eight years old, the light guided ships on Lake Ontario. If I were there for any other reason, I would have enjoyed seeing the changes.

I rode by an old seedy-looking boarding house and decided Mary Ann would never stay there. I noticed the foundations of homes that the British had burned in the War of 1812, and wondered if anyone would ever rebuild them. I rode on to the Mansion House. Now a tavern, it had been the only home that had survived the war. I decided to stop in for dinner and to ask where I might find a church.

"In Sodus Center. The Red Brick Church." The server seemed willing to talk.

"None here?"

"No, the Episcopalians own some property and they sometimes have services, but there are no buildings."

"Where would someone stay if they came here?"

"Alone? Probably the boarding house. But to tell you the truth, not many people come to stay."

I ordered and ate my dinner. It was getting late and the elders would notice if I didn't return soon. Convinced that Mary Ann would never stay in the boarding house, I hurried back to the farm. I would try again and look in Sodus and Alton, too.

As I rode home, my mind constantly replayed the scene that horrible day—Mary Ann walking away from the farm, alone and carrying a small valise with all her worldly goods. I had vacillated between my empathy for her, my anger at Eaton and my disgust that the elders refused to offer her a ride into town. That widened the crack that would destroy my belief in the Shaker philosophy. I didn't understand how righteousness could negate kindness.

A month passed before I had an opportunity to visit Sodus Point again. Elder John was feeling indisposed and asked me if I'd be comfortable running the deliveries on my own. I told him I would and passed the morning delivering honey and seeds to customers. When I stopped by the Bretton farm, I found Silas busy in his orchard. Silas had long been a customer and, like most of the farmers around, I found him to be friendly and open to conversa-

tion. Elder John has said that Silas was the most talkative of his customers.

"I have a question, Silas, and I don't know who else to ask."

"Go ahead and ask. If I know the answer, I'll tell you," Silas stopped working and took out his pipe.

"A couple of months ago, a young woman was turned off ... forced to leave our community. I heard she was hoping to find a place to stay in Sodus Point. I thought she'd go to a church, but there are none there. Have you heard anything?"

Silas looked at me and continued tamping tobacco into his pipe. He took his time lighting it, sucking in quick breaths to get a good draw. He appeared deep in thought and I didn't interrupt him.

"Why do you want to know?"

"What? ... Well, she was, or is, a friend of mine."

"If she's a friend, why wait three months to find her?"

I couldn't understand the harshness in his tone or words.

"I've asked before at the tavern, but didn't find out anything."

"Do you have a reason for wanting to find her?" Silas stared at me and I looked directly into his eyes, hoping to ascertain his thoughts. I hoped he saw my concern.

"Did the young woman have a name?" Silas said after another long drag on his pipe.

"Mary Ann."

"Aww, yes, I met Mary Ann," Silas checked his pipe bowl and took another draw. "I picked her up along the road and took her into town."

"Do you know what happened to her?"

"Look, son," Silas pulled the pipe from his mouth. "Are you the one responsible?"

"For her leaving?" I know my confusion showed on

my face. "No, she was turned off."

"I know that. Are you the reason she was turned out? I don't know any plainer way to ask this? Did you have your way with this girl?"

"No ... no, it's not what you think." I felt my face burn with shame. Surely I didn't have the look of a man who would forcefully violate a woman.

Silas seemed to be waiting for more.

"My friend, no, my ex-friend is responsible. He's forgotten all about her, but she was my friend, too. We were all friends until this. I can't quit worrying about her. She's all alone in the world."

"Yes, she is and I can't understand why you waited so long."

"So you know where she is?" Hope surged through me.

"Yes, at least where she was when I left her. She's at the boarding house here."

"But ... is it a decent place for her?" I thought of the look of the place and the stories I'd heard.

"Right now, she can't be choosy. Millie, the woman who runs the place, is a good, hard-working Christian woman. She took her in. About a month ago, she told me the girl is doing okay. She has melancholic days, but that's understandable."

"I need to go see her."

"I hope I didn't read you wrong, son. I wouldn't want to cause her any more misery."

"I won't hurt her. Thank you so much."

After I finished my deliveries, I walked over to the boarding house. A thin, middle-aged woman answered my knock. I suspected a smile may never have lit her face nor kindness relaxed her wooden posture.

"We don't need anything," the woman started to close the door.

"Wait a minute. I'm not here with any goods to sell.

I am looking for a friend of mine. Her name is Mary Ann and I was told she is here."

She looked me up and down. I stood there in my black knee breeches and black socks. It was obvious that I was a Shaker. My black coat and vest covered a white linen shirt. I had started the day clean, but after unloading so many deliveries, I may have looked dirty. One of the first things I learned living with the Shakers had been that cleanliness is next to Godliness.

"There's no one here by that name."

"But I talked to Silas Bretton and he said he brought her here a few months ago."

"Look, I've only been here a month and there's no one here by that name. Now I've got work to do." As she shut the door, I heard her mumble, "A good Baptist would never condone such behavior."

I wasn't sure what spurred her obvious disdain, but I suspected she was one of the town people who considered Shakers strange. I had heard stories of people ridiculing what they referred to as our "carryin' on" at our services.

CHAPTER FOUR

Present Day - June

People who fight fire with fire usually end up with ashes.

Abigail Van Buren
(from The Wisdom of the Midwest by Dr. Criswell Freeman)

ELLIOTT LIFTED THE BRIM OF his hat. Was that the new volunteer? Maybe the summer wouldn't be so dull after all. He hadn't stepped foot off the farm in the five days since he arrived. He needed some fun, and the company of a good-looking girl would help. The pickings were slim—mostly guys and older volunteers from around the area.

"Hi, I'm Elliott," he slapped his hat and watched the dust fly.

"I'm Claire. Nice to meet you."

"I'm here for a summer internship. You too?"

"Yes. I'll be working with Sara in the horse barn."

"Looks like we'll see a lot of each other."

"I suppose." Claire tried to deny a response to his charm as she turned and walked away. Maybe it was the too-blue eyes or the easy smile that warned her to beware. He had that look. She'd been there and done that but never again.

"Hey, wait up," he called. "Are you staying here at the farm?"

"Yes, in the Deacon's House."

"Great. I'm staying in the boarding house." Her apparent lack of interest surprised him. "See you around." He sauntered off toward the boarding house. Jeff, the operations manager, drove up and asked him to help Seth with some work in the cow barn. He wondered if he'd survive a summer of so much hard work.

"Hey, thanks for coming to my rescue," Seth grinned. "We're repairing the stalls and, as the saying goes, two hands are better than one."

"What do you need?"

"Right now, we have to finish unloading the lumber. I've already measured the lengths of the boards that need repair, so we'll be ready to cut them."

They stacked the lumber outside near the saw. Seth appeared to have the process organized so Elliott followed his lead. "Do you always work this quietly?" he asked. "No music, no conversation."

"Pretty much."

"Not even earphones?"

"Nope." Seth pointed to a stack. "This stack is the right length. We need to cut twenty boards for this other stack. If you hand them to me, I'll cut them."

Again they worked in silence. Elliott admitted it would be difficult to talk over the saw's noise anyway. By late afternoon, they had finished the repairs. As Seth assessed their work, Elliott asked, "Break time?"

"Yes, as soon as we pick up. Thanks for your help." Seth started picking up the tools. "You can stack the lumber scraps against that wall." He nodded toward the back of the barn. "Luckily, there's little scrap."

Elliott finished the task and wiped the sweat out of his eyes. What a long, boring afternoon. Even the animals offered more excitement than Seth. He probably hadn't spoken more than fifty words and they were all orders. All he wanted was a beer and shade. He'd learned the first day that there would be no drinking until they had finished the day's work. His dad and Uncle Gavin had certainly conspired against him. He'd get through the summer and show them he was ready for a leadership role in the company. Two old fuddy-duddies who still believed you had to start at the bottom and have no fun. They needed to move into the twenty-first century. He had more education and brains than either of them and he'd worked the grunt jobs for the last two years. They paid him so little he had to make up for it any way he could. Granted, that had caused trouble, but it was over now.

CHAPTER FIVE

The scars of abuse, be it physical or emotional, run deep and long.

CLAIRE STRUGGLED TO CONCENTRATE ON the horse's beautiful coat. She stroked her neck and uttered words of love. But Jake's angry face intruded. "I'm a coward for running away," she admitted.

"Jewel is loving that attention," Sara, her manager, smiled as she walked into the barn. "It's hard to believe how far she's come since she's been here."

"I love her name. She is a jewel, isn't she?" Claire smiled and patted her neck. "What happened to her? Was she abused?"

"Neglected to the point of abuse. Her owner developed dementia and completely forgot about her."

"So it wasn't intentional abuse?"

"No, but abuse nevertheless. Although the barn door was open, this poor baby kept going back out in the pasture looking for grass. Once the snows hit, she couldn't find food. When we rescued her, she was sickly and nothing but skin and bones. She couldn't even eat without getting sick. She wanted to lay down all the time so it was a constant fight to keep her on her feet."

"Does it hurt her to lie down?" Claire's heart ached at the thought of the horse's suffering.

"For a prolonged period, yes. Horses have to stand because of their weight. If they are down too long, it restricts their blood flow and can damage their organs. Then they have problems when they get up and the blood flows again. It's called repercussion."

"Does she have internal damage?"

"No, our vet thinks we saved her in time. Unfortunately, we have lots of stories like hers. Ask Cheri to tell you about Melvin sometime."

"I will. Thanks for giving me this opportunity. I know I'm going to love it here."

After Sara left, Claire cleaned the dandy brush and carried it and the currycomb back in the tack room. She looked forward to learning about caring for the horses. Right now, she felt more comfortable with animals than with people. The horses wouldn't ask for explanations.

She decided to walk down to the horse pasture before going back to her room. She wanted to learn each one by name and know its history. She watched the two hackney ponies. Sara had told her that Alvah Strong bought the farm in the 1920s and raised hackneys. These were the only two remaining of his bloodlines. Funny how time passes and only the land remains the same, she thought. This farm had been in existence in one form or another for nearly two hundred years. It puts my problems with Jake in a different perspective.

"Good evening." The greeting broke into Claire's thoughts. She turned to see a friendly face shaded by a baseball cap.

"I'm Seth. We were introduced your first day."

"Of course, I remember." She turned her head to hide behind that little white lie. Not really a lie. She remembered meeting people. She just didn't remember whether or not he was one of them.

"How's it going so far?" Seth recognized her discomfort but couldn't think of anything else to say.

"Fine. Lots to learn but I'm loving the horses."

"Yeah, they're beautiful. Wait until we have a new rescue and you see his improvement here. It will make you a lifetime supporter of Cracker Box Palace and all rescue efforts."

"I'm already understanding the value of the work we do here."

They watched two horses run across the far pasture. A gentle breeze ruffled the trees. Neither broke the silence.

"Well, it's about goin' home time." Seth said.

Claire barely noticed as the two horses took off running again. "Bye."

She loved how the green fields made a photogenic background for the horses. Whether they were black, shades of brown or white, the spring enhanced their beauty. She had always loved the four seasons, but this was the best she'd seen. Maybe because it was the first one spent in the country. She'd arrived in the middle of the apple blossom time, and nothing had prepared her for the vibrant pinks. Even when the colors faded into softer tones, she still responded to their beauty.

Later than evening, she wished she had her art supplies. Working with watercolors soothed her soul and filled her with energy, She could almost feel the brush in her hand. As she had gazed across the

RESCUED HORSES AT CRACKER BOX PALACE

pasture this afternoon, she'd had an idea for a new piece. But now, it brought Jake's face to mind. She had realized he had jealousy issues early on in their relationship. She had done her best to show him her undivided loyalty. That he'd be threatened by her art never entered her mind. After all, that was what had brought them together in the first place. Jake had been so gentle and kindhearted in the beginning. Falling in love with him had been too easy. He supported and admired her work and showed interest in her career. He even purchased a couple of her canvases and displayed them in his living room.

"I understand why you fell for him," her mother had said. He'd certainly turned on the charm when he met her. The more times she and Jake visited her, the more she pushed Claire to keep him.

When he asked, she had agreed to move in with him. They vowed their love and talked about forever. Then he began to change. Claire admitted she should have seen the signs. He didn't want her to bring anything but her clothes when she moved in. She put all her belongings in storage, thinking once they adapted to living together, she'd find room. That never happened. She had forgiven him the first time he had shoved her and smashed one of her paintings on the floor. She still didn't know which had hurt the worst. To have someone destroy your work cut deep into your soul. But he apologized, even cried. He promised never to touch her again. He even asked her to marry him. She might've forgiven him, but thank God she hadn't agreed to a wedding. She had pleaded for more time.

Jake was fine for a couple of months, then he slowly began again. The little snide remarks, the criticisms, the ridicule. Every little incident left a scar. He physically grabbed her arm and threw her around several times. Then one night, when she wanted to bring her art supplies into his house, he jerked her and dislocated her shoulder. He apologized again and built her a shed in back of the house.

A conversation niggled at her memory. The kind that should have warned her, but didn't.

"Now, you never have to leave here," Jake said.

"What do you mean?"

"You have everything you need—your art, our home, each other."

"I also have my mother and my friends. I enjoy my time with them. And I have my job."

"But you don't really need them. You'll see. You don't need to work. You have talent, a studio to work in and I make enough to provide for us." Jake took her in his arms, then turned her around to look at her new art studio. "See, it's furnished exactly as you wanted. We'll shop for anything more you need tomorrow."

Gratitude filled her. He did care and wanted her to be happy. She forgot their conversation. The next day, they shopped and by the time she put the finishing touches to her new studio, she'd already mentally sketched out her next work. She would use the large canvas and give it to Jake as a thank you.

When she gave it to him, he smiled and told her he'd like to hang it in his office at work. Pleased, she agreed. They celebrated with pasta and wine, followed by a Hallmark movie he chose. As the main character confessed her love and devotion to the man of her dreams, he turned to her. "You watch. He'll propose, she'll accept and they'll live happily ever after."

She should have known.

In the following weeks, she found her only real sense of freedom when she painted. She hadn't given up her job, but she did consider it. Then all hell broke loose. One evening Jake exploded because she was still working in the shed. When she insisted on finishing what she was doing, he hit her, knocked her to the floor, grabbed the nearly finished canvas, threw it on the floor and stomped on it.

"I gave you everything you wanted. You have the freedom to work here everyday. Is it too much to expect you to give me your full attention at night? I work hard and I come home expecting ..."

She tuned him out while she dabbed at the blood from her lip. She'd heard it all before.

That night after making sure he was asleep, she packed her suitcase and hid it under the bed. He left for work early. She had time to pack her computer, iPad, her chargers and a few clothes before leaving for work. She asked for some emergency time off. That evening she drove to Geneva. She scanned the Internet for a job, knowing that her savings would quickly be eaten up by hotel costs.

She had contacted her mother once and, as expected, her mother urged her to go back to Jake and try to work it out. She couldn't believe that he did the things Claire accused him of. She refused to tell her mother her whereabouts.

Then one day at the hotel breakfast, she heard people talking about a farm animal rescue center that needed summer help. She asked for the name and contacted Cracker Box Palace. The pay was little more than room and board, but it would see her through the summer and give her the option to explore new opportunities. She knew Jake would never look for her on a working farm.

CHAPTER SIX

Discover creative solitude.
Carl Sandbury

SETH FINISHED THE DAY AND drove in to his family's home in Sodus Point. He had the house to himself for at least a month so he made a ham and cheese sandwich, grabbed his fishing gear and drove to his favorite spot. After he set his poles, he looked across Lake Ontario. He'd never decided if he preferred the lake's New York or Canadian shore more, but both offered great fishing spots. His thoughts turned to stories of his great-great-grandfather and namesake. It always made for great conversation in the fishing community. It would be difficult to be a fisherman in New York and not know the name of Seth Green, the father of fish hatcheries. Rochester even had a street, trail, park and island named after him.

Seth never cast a line in the lake or river without wondering what New York would have looked like in his ancestor's day. The first Seth Green was born more than two hundred years earlier, in 1817. To think that he, the current Seth, fished today because the Seneca Indians taught his great-great grandfather their secrets all those years ago. He'd developed an interest in history after hearing that story. When he was young, he imagined having Indian friends who would teach him. He took pride in his heritage and wanted to make his own contributions to his home state. He felt that he could do so by working at Cracker Box Palace. He'd always been most at home in the outdoors. This job gave him the opportunity to help animals and spend his days on a farm.

With a couple of walleye in hand, Seth returned home in time to grill his catch and have a tasty dinner. He spent the better part of an hour catching up with his online courses from Syracuse University. Afterwards, he finished the book he'd been reading about Teddy

Roosevelt. He spent twenty minutes doing some stretching exercises, while reflecting on how he enjoyed his alone time. Seth couldn't see himself ever getting married and having a family. He enjoyed his own pursuits too much. He supposed he should feel some guilt for his selfishness but he never had.

The next morning he drove to the farm, refreshed and ready to meet the day.

RESIDENT OF CRACKER BOX PALACE

CHAPTER SEVEN

You don't choose your family. They are God's gift to you, as you are to them.
Desmond Tutu

"You know the history of the farm, don't you?" Eileen asked Claire.

"I know it has a Shaker heritage and later was owned by a man named Alvah Strong. Cheri bought it from Strong's grandchildren just a few years ago. That's about it."

"That's a start. There are legends about ghosts. Have you heard them?"

"No, haven't heard those stories yet." Claire smiled at the earnest expression on Eileen's face. She was a funny little thing—maybe seven or eight. Just a kid dressed in an old skirt and blouse with simple black slippers. Her straight brown hair hung down, almost to her waist. Where was her mother? She should be wearing jeans and boots.

"It's not a story, Claire. It's real."

"A legend means it may not be real. Who is the ghost?"

"Ghosts. There are several. I want to see them."

"Why? Aren't ghosts supposed to wish you harm?" Claire strove to maintain a straight face through this turn of conversation. She'd seen bad in this world, but she'd never seen a ghost.

"Not always. That's why I'm here." Eileen didn't understand her fascination with the spirit world but she'd felt it as long as she could remember. Even as a happy child before she'd found out she was adopted, she'd been the kid who loved ghost stories. Not the scary ones that kids share at Halloween, but the ones about ghosts that wander the world because their souls can't rest.

When her parents had told her they adopted her, she became convinced that her real parents still searched for her. She made up stories about her imaginary family. They were always ghosts that couldn't find her. She remembered the day she'd told Sharon, her best friend in fourth grade. Sharon had laughed. "Even if they were ghosts, they'd never be looking for you, silly," she taunted.

"Yes, they would."

"Why would they? They didn't want you then. Why would they want you now?" Shock and pain had ripped through Eileen's heart. She imagined a knife would have hurt less. Then the tears came. She sobbed and even though Sharon apologized, the damage had been done. They would never be best friends again. More importantly, Eileen would ever after have to wonder why her parents hadn't wanted her.

When she asked her adoptive parents, she saw the hurt and fear in their eyes. It was the fear that bothered her. Why? What were they afraid of?

The memories became jumbled. She remembered a farm, her dad's horse and buggy, and apples. She could still taste the juicy first bite each fall. There had been hayrides and a little schoolhouse. Then her memories changed. She saw an old car and listened to a radio. Everything became muddled into a past she didn't recognize.

Eileen recalled the first time she'd realized she was different. Her parents had taken her to a doctor who asked her lots of questions. Her father grew upset every time she told one of her "wild stories" as he called them. The doctor had cautioned him to be patient. "She has an overactive imagination," he'd told her parents.

Nothing had been the same since she contracted the fever. Eileen knew that she had died, but on days like today, she'd been able to assume her human form and talk to Claire. But nothing changed. She had no control of her appearances, only of her mind. Her past was still a jumble of nonsense and she still searched for her parents, especially for her mother.

"Eileen, are you all right?" Claire's concern reached her.

"Yes, I'm tired. I'll see you later." She turned around and noticed that she had been in a horse barn.

* * *

Claire shook the confusion from her brain. In the middle of a conversation, Eileen had clammed up and mentally gone somewhere else. Claire understood that people lost themselves in thought, but she'd never had someone so obviously leave the present. Should she be worried about her? Should she mention it to Cheri? She certainly didn't want to do anything that would hurt Eileen. She seemed lost.

CHAPTER EIGHT

Be cheerful, be cheerful, be cheerful!
Mother Ann Lee, founder of the Shakers

CORNELL UNIVERSITY. ELENA REYES STILL couldn't believe she had been accepted. Add to that the thrill of a summer job at Cracker Box Palace and life looked great. What a change. Last summer she'd spent her time on South Padre Island, enjoying the beaches and volunteering at Sea Turtle Inc. She learned about sea life and habitat loss for wildlife.

This summer she would concentrate on farm animals, apple orchards and Lake Ontario. She already loved the pastoral beauty of the countryside.

Her primary work would be with the goats, sheep and the lone alpaca. However, Cheri offered her the opportunity to assist Sara and Claire in the horse barn. She had helped clean the barn and feed the animals. Two of the goats tagged along wherever she went. She spent some time playing with them. She had time to go to the horse barn and talk to Sara before the day ended. When she entered the barn, she found Claire in the tack room.

"Hi, I'm Elena Reyes. Is Sara around?"

"She just left. Aren't you one of the new volunteers?"

"Yes, this is my second day. I've been assigned to the sheep and goats."

"I'm Claire and I've been assigned to the horse barn. Are you the one who's going to help us?"

"Yes. I guess I have to wait until tomorrow to meet with Sara."

"Feel free to hang out with the horses and me for a while if you want to. I'm still learning what to do. Where are you from?" Claire reached for a currycomb and dandy brush.

"Missouri. I'll be a freshman at Cornell this fall and I wanted to get a head start adapting to New York. How about you?"

"I needed a job and they were hiring. I really like it here so far. I'm finding horses are easier to deal with than people."

"Probably so," Elena laughed. "I've always loved animals. I want to major in biotech so I thought this would be a good summer job."

"I think you came to the right place. I already love it here. By the way, have you met Stormy?"

"No, who is that?"

"Stormy is our resident stallion. Come with me and meet him. He's one of our celebrities."

"I think I may have read about him in your literature. Wasn't he poisoned or something?" Claire grabbed some treats and they walked over to his pasture.

"Yes, he was moving up in the racing world before someone poisoned him and two other horses. They were all treated at the Cornell Vet College but he was the only one to survive. When his owner passed, his widow asked Cheri to take him in. He's getting older so he will live out his days with us here."

"He's beautiful, but doesn't he get lonely by himself?"

"No, stallions have their own territories. Besides, he gets plenty of attention. Just watch. When people visit, they almost always spend time with him and he loves the treats. See." Stormy nibbled the treats from Claire's hand.

"Maybe it's easier for animals than people." Elena tucked her long black hair behind her ears and adjusted her cap. "My parents live separately. They don't talk of being separated but Mom lives in Jefferson City, Missouri, and Dad lives in Kansas City. He travels a lot with his work. I've always thought both are lonely, but as a kid, I guess I didn't really understand their choice. They seem happy."

A pall of loneliness floated above Claire. She didn't have an answer for Elena because she had none for herself.

"I'm sorry for boring you with my family problems." Embarrassment flushed heat into Elena's face.

"You're not. I'm sorry. I was thinking of my own life. I left my boyfriend. That's why I'm here."

"Oh," Elena wished she had better conversational skills. She could think of nothing to say.

"Hey, we're getting too serious here. We better leave or we'll have to get more treats for Stormy." Claire turned away from the fence.

As they walked back to the horse barn, Claire shared stories of some of the other horses. They reached the horse barn just as

Elliott came out the door. "Claire, I was looking for you. Who's your new friend?"

"This is Elena, a summer intern. Elena, meet Elliott."

After exchanging pleasantries, Elena left to check on her goats and sheep. Claire wanted to finish her work, grab a cold bottle of water and head home to shower.

Elliott wanted company. "Would you like to drive in to Captain Jack's for a drink and dinner? It's a beautiful day to enjoy a sunset.'

"Thanks but I think I'll just have a quiet evening. I have some reading to catch up on."

"Come on, Claire. You have to have fun sometime."

"Maybe another time." She walked away but he followed her.

"I'm not going to give up, you know. Sooner or later, I know you'll have dinner with me."

"We'll see." *How do you get through to someone like him,* she wondered. *Is he that sure of himself?* He definitely possessed charm and good looks. Problem was, she had seen that same cocky look in Jake. She had fallen for it once, but never again.

RESIDENT OF CRACKER BOX PALACE

CHAPTER NINE

1841

A flower bloomed already wilting. Beginning its life with an early ending.
R.J. Gonzales (from www.wiseoldsayings.com)

EILEEN HURT ALL OVER AND she was so hot, hotter than standing in front of the fireplace. She couldn't lie still but it hurt to move. Where was her mother? She saw orange butterflies dancing around a beautiful lady in a blue dress. A butterfly lit on her shoulder. Eileen loved the orange on the vibrant blue. She felt sad when the butterfly flitted away. Maybe it would light again.

"Eileen, honey, can you hear me?"

Eileen heard the distant voice. Maybe it was her mother. She fought the lethargy to open her eyes. Her heart cracked when she saw, not the beautiful lady, but the woman who had lied her whole life. Until the last two weeks of her eight years, she believed this kind woman was her mother. But the woman wasn't kind, after all. Why had she pretended?

"Eileen, I need to give you a spoonful of water."

She closed her eyes and wished for the lady and the butterflies. She tried to block out her friend Sharon's words. "They didn't want you..." Where was the butterfly lady? Maybe she was her real mother.

"Eileen, your mother needs you to wake up and try to drink some water." A man's voice. Her pretend father? She had loved calling him "Daddy." She shoved back memories of riding on his shoulders. No, he wasn't her daddy. She didn't think much about her real father. It was always her mother—her beautiful and happy mother. If her mother were here, she'd take a drink of water. She would do anything to make her real mother smile.

"I'm so worried about her." Eileen heard the words but hardened her heart. She wanted to bring back her real mother and the butterflies. Maybe they could live in a butterfly garden. Her real mother would keep her from hurting and she'd fan away the heat. Then they'd dance together in the garden.

"The doctor will be here soon. Maybe he can get some water down her." The man who called himself her daddy brushed her hair away from her face. Eileen's heart almost melted until she remembered the lies. Why hadn't they told her? Why did it have to be her so-called best friend? She bet no other parents lied to their children. If only she didn't hurt so much, she'd ask them why again.

Her pretend mother had cried and her pretend daddy had tried to comfort both of them. "We planned to tell you when you were older," he said. "You are our daughter. We wanted you so badly and God sent you to us."

Eileen wished that were true. They had probably felt sorry for a child whose mother threw her away.

"Your mother died when you were born," her pretend mom said.

She didn't believe it. She would know if her real mother was dead. But if she wasn't dead, why did she give her away? Can people just throw away a baby? Eileen's head hurt. She didn't want to be sad. She didn't want to live with pretend parents. She wanted the butterfly lady to come back.

* * *

Jethro Barker had ridden hard to ask the doctor to come to call on his niece. He had visited his brother, Jonathan, yesterday, and found out that Eileen was sick with a fever. He had seen the fear in Jonathan's eyes. When Agnes came bustling down the stairs, he saw panic written all over her face.

"She's burning up. I've washed her with cold cloths over and over. We can't get any liquid down her." Tears spilled onto her cheeks. "She's our baby. We can't lose her."

"Now, now, Agnes. Surely God won't take her from us. He knows how hard we prayed to find a child."

"I'll ride into Sodus and get the doctor," Jethro offered.

"Thank you," Jonathan said. "You know we have a new doctor now that old Doc Montgomery passed on?"

"Yes, I haven't met him but I will find him and hopefully bring him back."

"I guess we should have told her how she came to live with us," Agnes dabbed her eyes with her apron. "I've got to get back upstairs with her. Please hurry, Jethro. Our little girl is terribly sick and I'm so afraid it's the deadly kind of fever. And to think she got sick right after that Sharon told her about the adoption."

"I'm on my way." Jethro buttoned up his coat, grabbed his hat off the rack and left.

Jethro rode his horse hard as he thought of that poor little girl. Eileen was the kind of child that brought sunshine into everyone's day. Happy and carefree, in a quiet sort of way. So different from his loud, rambunctious boys. Even they had fallen under her spell though. She could get them to sit quietly and read to her or listen to her stories. The girl had quite an imagination, too. Always talking about a little lamb that followed her around, that no one else ever saw. She named him Luke. When someone caught her talking to herself, she always claimed she and Luke were having a conversation.

A wet snow began to fall. By the time he reached the doctor's house in Alton, his coat was wet and his hat covered. He knocked on the door but no one answered. He waited and tried again. He stomped his feet to warm them and tried a third time. The doctor must be out on a call.

He rode his horse down the road to the tavern, only to find out from the owner that Doc Godfrey had been called out to a problem birthing in Sodus.

"When will he be back?" Jethro knew that was a question with no answer.

"Don't know. Want to leave a message?"

"Yes, my brother's child is bad sick with the fever. His name is Jonathan Barker and he lives on a farm between here ..."

"I know him and I know his farm. He brings tomatoes in all summer and peaches in the fall. I know his place. I'll let Doc Godfrey know as soon as he gets back."

Jethro rode back to the farm laden down with the fear the doctor would be too late for Eileen.

* * *

Jonathan held Agnes in his arms. "God will look after her now." His darling Eileen looked beautiful, but he knew she'd breathed her last. The pain left her face and her fevered tossing and turning ceased.

Agnes's huge gulping sobs broke his heart again. Funny how a man can survive such pain. He knew he had to get out to the barn and take care of his chores. Life hadn't stopped, even though their little world had collapsed. He helped Agnes to their bed and told her to lie down and rest. There would be plenty of time to lay out the girl when he finished feeding the livestock.

On the way out to the barn, Jonathan saw a white lamb standing below Eileen's window. He called to it but it didn't move. Well, if it didn't follow him to the barn, he would come back and get it. When he finished his chores, the lamb was nowhere in sight.

He walked into the house to help Agnes with the most horrible of chores that a couple could face—the laying out of a beloved child.

RESIDENT OF CRACKER BOX PALACE

CHAPTER TEN

Present Day

The most important history is the history we make today.
Henry Ford

CHERI ROLOSON STEPPED OUT ONTO the back porch of the boarding house. She smiled as she watched two horses playing in the pasture. She and Burt had come so far with this dream of theirs. It was June, the air still cool but the warmth of the sun coaxed the flowers into bloom. A perfect day to dream about the future and give thanks for the crew they had assembled for the summer. God bless volunteers and interns! When money was tight and need was great, they kept the dream alive.

Cheri thought about her dad. She'd inherited her love of horses and empathy for all animals from him. He'd taught her so much and he planted the seed for the dream she and Burt shared today. Watching the horses play reminded her of Melvin. Had it only been twenty-some years? It seemed like a lifetime—and only yesterday!

She walked back to her makeshift office, brought her computer to life and continued editing the grant material. How many times had she told the story of Melvin? It always sounded the same but each time it brought a new sense of purpose.

Cheri read over the material already written:

"One day in the early 1990s, Walt Roloson, a lifelong lover and trainer of horses was called on to help a group of Saddle-bred horses. At that time, Walt had been working with green and troubled horses for about 50 years. The owner of this once spectacular farm was aging and suffered from Alzheimer's and the horses had fallen

into neglect, shut into a barn from which some had never come out. They actually had to be taught to leave their stalls. Walt brought with him a few helping hands for the task. Among them were his daughter, Cheri, and her husband, Burt Madison. Among the horses they taught to accept and lead on a halter that day, was a young colt."

"Cheri, are you in your office?"

"Yes, I'll be right out." Burt had finished his work early. They'd have some time together. Maybe they'd go in to the Franklin House Tavern in Sodus Point for an early dinner. It was fish fry night and a favorite for both of them.

After they found a table and placed their orders, their conversation turned to the farm.

"What were you working on today?"

"More PR material. I was editing the last flyer when you came in."

"The story's still the same," Burt laughed.

"I know but we're getting ready to advertise for Moosic Fest. Just looking for some fresh ideas for our flyers. The first horse camp is over and the kids loved it."

"Some of them know nothing about horses when they get here. It's a great experience for them."

"We have a couple more weeks scheduled. I hope they go as well." Their fish dinners arrived and conversation slowed. They relished the time to relax away from the farm, but it was never far from their minds. Raising money to support their work occupied most of Cheri's time these days. "I'm so happy with the staff we have now. I feel comfortable turning over responsibility to them."

"And it looks like this year's new volunteers are working out. What's the story on Elliott?"

"He's here at the insistence of his dad and uncle. I was afraid he wouldn't work out but so far, he's okay. I think it's a real lifestyle change for him."

Burt laughed. "Yeah, I'd say so. From the CEO's kid to just a farmhand shoveling manure."

"The harder they fall, huh? He's got a lot to learn but so far, no complaints. Sara thinks he's full of himself."

"How is Claire doing? She's quiet, isn't she?"

"She's doing fine. She loves the horses and has fallen for Jewel. That's great because Jewel still needs lots of attention to continue her healing." Cheri's mind flashed back to the first time she'd seen the poor horse. She hadn't been sure they could save her. Now it looked like Jewel would be another of their success stories.

"Jewel reminds you of Melvin, doesn't she? She's even close to the same copper color."

"Yes, but she's missing that white stripe down her face. There will never be another Melvin." Just the thought of him served up a heaping dose of nostalgia. He was the horse that started it all. "I wonder if there'd even be a Cracker Box Palace today if we hadn't rescued Melvin."

Burt shook his head. "I think so. There are so many farm animals that need to be rescued. I think you and your dad would have found a 'Melvin' somewhere."

"You're probably right," Cheri agreed. But she couldn't picture their lives without Melvin in it. She smiled at the thought of his funny ears, the way they curved in. The smile faded as she recalled how near death he had been. He'd been so weak when they found him that he couldn't stand long enough to trim his hooves. They'd brought him home and nursed him. In return, he changed their lives forever.

Burt and Cheri drove home sharing memories of some of the animals they had passed through the farm. Some had gone to new homes but some had spent their remaining days at the farm. "I'm so glad we have the memorial grounds. It's such a peaceful place."

"Me too. We've come a long way, haven't we?" Burt said as he turned in their driveway.

The phone disrupted their quiet conversation.

"The main house is on fire again!" Jeff shouted. "I've called the fire department."

"Is everyone all right?" Cheri heard the panic in her voice. "How bad is it?"

"If help gets here, I think we can put it out before it spreads."

"Be there in a few minutes."

"I heard," Burt said. He turned the truck around and headed for the farm.

Jeff had organized a crew by the time they arrived. Flames licked the walls and the roof but it wasn't the horrible roar of fire that had totally destroyed the third floor in 2009. The house had been uninhabitable since then but the main danger now would be the threat to the nearby barns. The farm had seen its share of fires since the days of the Shakers.

The fire truck arrived before Burt had turned off the engine. They both jumped out and ran to Jeff.

"I think it's dying down already," Jeff yelled.

The crackling of burning wood filled Cheri's ears. She looked up at the flames licking upward toward the trees. Thank God it had rained yesterday. She watched, through a daze, as the firemen unrolled the hose and water began to spray toward the flames. The frightened neighing of horses penetrated her consciousness. "Where's Sara?"

"In the barn," Jeff yelled.

Cheri ran toward the barn. There was nothing she could do to stop the fire but she could help calm the horses. A loud cacophony of animal voices filled the air. "Please help the animals," she called to the volunteers who stood watching the flames.

"A cat. I see a cat in the house, inside the door," Claire yelled. "We have to get the cat." She ran toward the house. Two big arms grabbed her from behind.

"Stop. You can't go in there."

"The cat. I have to ...".

"I'll go," Elliott ran past her. He stumbled on the first step.

"Stop!"

Elliott turned and looked into the face of a fireman. "Get back. I'll get the cat."

"I ..."

"Don't be a fool! Get back." The firemen pushed him aside and ran across the porch. He opened the door and saw the cat was little more than a frightened kitten. It's hiss and self-defense was weak and he quickly picked it up and ran back out the door. The heat was unbearable but the noise was less than when they arrived. He judged they already had the fire under control. He handed the kitten to Claire. She ran back away from the house, sat on the grass and stroked the shaking kitten. "It's Jenny," she said as Elliott sat down beside her. "She'll be all right."

"Thank God you saw her in time." He tentatively patted Jenny's head. The kitten backed away from his touch. "Sorry. I guess she's still scared."

"She just needs some quiet time to readjust. I'll sit here and hold her until she's calm and then I'll let her go. I'm sure she has her own safe place to hide." Claire continued to gently stroke Jenny and murmur soft words. Claire looked up to see the flames were no longer in sight.

The firemen continued to hose the fire. Jeff and his crew had left to help with the animals. Slowly the noises from the barns and fields quieted as the animals sensed the danger had passed.

Elliott stayed by Claire's side.

"Why aren't you helping with the other animals?" She immediately chided herself for being unkind. After all, he had been willing to risk his own safety to rescue Jenny. "I'm sorry. I shouldn't have said that."

"That's okay. I'm just worrying about this little kitten and hadn't thought about anything else."

"I know. I appreciate it. The poor little thing had to be so frightened. I can't imagine the heat and smoke that she endured. Thank you for trying."

"She'll be all right because of you. I don't think anyone else saw her." He didn't mention that the fireman would probably have checked the building anyway.

"Oh, and thank you for stopping me. I acted before I thought."

"That's okay but I didn't stop you."

"But ... I thought it was you." She could still feel the strength in the arms that had stopped her. She wished she knew who to thank.

The firemen remained at the house until well after dark. The fire was out but the acrid smell of embers and burnt wood still signaled danger. It was too dark to assess the damage but at first light, they would have someone out here to study that and the cause of the fire. The old Shaker-built house may be beyond repair.

***

I didn't start this fire. I admit that I've caused trouble on the farm before, but I suspect this fire was an accident. Not only am I not guilty, but I actually stopped a probable injury. Today I have been reliving some of the Shaker history, hoping to restore my faith and turn my thoughts to the love I once had for this piece of land.

We accomplished a lot in the few short years we lived here. I had not yet united with the Shakers when we first packaged seed but it became a thriving business. I loved the days I helped deliver the boxes of seeds to the surrounding towns. I once helped deliver a wagon load of boxes to the Erie Canal, where they were shipped to Rochester.

New Yorkers grow up on fresh fruits, and we produced some of the best I've ever tasted. I worked the apple orchards several times during picking season. I actually looked forward to those fall days and the apples that tasted like a cool breeze on my tongue, hinting of the winter winds to come.

Maybe it was the fire that started me thinking about the blacksmith shop. I dreaded the work. The heat from the forge scorched my skin right through my clothes as we made the shoes for the oxen. Making the shoes was harder than fitting them on the poor beasts. I never mastered working the red hot, soft metal into shoes or tools. I was always thankful when I rotated out of that work into another. There's good and bad in the way the Shakers scheduled our work. Every month we would move from one assignment to another. The good was that we learned about all functions of the farm. The bad was that we learned about those we either hated or had no talent for.

I still laugh at the thought of our gift exchanges at Christmas and throughout the year. We gave and received imaginary gifts. It sounded crazy when it was first explained to me, but I grew to love it. Never a graceful dancer, I appreciated the 'gift' of a pair of socks to 'put warmth and grace into my dancing.' The most meaningful gift I gave was to Mary Ann. I handed her an imaginary sunflower to 'bring sunshine and beauty to her day.'

Those first years with the Shakers filled me with happiness, faith and hope. I never dreamt it would end as it did.

* * *

"Fire is the gift that keeps on giving here," Elliott announced on the boarding house porch. "Seems like it's another wiring fire. Something ate through the wire, probably a rat."

"Who told you that?" Seth asked.

"Cheri. That's the report from the fire chief. Bad wiring."

"I guess that's better than ghosts setting it," Sara laughed.

"Ghosts? Do we have ghosts here?" Elena found it hard to contain her excitement. She remembered the ghost she had seen several years ago at the Missouri State Penitentiary. "I hope it's a ghost we can communicate with."

"You've been reading too many novels," Elliott scoffed. "There are no ghosts."

"Oh, but you're wrong," Sara said. "This old farm has its ghosts, supposedly dating back to the Shaker days."

"Have you seen them?" Elena asked.

"No, but others have. Cheri says the former owner, Griff Mangan, has dealt with them. He was convinced one of them set the big house on fire back in 2009."

"Wow, Griff Mangan? Paragraphs on South Padre Island?"

"What?"

"I know Griff. He and his wife, Joni, own the bookstore on the island. I knew he was from New York, but I never made the connection. Wow, that's unreal! He saw the ghosts?"

Claire walked up to the porch. "What am I missing out on?"

"Ghosts. Did you know this place has ghosts?" Elena's excitement brought a smile to Claire's face.

"I heard something about it, but I don't really believe in ghosts," she answered.

"I do. I've seen a ghost before and I know they are real people, or the spirits of real people. I've researched it and our world is filled with spirits that move back and forth between their time and now."

"And why would they do that?" Elliott asked.

"Unfinished business, in most cases. Or loneliness or revenge. There are many reasons. You have to look at individual cases to understand."

"Right. So I need to find a ghost and ask it whether it's lonely or revengeful? Give me a break."

"Calm down, Elliott," Seth said. "It sounds like Elena is really interested. Tell us about the ghost you saw at the prison. Where was it, Montana?"

"Missouri. It was the ghost of a woman who had been murdered. I think ghosts need closure of some kind before they can move on."

"Or maybe they come back for a reason." Claire hadn't had time to think about ghosts but she'd learned the hard way that anything is possible. A few years ago she would have sworn that a loving boyfriend could never turn into a mean, abusive man.

"I think you're right. Has anyone here seen them?" Elena waited.

Her phone rang. It was her dad. She answered it, wishing she'd had more time for someone to answer her question. She walked down the stairs and down the driveway as she filled her dad in on her day at the farm.

"The animals are so sweet, Dad. I'm working with the sheep and goats. We have the cutest alpaca. I took a picture and I'll message it to you. I know you'd love it here."

"It certainly sounds like you are adapting to New York."

"I am. The barn where the goats and sheep live is an old Shaker barn. It was built in the 1830s. Can you believe that?"

"What an opportunity for you to learn some New York history too. Listen, I wanted to tell you that I'm headed back down to South Padre Island. I hope to see Hap and Peg while I'm there."

"Awesome! I wish I were with you. Tell them I miss them. And go to Paragraphs. This farm once belonged to Griff's family. Can you believe that?"

"What a coincidence. I'll be sure to talk to Griff, and I'll tell Hap you're too busy to do research on another murder investigation. You need a relaxing summer."

After she told her dad she loved him, she hung up. She hadn't thought of Hap and Peg Lynch since she'd been here. Luke, their little white Bichon, would love the farm. She could picture him chasing after the goats.

She sent a quick text to Hap before she stuck her phone back in her pocket. "Call me when you have time."

* * *

"Elena just texted me," Hap called out.

"Any news?" Peg walked out onto the porch. "Where's Luke?"

"He's out in the yard checking out the ducks. No news from Elena. She wants me to call her when I have a chance."

Peg laughed, "What better chance than now?"

"I'm thinking about it. Seems like there's always trouble after I talk to Elena."

"You're just enjoying doing nothing, for a change."

"Truthfully, I am. I always have that itch to get involved in a case but this quiet time is great. I think Luke is enjoying it too."

"Go ahead and call Elena. I just want to make sure she's okay."

Hap set down his iced tea and picked up his phone. Elena answered on the first ring.

"You live with your phone in your hand?"

"Nice to talk to you too, Hap."

"Peg's worried about you." He didn't want to admit how much he enjoyed talking to her.

"I'm fine. I'm loving Cracker Box Palace and I've only been here a few days. I adore the animals. They are so special. Some of them had been horribly abused. You would love the people here. Cheri is the owner and she's great. She cares so deeply about the animals. New York is gorgeous. The greens are greener and the trees are bigger. I hope I can help some of them before school starts. You know how excited I am about Cornell. Can you believe I'll be there?"

"Whew, slow down, girl." Hap wished he had half her energy. The girl did love life. She was smart, too. She had helped him out on a couple of cases since he'd met her in Jefferson City a few years ago.

"I just remembered why I texted you. Dad's headed back down to South Padre. I hope you get to see him. By the way, how's Luke?"

"Luke's fine. He's watching the ducks right now. I can't believe he hasn't chased one yet."

"He's probably afraid they'll chase him back." Elena remembered laughing at Luke as he bounced through the grass as fast as his little short legs would carry him. "I miss Luke. You and Peg, too. I wish you could visit here. New York is beautiful and the people are so friendly."

"I'm happy your summer is off to a good start. Sounds like you'll be a lot cooler than your dad will be down here. Tell him to give us a call. I have a fishing trip booked in Canada, but other than that, we'll be home."

"I'll tell him. Oh, you do know that Griff used to own this farm, didn't you?"

"No, I knew he was from up there, but I didn't make the connection."

"His family owned it, and sold it to Cracker Box Palace."

"She's fine," Hap filled Peg in on the conversation. "Full of energy, as usual. Hard to keep up with her, even on the phone."

"The world is small, isn't it?"

"Definitely. I knew Griff and Joni lived in New York before they moved to South Padre and opened the bookstore, but I never made that connection."

"Me neither," Peg said. "I heard him talk about the family farm several times. I think his grandfather bought it and when he died, Griff and his mother ran it. I'm happy they moved to Texas and opened Paragraphs."

"I agree."

* * *

Elliott watched Claire, and liked what he saw. Maybe it was the long wispy caramel-colored hair or the slender figure. Whatever, she possessed a fragility. She needed someone to take care of her, to cherish her. It might make for an interesting summer. He followed her down to the pasture.

"Do you know how many horses we have?" he asked.

"Sara said we have thirty-four now. I guess they come in and then get adopted out."

"That's a good thing, isn't it?"

"To be adopted, yes. But the reasons they came here, not so sure."

"What do you mean?"

"Most are here because of neglect or abuse. No animal should suffer either of those."

"I see what you mean." Elliott had never thought about the animals. He'd been sent here as punishment, so in a way, they were like him. All in a place they never would have chosen.

"Look at those two playing," he pointed to a couple of horses running along the fence. He slipped his other arm over her shoulders.

"They're so graceful." Claire didn't appreciate Elliott's forwardness. She shrugged out from under his arm and moved away. He followed.

"Sorry," he said. "Just being friendly."

"Please don't. You made me uncomfortable."

"Are you shy?" He pictured himself drawing her out of her insecurity. Timid girls loved attention and he was willing to shower Claire with plenty of it. The prize would be worth it.

"Not really. I just like my privacy."

"Understood." Elliott kept talking about the horses as they walked back to the barn. He had time.

Sara was busy cleaning a stall when they entered the barn. "Just in time to help," she motioned to another pitchfork and a bucket filled with water.

"Guess I'd better get back to work," Elliott hedged.

"There's plenty of work here if you want to lend a hand."

"Thanks, but Jeff is probably looking for me."

Sara watched him leave. Was that relief she noticed on Claire's face? "He's not a problem, is he?"

"Nothing I can't handle." Claire shrugged off the earlier encounter.

After finishing in the barn, she decided to go back to her room. She noticed Eileen walking toward the old house. She called her name at the same time a car drove in. The driver asked if he and his daughter could look at the goats. "Sure," she said. They got out of the car and Claire pointed to the goats.

"Oh, we've been here before. Thanks." They walked toward the goats.

Claire looked for Eileen but she was nowhere in sight.

* * *

After dinner that evening, Cheri asked the new staff members, "Do you know about the Shaker history?"

"I read on the website that it was called the Shaker tract because they lived here back in the 1800s," Elena said. "I read a little bit about their religion."

"What about you, Claire?"

"No, I haven't read anything."

"Before the summer's out, you're sure to hear the story. The Shakers bought the farm in the 1820s and lived here about ten years before they sold it."

"Why did they sell it?" Elena asked.

"The Erie Canal opened in 1825 and some men wanted to build a canal that would connect it to Lake Ontario. The Shakers didn't want their farm divided so they sold it and over the next couple of years, moved to Groveland, about fifty miles from here."

"Where did the name Shakers come from?" Claire asked.

"Their dancing. I guess today we would call them Pentecostal. They were very demonstrative, singing and dancing. In their fervor, their dancing would become frenzied."

"Sounds a little strange. Were they Christians?"

"Yes, they believed in Jesus, but they felt that their leader, Mother Ann Lee, represented the female side of Christ. They believed in complete equality of the sexes years before the legal system recognized it. They lived in a communal society, preaching peace and hard work. They became known for their woodworking and their farming. They were the first to package flower seeds and distributed them throughout the area. They also invented several tools, such as the circular saw and a flat broom. I think they invented the clothes pin too, but I'm not too sure you young people even know what a clothes pin is." Cheri smiled at the thought.

"I can't say I ever used one, but I know what they are," Claire said.

"Didn't they believe in celibacy? Makes you wonder how they could keep the church alive." Elliott's joke fell flat.

"Conversions! That's how. There were plenty of people searching for life's answers and the Shakers appealed to many of them." Cheri answered. "But you're right. They practiced celibacy. Men and women lived in separate quarters and most of their functions were divided as well."

"Can't believe that worked," Elliott responded.

"It did for some, and not for others. While they were here, they had lots of people join and then decide the life was too hard for them. Communal living can be hard, too. People don't own anything, even the clothes they wear. It all belongs to the group."

"I couldn't live like that," Elliott laughed.

"I don't think I could either, but you have to respect those that did. They had enough faith to make the necessary sacrifices," Elena argued.

"Whatever," Elliott shrugged.

"In any case, their history has been kept alive because they left their mark on the area. Because of the buildings they constructed here on the farm, we are listed on the National Register of Historic Places."

"I had no idea of the history here," Claire said.

CHAPTER ELEVEN

Horace

Revenge is a mean pleasure.

Henry C. Blin, Canterbury, NH
(from Simple Wisdom by Kathleen Mahoney)

I wandered around the old house. Ever since the big fire, the one in 2009, I've been depressed. Everything I had done had been for Mary Ann. How did you right a wrong after so many years? Sure, I'd get mad and do something stupid but that never solved any problems. If only Mary Ann would confide in me, I could help her. Whenever we crossed paths, which was seldom, a cool-ness swept through the air. I longed to reach out and touch her, to hold her like a child and comfort her, but I recognized the impossibility.

As the years passed, I had grown to hate Eaton even more. I found it difficult to comprehend how we had ever become friends. I could blame Eaton for every bad act I committed, but I knew the guilt lay with my inability to control my anger. I no longer knew if the anger was direct-ed toward Eaton or myself. I should have spoken when I saw their attraction deepening. I could have warned Mary Ann, but I became tongue-tied every time I tried.

Our whole world would have been different if I hadn't been so gutless all those years ago. Depression once again darkened all my thoughts until I could only think of disap-pearing into nothingness.

The spirit world was alive with noise today. Ha, poor choice of words, definitely not alive. No, it was the mournful calling out from other spirits. I have always been so caught up in my own angry world that I have failed to notice the pain of other spirits. Each of them would have a story of why they couldn't let go. I suspected sometimes it was their choice and other times, God's. I wondered how many of them were Shakers. So many had joined and so many had left. If the spirits belonged to Shakers, would they be the ones who left? I believe any faithful Shaker would enter the kingdom of God immediately after death. If that were true, then only the sinners remained.

FARMHOUSE

CHAPTER TWELVE

Abusive people don't change no matter what they say.
www.seethetriumph.org

JAKE VACILLATED BETWEEN REMORSE AND anger. Sure, he was sorry he had hit Claire hard enough to make her fall. But it had been her fault. She had a smart mouth and she had gotten caught up in all this liberal thinking. He worked hard to make her happy and then she gets those crazy ideas about an art career.

He needed to find her. He would teach her not to leave again. She'd promised never to leave him. Yet, a little disagreement and she's gone. At least she hadn't run home to mama. Her mama would be on his side. He had learned long ago to turn the charm on for a girl's mother. Rebecca thought he was the perfect match for her daughter. He bet she spent half her time planning a wedding. That would happen when he was ready, and not before. Now, he had to find Claire and bring her home. He knew the drill. Plenty of apologies, flowers and a nice dinner. A few days of undivided attention and she'd be back where he wanted her.

He remembered when they had met. Claire was the featured artist in a Syracuse gallery. He had stopped to ask her about her intricate paintings. She actually did nice work, but it had been that red top that flowed down past her slender hips that interested him. Or rather what was underneath. Red highlights in her light brown hair added to the appeal. Just a shade deeper than strawberry blonde. He had hung around till the end of the show and she had agreed to have a cup of coffee at the diner down the street.

For their first date, they drove to Letchworth Park, spent the day and then drove back to Syracuse for dinner at a barbecue restaurant. For another date, he had taken her to Dinosaur BBQ in Rochester. Soon they were meeting along the Erie Canal for evening strolls.

Couldn't get anymore romantic than that. Within six months, she had agreed to move in with him. He'd kept her so busy she had very little time to work on her art. He had wrongly assumed that he was more important to her than some crazy hobby. For the first couple months she had been content to re-decorate the apartment. Jake had to admit she had an eye for design. At first he had been afraid she'd add clutter, but her taste ran to simplicity and class. He had to hand it to her. She had turned his home into something that could be shown in a magazine.

Then she wanted to move in all her supplies. When he objected, she cried and he relented. He ended up building her a "she-shed" in the back yard where she could keep all the junk she wanted. The trouble began when she started spending hours out there. He argued that she should only work on her art when he was busy. Once he came home, she should spend her time with him. She argued that she only got home an hour before him.

He hated thinking about her. She should be here, and she would. He'd find her and bring her back. She belonged to him.

CHAPTER THIRTEEN

Those who scatter seeds of courtesy and kindness
Reap the blossoms of friendship.

FRIENDSHIPS FORMED BETWEEN THE VOLUNTEERS and staff as the days flew by. Everyone loved the days when one of the animals would go to a new forever home. They dreaded the days when a new animal would arrive, abused or neglected. Often the animal would be afraid to leave its stall or to eat.

"This poor horse is skin and bones. How will we get her to eat?" Elena stood outside the stall.

"Lots of love and patience," Sara said as she slowly entered the stall. "Her name is Diamond. Cornell just released her to us and we have a lot of work to do. She is healed physically but now we need to help her heal emotionally. First, we have to get her to accept our touch. Cheri says she was abused, almost killed, by her owner. She panics whenever a man comes near her. It will be up to Claire, you and me to calm her. Once she accepts our touch, she should start to eat, too."

"What can I do now?"

"Stay where you are and gently talk to her. Let her hear the kindness in your voice. Don't yell or talk loudly in the barn. Also, silence your phone. Unexpected noises can frighten her even more."

"Diamond, I love your name. I think you are going to be happy here with us." Elena began a quiet one-sided conversation. She talked while Sara stood quietly in the corner of the stall.

Claire walked into the barn and stood beside Elena. After a few minutes, Sara left the stall. She put a treat on the railing and they walked away. "We'll do this every hour or so throughout the day. Each time you walk by, check on the treat. Hopefully, hunger will drive her to accept it."

They walked over to the porch. Cheri was explaining something to Jeff, Elliott and Seth.

"Hey, did you know we had two cows delivered today? They came from a local farm. I was filling the guys in on the details."

"Are they all right?" Elena asked.

"Yes. Their owner is moving and can't take them, so he called us. Hopefully, we'll let them adapt to their new surroundings, make sure they are healthy and then put them up for adoption. They will probably only be here a few months. How are we doing with Diamond?"

"We are making introductions at this point," Sara answered.

"It will take some time with her, but we have the patience." Cheri thought of the many times they'd replayed this same scene. This one would most likely involve a court case, since it was an obvious case of physical abuse. Animals like Diamond always renewed her commitment and energy.

An anonymous donor had saved Diamond from being put down. He spared no expense in her treatment and sent a $10,000 donation for her care. Everyday Cheri thanked God for the donors who made Cracker Box Palace possible.

* * *

Elena rubbed the tension from her neck as she walked out of the barn and turned toward the goat pasture. She needed to see the expressive faces. Just thinking about the goats brought a smile. Claire, Seth and Elliott, all leaning against the fence, must've had the same thought.

"How are you and the goats getting along?" Seth asked as Elena joined them.

"Fine. These silly guys can be so funny. I can't believe how much they like people. The sheep pretty much ignore me, but the goats think they're my best friends."

"They probably will be by the time the summer is over," Elliott said. "Claire, I need to walk down to the cow barn. Would you like to join me?"

"No, thanks. I have to finish my chores and I want to visit Diamond again."

"Let's drive into Sodus Point after you're finished. We can walk the beach at sunset."

"Not tonight."

"I'd love to go," Elena said.

"Uh ..., anybody else?" Elliott looked around.

"I'll go," Seth said. "Sounds relaxing. Might even take my fishing pole."

"It's going to be fun. Please, Claire, join us. We haven't visited the beach yet."

"All right," Claire laughed. "You convinced me. I'll go. Maybe Seth can catch us tomorrow's dinner."

Elliott confirmed the plans and they all left to finish their work. At least, Elliott thought, I learned how to get Claire to leave the farm with me.

It turned out to be a perfect summer night in Sodus Point. The deck at Captain Jack's offered a beautiful and relaxing view of the bay.

"Have you heard Melvin's story?" Seth asked, after they placed their order. "Cheri went with her dad to rescue some Saddlebred horses that had been seriously neglected. It had gone on so long that they didn't want to leave their stalls. One of them, Melvin, captured Cheri's heart and she spent the next three years rehabilitating him. Then her dad, his name was Walt, decided it was time for him to be put up for adoption. Cheri couldn't let him go. Melvin gets the credit for planting the seeds of Cracker Box Palace in Cheri's mind. It wasn't long before she found other animals that needed her."

"Is Melvin still around?" Elena asked.

"No, but you can bet Cheri thinks of him often. Have you visited the memorial gardens down past the horse pasture?"

"I haven't," Elena said.

"Yes, it's peaceful and I liked reading the names of the animals that are gone," Claire said.

"Good. Elena, check it out. It shows Cheri's respect for the animals who have lived here."

Their burgers arrived and for a while, conversation ceased. As they finished their meals, the talk again centered on the farm until the evening light began to soften the sky. They left and hurried to the beach. Elena wanted to walk the pier out to the lighthouse, so they all joined her.

Elliott cornered Seth. "I want some time with Claire. Can you keep Elena busy?"

"If Claire wants time with you, you won't have to arrange it."

"Come on, buddy. I need your help. I know that once get her alone, she'll warm up to me."

"I don't think so, but I'll help you out this time."

"Thanks, pal."

Seth turned away before he said more than he should. He and Elliott were no pals, but they needed to get along for the sake of the farm.

"Elena, let's just hang out here at the lighthouse and watch the sunset. It's a great place to watch the boats coming in and out of the bay."

"Sounds super, but Claire wants to find the best spot for a sunset photo."

"Elliott is going to drive her up to the old lighthouse. She can get a great shot from there."

"It's beautiful right here. Does she want to go?"

"Sure. If she doesn't, she won't go."

Claire didn't want to leave the others but Elliott raved about the view from the old lighthouse. Before they left the farm, he had quickly looked up the history of Sodus Point and filled her in as he drove.

"There's a historical marker about the War of 1812. I'm not sure why they called it that since they attacked here in 1813. The British landed one night in June, but we repelled them. Then the next morning, they landed again in another part of town and burned almost every building."

"I don't know anything about that war. I hope I have time to read the marker and still get the photos."

"You will. Also, that lighthouse was built in 1825, back before the Shakers came to the farm."

"I read some of that history. I had heard of Shaker furniture but knew nothing about the religion. I find it fascinating that so many forms of religion sprang up in New York. I was brought up in a traditional Protestant home and learned very little about other religions."

"Me, too. Anyway, it's all a part of Sodus Point history. I guess Cracker Box Palace will be written in the history books someday."

"I hope it's around for a long time. The work Cheri does is desperately needed."

"Right, but enough about work and history. We're here so let's enjoy the scenery."

Claire wished she were here alone with her camera, but Elliott followed her every step. "You're giving me claustrophobia," she said.

"Funny."

Claire hadn't meant it to be funny. She concentrated on the magnificent show nature presented over the horizon and took shot after shot. She stayed until the last vestige of color left the sky.

Elliott took her arm and led her back across the lawn. When they got in the car, he turned to her. "Claire, I really like you and I want us to go out together, just the two of us."

"Look, you've been very nice to me, but I'm don't want to get involved in any relationship right now."

LIGHTHOUSE ON SODUS BAY

"I'm just asking for a date. We don't have to get involved if you're not ready. The summer is flying by."

"I know it is, and I am enjoying it. How about you?"

"Changing the subject?" He tried to keep his tone light. "I'm enjoying it since you're part of it. It was my dad and uncle's idea, not mine. I do like the crew we have. But back to you and me."

"There is no 'you and me' and there won't be. Please accept that and let's be friends. I'm sure Elena and Seth are wondering where we are."

"I'm not giving up." Elliott calmed himself. He had never worked so hard to get a girl's attention. Why was he wasting his time on Claire? They made the drive back to the beach in silence and found Seth and Elena sitting on a park bench. Elena carried the conversation on the ride home.

* * *

Each day Claire spent as much time as possible with Diamond. On the third day, she had eaten the treat they left on the railing. Sara considered this a good sign. As she entered the stall, she put another treat on the railing and held one in her hand. She knew Diamond wouldn't take it, but she wanted her to begin to associate her hand and the treat. She spent more time in the stall but didn't directly approach the horse. The fact that Diamond no longer cowered in the corner proved they were making progress. Sara invited Claire into the stall with her.

On the fifth day, Sara walked toward Diamond but didn't touch her. She held out her hand with the treat. When she left, she put the treat on the rail. The horse was beginning to munch on the hay in the stall. Although she had left a bucket of feed each day, it had not been touched.

By the end of the first week, the feed disappeared and Sara had been able to touch Diamond. Claire fell more in love with this wounded horse each day. "I think we're kindred spirits," she told her.

Diamond didn't answer, but Claire understood. She knew the fear and lack of trust that accompanied abuse. She had been there, too. She wanted to spend all her spare time with this horse, and to teach her about love and trust.

"I think she likes you."

Claire turned and found Eileen standing by the next stall. "I haven't seen you around. Where have you been?"

"I've been here. I've seen you."

"Have you been watching Diamond? She's beautiful and I want to help her."

"I know. There are lots of animals here that need help."

Diamond shuffled her feet nervously.

"I wonder what is making her jittery," Claire said.

When Eileen didn't answer, Claire turned to find her gone. She couldn't believe how quiet she was for a kid. She had forgotten to ask Cheri about her.

Seth was walking by when she left the barn. He waited for her and they walked to the boarding house together. He took a couple of bottles of water out of the fridge and offered one to her. As they drank, she filled him in on Diamond's progress.

Later Seth went for a walk, and Elliott caught up with him. "I see you're making time with Claire."

"Sharing water and conversation is hardly making time," Seth answered.

"Well, she's going to be mine before the summer's over."

"Does she know that?"

"I'm just giving you fair warning. So hands off."

"Maybe she doesn't want you, ever think of that?"

"She's playing hard to get. I've known girls like her before. They like to play the game. Claire doesn't realize that I play to win, and I always do."

"Whatever." Seth turned and walked back to the boarding house. He hated Elliott's arrogance. The guy had an ego bigger than New York. Somebody needed to knock him down to size.

* * *

I once valued friendships, before I tasted the bitter dregs of betrayal. In fathering a child with Mary Ann, Eaton had ended the circle of friendship that had meant the world to me. In the early days with the Shakers, I frequently requested joint work assignments with Eaton. It brightened many a day to enjoy his sense of humor while we worked. Especially in the drudgery of assignments such as the blacksmith shop. When I worked in the fields, I enjoyed working alone or with others. I paid scant attention to Eaton's bantering on those days. I couldn't count the times that Elder Joseph had reprimanded Eaton for his jocularity. I would listen and then hide my smirk behind my hand. Eaton never let a rebuke darken his thoughts for long. As soon as Elder Joseph was out of earshot, he'd grin and take up where he left off.

Occasionally, Eaton's humor irritated me. When he crossed the line between teasing into snide, hurtful remarks, I would flinch and close my mind to him. I never rebuked him, because it was easier not to cross him. I had never thought deeply enough to realize that cowardice became my way of holding on to our friendship.

Even after Mary Ann's shaming, it took me days to stand up to him. I held my anger inside. When I finally confronted Eaton, I struggled to hide my emotions from the others. Looking back, I realize they saw much more than I thought.

My rage turned to guilt everyday when I walked into the meetinghouse. I sang out louder as I needed to convince God that I remained faithful to his teachings. I danced with an energy derived from emotion and anxiety. I would catch the elders observing me and try to refrain from my frenzy. Usually it worked. I didn't admit to myself that God saw much deeper into the rot that infested my heart. No wonder the elders eventually diagnosed me as deranged.

CHAPTER FOURTEEN

Whatsoever a man soweth, that shall he also reap.
Galatians 6: 7-9

Elliott answered his phone.

"Hello."

"I'm still waiting on the money."

"I'm working on it." Elliott couldn't believe that Dominic had discovered his new number.

"My patience is coming to an end."

"I know. I've been busy and haven't had a chance to call." Elliott wished he had planned a better excuse.

"Sure. Now we've talked. I'll call again in three days and I expect you to find the money by then. This time we won't be kind."

"Okay. I will." Elliott grimaced at the sneer in Dominic's voice. He would agree to anything to end this conversation. He remembered the beating he received on a previous visit from Dominic's friends. It had taken him a week to recover.

"Remember, three days! And don't think you can just ignore my call."

"I won't. I'll be here."

"It'll be better for your health, for sure." Elliott winced at the threat.

He'd left his old phone at home and purchased another one at Walmart. No one had this number except his family. He couldn't tell Dominic his dad had shipped him out of town, where he had no access to money. Three days only gave him until Saturday. He needed an excuse to make a trip home before then. Hopefully, his dad would be out of town. Maybe he went to Vegas with Uncle Gavin again. They made that trip half a dozen times a year.

He called his mom and luck was on his side. His dad was in Vegas and wouldn't be home until Sunday night.

"Elliott, I'd love to see you, but can't you wait until your dad is home? He'll be so disappointed to miss you. How is your summer so far? I miss you."

Yeah, right, Elliott thought. *So much so you let Dad kick me out of the company for the summer.* "Sorry, Mom. I have Saturday off and I don't know when I'll get another day. We're busy here, with new animals coming in all the time."

"I'm happy it's a rewarding experience. Your dad said it would be good for you, and it sounds like you are enjoying it. Can you come Friday evening? We'll have a quiet dinner together."

"I'll try, Mom. You know, it's nearly a three-hour drive. Depends on what time I can get away."

"Please try. I have a meeting Saturday morning, but then we can have a nice lunch." Virginia Werner wiped her eyes. She had hated it when Charles and Gavin decided to send him away for the summer. The thought of spending time alone with Elliott brightened her day.

"I'll try." The last thing Elliott wanted was a quiet dinner with her. She was clueless about his life and she wouldn't believe the mess he was in if he told her. That might play to his advantage. Maybe he could get the money from her without going through his dad's office.

Thursday morning, he walked in to Cheri's office only to find it empty. He looked around her desk and found one of the brochures she was working on.

WE ARE A NO-KILL SHELTER WHERE OUR RES-
IDENTS CAN SPEND THE REST OF THEIR LIVES
LOVED AND IN PEACE....

He flipped the brochure over. Cracker Box Palace is funded by donations ... An idea took root.

WE RELY ON OUR GENEROUS CONTRIBUTORS AND OUR HEARTY
VOLUNTEERS.

Bull's Eye! That would work. He could play the role of the hearty volunteer and come back with a generous contribution from his mom. He only owed $10,000. As he walked out, he ran into Cheri in the hall.

"Sorry. Did you need to see me?"

"Yes. I just talked to my mom. She's alone this weekend and begged me to come home Friday night. If I could leave about three on Friday, I could be back Saturday night."

"No problem. If your mom needs you, you better go. Make arrangements with Jeff and we'll plan on you being here on Sunday.

Have you checked on the new cows today? I had to run into Alton and I just got back."

"I'm on my way down to the barn now. Thanks a lot. I appreciate your help."

"No problem. See you later."

He's such a nice young man, Cheri thought. She didn't understand his problem with his dad and uncle but they had made a significant donation so she would accept him for the summer.

The workday calmed Elliott's nerves. Dominic's threat dimmed. By afternoon, he decided to arrange more time with Claire. First, he needed to find Elena.

"Elena, wait up," he spotted her at the sheep corral.

"Hi, I'm giving them their afternoon treats," she answered. "They all want attention. Come on down and help me." She handed him some treats when he reached the fence.

"Those goats are crazy, aren't they?" He knew how much she loved them.

"They are, but they're so cute, too. Look at their eyes. I can't get used to them. They are like a cat's, only sideways. I read that helps them to see peripherally when they are grazing."

"Oh, yeah?"

"Nature is amazing, isn't it?"

"Sure is. Hey, what are you doing tonight?"

"Nothing, why?"

"I thought we might get Seth and Claire and go explore the waterfalls on Second Creek."

"Sounds great. I haven't seen it yet. Have you talked to the others?"

"No, I thought maybe you could ask them. I have some work to do before then."

"Okay. Plan to meet at the boarding house?"

"Sure."

Elena wished she'd brought her Canon but her iPhone should capture a good picture of the falls. She texted both Claire and Seth and they agreed to meet at six-thirty.

Seth loved the waterfalls. The thought of showing it to Claire enticed him to say yes. Too bad Elliott would be along. He enjoyed Elena's enthusiasm. It would be a fun evening.

The weather cooperated and they all enjoyed the hike to the falls. Claire brought her camera and they took turns posing for pictures. Elena immediately posted her best shots to Instagram.

"Hey," Elliott pulled Seth away and whispered. "Can you make some excuse and walk Elena back? I'd like to explore some more photo ops with Claire."

"Yeah, I'll bet."

"Please. It's so hard to get any alone time with her."

"Sorry, bud. I'm not pimping for you."

"Claire wants to take another picture," Elena called as she waved to them.

Elliott fought to hide the fury that threatened to spill out. "Sure, I'm coming."

"You'll be sorry for that comment," he hissed at Seth.

Seth followed along, determined that this would be the last time he agreed to anything that involved Elliott. He had watched Claire side step around every move that Elliott made, but the guy was too stupid to get the hint. Or he was too conceited to notice.

After the last of the pictures, they all walked back together. Elena, oblivious to the tension, kept up a running dialogue. She and Claire pointed out nature's wonders on the farm while the guys attempted to cover up their antagonism toward each other.

Back in his room, Elliott slammed his door and kicked the cabinets. He popped a beer and chugged it. On the second one, his temper calmed to a slow seething of resentment. Seth would pay for the trash talk.

Friday, Elliott worked alone as much as possible. He needed to channel his inner charm and lose the anger before he saw his mother. Spending an evening with her was a bore, so he needed to start with a positive frame of mind. He did make sure that Cheri saw him working when she arrived. At two-thirty, he went to his room and took a quick shower. He was on the road by three. I-90 traffic had the usual number of trucks and construction slow-downs but he made it home before 6:30.

CHAPTER FIFTEEN

Change your thoughts and you change your world.
Norman Vincent Peale

I realized I was becoming involved with the Cracker Box Palace group. I preferred to stay away from current happenings because I had never solved my own problems. But it would take a blind person to not see the friction between Elliott and Seth. I had ignored them at first, like I did most guys. I focused my energy on women.

I felt a kindred spirit with Claire. She was fighting against something in her past. I could see it in her actions. I often smelled fear when she was near. Something, or more likely someone, had hurt her. She reminded me of Mary Ann. I had failed to protect her when I should have. I vowed I would not fail Claire. I would watch over Elena, too. She was young and full of life. That was as it should be.

Then there was Mary Ann. I hadn't seen her in days and that always worried me. I knew she fought a depression even more severe than mine. If only she would communicate with me.

Over the decades, I occasionally engaged with the farm's current inhabitants. I most often interfered because someone's actions angered me. It was as if I had to explode periodically and do something spiteful. When I pondered it later, I realized it was never about the current situation. It always went back to the Shakers and Eaton.

***

Sara and Claire entered Diamond's stall. The horse became more comfortable every day. She was eating now and starting to gain weight. Sara brushed her for the first time. "She has a sweet disposition. I think when she's totally comfortable, she will be friendly to everyone."

"And maybe a little bit feisty," Claire added.

"I certainly hope so. She needs some sass."

"Do you think I'll be able to brush her soon?"

"When I leave, you come in. If she lets you close, just stroke her neck. If she accepts that, we will both brush her tomorrow. Be sure to bring her a treat."

Sara left and Claire slowly entered the stall. Diamond stood still but didn't cringe when Claire reached her. She stroked her neck with her left hand and offered a treat with her right. Diamond took the treat and accepted Claire's presence.

"Thank you." Claire wiped the tears from her eyes. "I am so thankful you are healing. You are a beautiful lady, and I know you're strong too."

Diamond listened.

"I know some man abused you and I understand that. We're alike and we're both survivors." Claire leaned her head against the horse's neck. "You understand what I'm saying, don't you?"

Sara walked back toward the stall. She stopped when she saw Claire hugging Diamond. There was a depth to Claire. Sara wondered what she and Diamond had in common. Maybe someday Claire would share. Until then, it was none of her business.

* * *

Eileen watched from the barn door. Claire hadn't noticed her yet. She liked Claire and wanted to spend some time with her, but she wasn't sure what to say or do. She had never mastered carrying on conversations with adults, but Claire had been kind when they talked before.

She longed to talk to someone about her mother.

She sensed a presence behind her but when she turned around, she saw no one.

* * *

I've noticed this young spirit before. Should I try to

connect with her? No, I think I will keep an eye on her. She's new to the farm, in fact, the only new spirit I've seen in many decades. Is she from the Outside World? We always had visitors that attended our meetings. That's how we recruited new souls into our community. Maybe she came here and died, but then surely I would have seen her before now. No, she must be an outsider. She wears the clothing of years gone by. I am fascinated by her ability to relate to living souls.

I need to clear the resentment away, and open my mind to the other lost souls. I suspect we all drink from the same bitter cup of loneliness.

* * *

Elliott submitted to his mother's hug.

"It's so good to see you, son. I miss you."

"I miss you, too. It's a long drive and I'm thirsty."

"I'll get you a beer. Or better yet, you pick what you'd like. I think I'll have a glass of wine. I have been so busy this summer already. One charity event after another, and I'm on the planning committee for the art festival in September. I'm so happy you'll be home for that."

"I hope I will, if Dad thinks I've paid long enough." He tried to keep the anger tamped down.

"Now, son. You know your dad. He's only trying to do what he thinks is best. I'm not sure what happened between you, but I'm sure you'll work it out."

Elliott opened his beer and took a drink. How did one deal with a clueless mother? Apparently his dad hadn't told her anything, because she would have found excuses for her baby boy. Step easy, he told himself.

"You're right. Let's enjoy tonight. I have so much to tell you about Cracker Box Palace. They are doing much-needed work and I'm learning there is so much abuse and neglect in the world."

"I'm sorry you have to find out about the seedier side of life, Elliott." He nearly spit out a mouthful of beer. Had she really said that? No one could be that naive. He hoped she never found out about Dominic. Another reason he had to get the money. He realized he made a mistake when he ran up his gambling debts. Why hadn't he realized his dad would refuse to help him? He had begged.

"Where would you like to go for dinner?"

"Let's drive over to Skaneateles for dinner. We can eat at the Blue Water Grill and enjoy the lake." Elliott knew how his mother loved lakeside dining.

SPIRITS OF THE SODUS BAY SHAKERS

He kept the conversation light as they drove, asking about his mother's charities. Once they were seated at their table, the waiter brought two glasses of water. His mom ordered a glass of Chardonnay, Elliott a beer.

"I am so busy, but it's all worth it. I'm now working with the humane society. So many animals and not enough donors. I am working on a benefit later this summer. They desperately need larger facilities."

Awesome, Elliott thought. Help the animals. "That's part of the problem we have at the farm, too. The upkeep is so expensive. Many of the rescued animals will never be adopted."

"Oh, my. What happens to them?"

"Cheri and her team are dedicated to letting them live out their lives at the farm. You should visit the farm. I know how you love horses and we have more than thirty."

"I would love to, but I don't have the time now. Maybe someday."

Their drinks arrived and they placed their orders. Elliott ordered the chicken tenders with fries. They had been a favorite of his for years. His mom ordered a salad.

Elliott knew that his mother's someday visit would never come. The farm would never give her the same social status as her local charities. She loved the visibility on the local scene. "Maybe you could help another way."

"What do you mean?"

"Mom, the farm may not survive if they can't raise money. I know you donate to so many charities, but this one already means a lot to me."

"I'm so happy to see you involved in helping others. Sure, I'll make a donation. How much?"

Elliott thought about the best way to get his mom to think in large numbers. "I think it takes at least twenty-five thousand a month to care for the animals."

"Surely, they don't need that much. I'm not prepared ..."

"Of course not. I wanted to give you an idea of their budget." He patted his mom's hand. Here goes the negotiation. "Half of that would solve the existing crisis."

"That's still more than I can do."

"Look at it this way. That money could keep the place alive for the rest of the year. I can spend the summer scouting out other ways to raise money."

"You're so kind-hearted. I know you mean well, but I can't and won't donate that kind of money without asking your dad to research it."

"Whatever you think is best. I was hoping I could go back to the farm with a substantial gift. Since I've been there, we have rescued a badly abused horse and several cows. I am concerned with their future." Elliott needed ten thousand to pay off Dominic. He had counted on softening his mother's heart.

"I'll give you a couple thousand. That should help with an immediate need."

"Mom, that's wonderful but it's just a drop in the bucket. I wish I had taken a picture of that poor horse. Her name is Diamond and she's a beauty, but she is taking lots of extra care. And there are the massive vet bills." He had no idea of how many times the vet had seen Diamond, if at all, but hopefully, it would create sympathy.

Their dinner arrived and they watched a group board their boat. Elliott wished he were with them. An evening cruise with no stress sounded like a dream. Instead, his stress level skyrocketed at his mother's refusal to donate money to the farm.

"Mom, can you spare ten thousand or maybe eight? Then have Dad research it when he gets home."

"No, but I'm contemplating what I should do. Let's enjoy our dinner and talk about the fun times we've shared on the lake. I know you miss being here for the summer crowd."

Elliott's expertise was in small talk and idle chatter, so he regaled her with some of his favorite memories. He made sure the best ones included times he spent with her.

After dinner, they drove home and watched a couple of episodes of Downton Abbey, her all-time favorite series. She mourned the demise of the series over several more glasses of wine. She asked Elliott to lock up the house as she tidied up the kitchen, then she went to her room.

Elliott spent the night plotting new ways to convince his mom.

Saturday morning, she left for her meeting with a promise to be back in plenty of time for lunch. Elliott suspected he might find some cash in the house and used the time scouring her rooms. He came up with the grand total of four-hundred-and-thirty-eight dollars. Not enough to do much good, but he took it anyway. He hoped his mom's scatter-brained tendencies extended to spare cash.

His mother opted for Andriaccio's for lunch. He loved their pizza so her choice was good. Although he tried, he found it almost impossible to bring out his inner charm. He needed that money and he needed to take it with him.

"Mom, I promised Cheri I'd be back in time for the early evening chores. I plan to drive you home, pack and head back."

"I understand but I hate to see you go so soon."

"About our conversation last night,..."

"The money. Yes, I've been thinking about it."

Elliott's spirits rose.

"I will give you four thousand. That should help with this month's feed bill. I am sure the owner, ... Cheri, is that her name ... will be grateful for that much."

His heart sank. He knew Dominic would never settle for less than half the money.

"Mom, ..."

"Don't say anymore, Elliott. I will talk to your father. I'm proud that you care so deeply about the farm. I think he will be, too. Maybe he was right to send you there for the summer."

Squelching the urge to tell her he was twenty-five and too old to play his parents' games, he nodded. Too old or not, the person who holds the money wins.

Anxious to leave, he found it difficult to hug his mother goodbye, even after she handed him a check for four thousand dollars—made out to Cracker Box Palace. He was screwed.

Dominic's face might as well have been plastered on the windshield. He could hardly see to drive home because his mind saw Dominic's angry eyes far clearer than the road ahead. It had all started so innocently. Just a few fun nights playing poker in the frat house. He'd loved the challenge and the anticipation. One thing led to another and he found himself playing with money he didn't have at Dominic's casino. His dad had bailed him out a couple of times, but each time threatened it would be the last. Elliott hadn't realized the biggest gamble was betting on his dad's support.

The amounts grew and with that, his dad's generosity shrank. Uncle Gavin played a part in his dad's refusal to bail him out once again. He'd used a poor performance review to convince his dad. Never mind that Uncle Gavin had conducted the review. Elliott hated him!

CHAPTER SIXTEEN

We trust that God is on our side. It is more important that we are on God's side.
Abraham Lincoln

MARY ANN FOUGHT AGAINST THE despondency that shrouded her. She had hidden in this never-land zone for far too long. Although she had never given up hope of finding her baby, she knew the chances grew slimmer. Maybe the baby had died. Maybe she had been wrong all along. Had she lost her chance of Heaven for her foolish refusal to accept God's will? She had never seen the bright light since the day the baby came.

The Shakers believed that pacifism required one to fore go bitterness and revenge. She had sinned grievously. She could find no way in her heart to seek the highest good for Eaton, not after he left her to face her shame alone. She acknowledged the need for forgiveness and her inability to do so. No wonder she had been shut out of the community. She had been a dismal failure, displeasing God.

Maybe she could never have reached the light, even if she had tried. Was she cursed to spend eternity searching for an impossible goal?

In a way, she missed Horace. She didn't understand why she still saw him, and her guilt kept her from acknowledging him, but his presence comforted her. She had no idea why he was still here.

A memory from her childhood religion came to mind. The guardian angel. Every child had an angel that guarded against harm. That proved to be ludicrous. Her baby certainly never had a guardian angel. There were days her anger at God outweighed her bitterness at Eaton. Both had wanted her—Eaton her body and God her soul. But both had failed her.

* * *

Elliott drove back to the farm. He was out of options and he knew it. He could think of no way to get that money. He would have to hand over the check to Cheri. Tomorrow Dominic would call. He wasn't sure what he would do, but he believed Dominic when he had said he'd be sorry if he didn't come up with the money and pay his debt.

He arrived at the farm in time to help with the chores. Cheri was in her office but he avoided her. There had to be another way. Jeff and Seth kept him busy for a couple of hours. Cheri caught him before he climbed the boarding house stairs.

"I hope your mother enjoyed your visit."

"Yes, fine." He walked up the steps.

"Is everything all right?"

"Sure, just tired. I think I'll take a quick shower before dinner. That should revive me."

"I'm headed to the cow barn to check on our recent arrivals. See you later."

Elliott stood under the warm water, hoping it would wash away his misery. But it only replaced it with desperation. He had to find money. A thought occurred. Cheri kept money in the office. He had seen it before. Even though it was Saturday evening, she might have enough stashed away to solve his problem, at least to make a down payment to Dominic. Energized, he jumped out of the shower and dressed quickly. With luck, Cheri would still be out with the cows. If she had locked the office and left, he'd have to figure out a way to break in. Next time he saw Cheri, he'd give her the check. That should allay any suspicions she might have. No one would give her money and steal from her at the same time.

Cheri had locked the door before she went to the barn, but she hadn't set the deadbolt. He had learned how to jimmy an ordinary door lock from one of his high school friends. One night when they'd been drinking, they had broken into the football field office. The coach would often confiscate drugs and lock them in his desk. They hadn't found what they were looking for, but they had gotten away with the break in.

Elliott opened drawers and looked inside manila envelopes. He searched the closet and the file cabinet. Where would she hide cash? Surely she had to keep it on site in case she needed it. He found a petty cash box, and that's what it contained. Petty cash. About fifty dollars. He wanted to throw the box and trash the room. He needed to get out before he lost control. He barely made it back to his room before he heard Cheri in the hallway.

After a sleepless night, Elliott decided his only option was to lose his phone. He drove the Gator down past the horse pasture and threw his phone into the timber. He would find time to run down to Newark to Walmart later in the day. He hadn't solved anything but at least he'd postponed it. Today, he'd concentrate on Claire.

* * *

I followed Elliott and watched him dispose of his phone. It didn't take much to know that Elliott was in some kind of trouble. I will keep him under surveillance. I feel no special compassion for him, but I still possess the Shaker values of peace and non-violence.

* * *

Eileen fought against the lethargy. She was so tired of searching. All she ever wanted since that fateful day Sharon had turned her world upside down, was to find her mother. So many people had passed through her awareness since then, but never the one she wanted. She had accepted the fact that her human life was over, but her pretend parents had taught her about God and salvation. She remembered their lessons that He encouraged love, kindness and forgiveness in everyone. She assumed that still pertained to her.

She had struggled with it, but she had finally forgiven Agnes and Jonathan Barker. She knew they loved her and had given her a home when her real mother didn't want her. She couldn't continue to blame them for something they held no responsibility for. She had to find her mother and discover why she had given her away. Strangely, once she thought of the Barkers without malice, she changed. Before she had wandered around New York completely invisible to all life forms. Now, she sometimes felt her body as it had been before the fever and resentment took her. The joy of talking to a living human was the first bright spot in her spirit life.

Eileen didn't understand or care. Simply talking to someone gave her hope and the courage to continue. Claire had seen her and they had a conversation. She knew Claire had looked for her but somehow Eileen couldn't make her body appear. She had no control of that. She attributed her lack of understanding to her youth. A child had so little knowledge about the world and she had never progressed on to adulthood. Even after a couple of centuries, she still knew herself as the lonely eight-year-old who needed to find her mother.

CHAPTER SEVENTEEN

Control your emotions or they will control you.
Chinese Proverb

SUNDAY MORNING BROUGHT BLUE SKIES and sunshine. Seth had the day off and wanted to take advantage of it. He had heard about an Irish restaurant in Syracuse. Coleman's had a great reputation as an authentic Irish Pub. He already had it planned. A Guinness and Shepherd's Pie. All he lacked was good company.

He walked across the road to the Deacon's House. Before he reached it, Claire opened the door.

"Hey, I was coming to find you."

"Good morning to you, too." Claire was looking forward to a day of reading and sketching.

"We're off today and I have an idea. I've never spent any time in Syracuse and I thought today would be a great time to check it out. I've heard about Coleman's, an old Irish pub." His voice trailed off at Claire's expression. "What's wrong?"

"Nothing. I was thinking of something else. I had planned to spend the day relaxing and reading. I don't think I'm up for Syracuse." She fought the panic in her voice. She knew she could never go there again. Jake would find her if she did. And Coleman's. It had been one of their favorite places when they first dated. Any Irish girl from Tipperary Hill knew every item on the menu. A wave of homesickness struck her, but she couldn't go back.

"Are you all right? You seem stressed."

"Tired, is all. That's why I want to spend the day reading. Why don't you ask Elena and Elliott?"

"Are you sure? It would be more fun if we all go."

"Thanks, but I'm sure. Maybe some other time. I'd like to go to the Strong Museum of Play in Rochester some time. Maybe we can do that."

"Okay, I give in." Seth accepted her refusal with good grace. He had anticipated Elena's enthusiastic response before he asked her. He didn't want to ask Elliott but he didn't want to leave him here with Claire either.

He found Elliott on the boarding house porch. "Elena and I are driving into Syracuse today. Want to join us?"

"Sorry," Elliott lied. "I told Cheri I'd work today to make up for Friday. Is Claire going?"

"She wants to spend the day alone. She's tired."

Good deal, Elliott thought. I lucked out on that. "Well, have fun. I'll be here slaving away."

"Yeah." Seth knew he'd do as little work as possible but take credit for running the farm. At least Jeff would be here with him. Maybe he'd keep him busy.

Seth drove Elena through the Syracuse University campus. She wanted to take pictures, especially of Carrier Dome.

"Is it true that it's the largest domed stadium on any campus?" Elena snapped another shot.

"I've heard that. I do know that it's the home of both football and basketball."

"Also women's basketball. I plan to come up for one of their games."

"You'll become so enchanted with Cornell that you'll never want to leave Ithaca."

"I hope so." Elena had fallen in love with the Cornell campus on her first visit. She was looking forward to four awesome years there. "I'm starving. Are we still going to Coleman's?"

"Sure, but first I want to show you something near there."

As Seth drove, he filled her in on the story of the green-on-the-top traffic light. She couldn't wait to see it.

"Did those boys really break the red light out every time it was replaced?"

"They sure did. You know the Irish. They take pride in their heritage and love their green. They wanted the green light on the top. Finally the city gave in, and now it's the only traffic light in the country with green on top and red on the bottom. At least that's what I've always heard."

"That is awesome! And we'll see the statue too?"

"Yep, it's right on the corner."

Seth laughed as Elena took multiple photos, including selfies, of the light and the statue.

"That's a great story. Now I'm ready for Irish food."

After more selfies with the Leprechaun phone booth and at the bar, they finally found a table. Seth didn't even check the menu. He ordered a Guinness and the Shepherd's Pie. Elena opted for a Diet Coke and the beef stew because she'd read about it on TripAdvisor. Their conversation drifted to the farm.

"I'm loving my summer so far," Elena said. "I really like working with Sara and Claire."

"It's a great place to work and we do a lot of good."

"I know. You should see Sara and Claire with Diamond."

"She's the new horse that was an abused case, right?"

"Yes, and they have made so much progress with her. At first she wouldn't leave the corner of her stall, not even to eat. But now they can comb her and she is eating. They are ready to try taking her out to the pasture. I want to be there when that happens."

"It's always rewarding when an animal recovers from their past. Let me know when they plan to take her out, and I'll watch it with you."

"Sounds awesome." Elena cleaned up the last of her stew. "That was so good."

"Mine, too. Are you and Claire becoming friends?"

"Yes, I think so. It's hard to know with someone older than you."

"Elena," Seth laughed. "Everyone there is older than you."

"Well, Claire isn't that old, but she's at least ten years older than me."

"You're probably right. I don't know much about her. She hadn't been here long before you came. She's smart and learns quickly. I hope she stays. Cracker Box Palace needs people like her."

"I think Elliott likes her, but she's ignoring his attention." Elena thought Claire could do a lot better than him.

"He's making himself a pest."

Neither noticed a guy at the bar until he came over to their table. "This Cracker Box Palace, what is it?"

Seth noticed the intensity in the guy's eyes. "It's a farm animal rescue organization. Have you heard of it?"

"No, but I couldn't help overhearing your conversation. They rescue horses, huh?"

"Yes, and all kinds of farm animals."

"Where is it?"

"Alasa Farms, near Alton."

"That's not too far from here, huh?"

"Not at all. Do you have a special interest?"

"No, I just like animals."

"They welcome visitors," Elena said.

Seth paid the bill and they left. On the drive home, he and Elena raved about their dinners and the bar's decor.

* * *

A restlessness ran through me. I watched Seth drive away with Elena. I felt an anger seething just below the surface. I had tried to deny it for days but something was bothering me. With no sign of Mary Ann in recent days, I spent too much time watching the farm's happenings.

Cheri left to spend the day with Burt. Sunday should be a quiet day. As the day wore on, I relaxed a little. I should have known better.

* * *

Anger and anxiety warred inside Elliott. How dare his mother let him down. She had always been there to wipe away his problems and pick up the pieces. He blamed his stress on her refusal to help. He didn't know how long he had to come up with the money before Dominic found him. He finished his chores and took a long walk around the farm. Nothing helped.

When he passed the horse barn, he heard Claire's voice. She was talking to that damn horse again. She certainly didn't give him that much attention. He stopped and listened.

Then he realized she was the one thing that could take his mind off his problems.

"Hey," he greeted as he walked into the barn. He glanced around to verify that no one else was around.

"Hi."

"You and Diamond have become best buds, haven't you?"

"Yes. I love her. It is awesome to see her improvement every day. Sara knew exactly what to do to encourage her."

He watched her lovingly stroke the horse. "You talk to her, too. I heard you."

"Can't deny it. She keeps all my secrets."

"You have secrets. I would keep them, too." He opened the stall door.

"I'm not sure you should come in. Diamond seems to be afraid of men. I think it may have been a man who abused her. As for secrets, I think they are safer with Diamond than anyone else."

Elliott walked into the stall.

"Please don't come any closer."

"Then you come out here and talk to me."

Claire looked at the door. Where was Sara? "I'm busy. I'll come out after I finish combing her."

Elliott couldn't stand another refusal. Why didn't anyone respect his wishes? He continued walking toward her. He reached over her shoulder and put his hand over hers on the dandy brush. "I'm like Diamond. I need a friend, too, and I want the same loving care."

"Sorry, it's not part of my job description."

"I get what I want, Claire. You can fight me or not, but I will win either way." He liked the fear in her eyes.

"What do you want?"

"You know exactly what I want."

Claire struggled to get away but he held her. Claire could feel the jittery reaction in Diamond. "You're scaring her."

"That's your choice. Stay here or come out with me. You name it."

"Neither."

He reached for her and Diamond reared up. She shook her head and brought her front legs down again and again. Fear seized Elliott. He knew nothing about horses except that he hated this one. In fact, he hated everything about farm life. He backed out of the stall, never taking his eyes off Diamond. Once outside, he threw the stall door closed. "It's not over, Claire."

Elliott cursed his dad, his mom, Claire and the farm. Then he uttered a special obscenity for Diamond. But Dominic was the real enemy. His anger paled in comparison to his fear. He saw no way to solve his problems.

* * *

Claire finished her work and went to her room. She debated whether or not she should report the incident to Cheri, but decided to wait. Elliott was a problem. He didn't accept rejection, or else he lived with the fear of it. She had neither the time nor desire to psychoanalyze him. He posed a threat requiring her constant vigilance.

* * *

I went back to the barn later to apologize to Dia-
mond for prodding her with the pitchfork handle. Neither
Claire nor Elliott had noticed the pitchfork, but it had
caused the desired reaction. Diamond was in no mood to
accept my apology. She recognized me for what I am and
I frightened her. I left the barn with my apology running
through my mind. I never intended to hurt the horse.

* * *

Elliott drank another beer. With each one, his anger rose and his fear dissipated. Dominic wouldn't come after him here. There were too many people around. He would stay on the farm, and continue his game of pursuit with Claire. He got up and went to the fridge for another beer, while thoughts of Claire played in his head.

It only took a couple more to garner the courage to do what he wanted. And he wanted Claire. He looked out the window and saw her sitting on the porch. She was alone.

"Hi," he called as he crossed the road.

"Hi. I guess it's getting late and I better get to bed." Claire stood up and moved toward the door.

"Wait, I need to talk to you just for a minute."

"You've been drinking," she had heard his slurred words.

"No, well, I just had a beer. I just want to ask you a question."

"What is it?"

Elliott reached the porch. Claire looked at his disheveled clothes and his alcohol-induced silly grin. "Ask your question so I can go inside."

"Okay. I need a favor and I don't know who else to ask."

Claire waited. Elliott moved closer. "Someone is coming after me and I need your help."

"With what? Who's coming after you?" Her patience ran thin.

"I...just someone I owe money to."

"Sorry, I can't help. I have no money."

"It's not money I need from you." He moved to position himself in front of the door.

Claire's heart raced. Should she call for Sara? If she were in her room, she'd hear her. She opened her mouth and Elliott's hand slapped over it. "Don't."

"Take your hand off me. I'm going inside."

"Your 'hard-to-get' game is getting tiresome. It's time we had some fun."

"You're drunk."

"Not as drunk as you think. You can come with me quietly or we can make good use of that chair."

Claire panicked. He sounded just like Jake. She had suffered enough bruises and injuries to know the cost of refusing him when he had been drinking.

"Where do you want to go?"

"Let's go check on the horses."

"Not this late. I don't want to disturb them."

"I thought I heard Diamond. It sounded like she was in distress." Elliott grabbed her arm and pulled her along.

She worried about Diamond, but she didn't trust Elliott. Maybe if she got to Diamond's stall, he'd leave her alone. As they walked, he rambled, some story about his mother refusing to help him and his dad sending him away. How they and some guy named Dominic, who threatened him for something, had treated him unfairly. None of it made much sense, but she kept quiet and listened.

They reached the barn. He opened the door and they walked in. When she headed toward Diamond's stall, he stopped her. "Not there."

"You said something was wrong with Diamond. I'm going to check on her."

Elliott grabbed her arms and his lips assaulted hers. She bit him and he yelled. He jerked her arm and pulled her down on the ground. Anger overtook reason as he tore at her top. She squirmed out of his hold and sat up. He lunged to push her down. Out of the corner of her eye, she saw the dandy brush crash into his head. She heard his scream of pain and saw the blood ooze out of a cut just behind his temple.

She looked around and saw no one. Where did the brush come from? Nearly paralyzed by fear, she managed to stand and run out of the barn. She never looked back. Later that night, she lay in bed puzzling about the brush. If someone was watching, why didn't he help her? Elliott's intentions were clear.

CHAPTER EIGHTEEN

True redemption is...when guilt leads to good.
Unknown

This time I have not failed. It doesn't undo the injustice to Mary Ann but it makes me realize there is redemption. Maybe God has not forsaken me after all. I had gone back across, looking for Mary Ann on the other side. I hadn't found her. The spirit world is beyond the imagination of the living. There is as much unknown now as when I first transitioned. I wish I could change people's thinking. We don't just die or pass away. We cross over. I've never decided if it's a curse or a blessing that I have been able to transition back and forth between the two realities.

But I am thankful that I didn't stay on the other side. I came back to the farm in time. I know that I will ponder the possibility that God guided me back.

I stopped the crime, for that is what it would have been. Elliott intended to commit a violent crime against Claire. I found the rage taking over and I couldn't tell the difference between Elliott's face and Eaton's. There is one thing I know. I never punished Eaton for his sins. I will not make that mistake again. I realize there are those who would tell me I am not the judge and jury, but I believe that God has given me the responsibility to right such wrongs.

When I united with the Shakers all those years ago, I admired their recognition of the equality of the sexes. But I have learned they were wrong. Women have a courage and purity of spirit that men will never be able to achieve. I believe that God intended them to remain superior.

CHAPTER NINETEEN

Whatever is begun in anger, ends in shame.
Benjamin Franklin

JAKE LEFT COLEMAN'S WITH NEW hope. A girl named Claire worked less than an hour's drive away. He felt in his bones that it was his Claire. He wanted to jump in the car and head over there on the spot, but he had learned a dabbling of patience. He needed to plan his approach. If it was his Claire, he wanted her to willingly come back home with him. He would play the game and sweet-talk her into it. She had fallen for that every time except once. He'd get her back and never allow that to happen again. But first, he had to verify that she indeed worked at that farm. She'd always liked animals, so it would be a natural for her.

At home, he opened his computer and typed in Cracker Box Palace. Sure enough, there it was. Far enough away that she probably thought she'd escaped, but it was only a matter of time. He didn't want to act hastily so he promised himself he'd wait for two days. Then Wednesday morning, he would get up early, shower, find clean clothes and drive to the country.

People told him the New York countryside was beautiful, but he failed to see it. He loved the city, the many bars and the nightlife. He liked living where it was easy to find jobs and rewards. Sometimes, he crossed the line of legality, but a guy had to make a living. He never hurt anyone unless he had to. He had been hired to do some break-ins, but he didn't do robberies. A guy had to draw the line somewhere. He didn't want to carry a gun or have to hurt an innocent person. As a bouncer, he learned that he had no problem getting physical with someone who deserved it. He always strove to live up to his code. Claire had never understood that. He loved her and he had been faithful. Yes, she would see that and come back where she belonged.

That evening he did his laundry, out of necessity because he had no clean clothes left. He cleaned and washed the dishes in the sink. He wanted the house to look pretty for Claire.

Wednesday morning, he left the house at nine. He figured it should be break time when he arrived. He had no idea of how farms scheduled breaks, but it wasn't really important. If his Claire was there, he intended to bring her home.

* * *

Claire spent a sleepless night on Sunday. Monday morning, she vowed to carry on and not let Elliott ruin her summer. As she finished her morning chores and left the barn, she saw Eileen near the house. She called to her but the girl disappeared behind a bush. By the time she walked over there, Eileen was nowhere in sight.

She brushed the spider webs away from the porch steps and sat down. She was tired and it was still morning. To keep from recalling yesterday, she focused her attention on the house. She remembered Eileen's story about the Shakers and ghosts. She had read about the Shakers in some of the literature. Then she found more information about them on the Internet, on a site about historic Sodus Bay. At the time, she had thought the religion was strange but now, maybe not. Separation of men and women. Based on her recent experience with men, the idea appealed to her.

She relaxed, enjoying the peace and quiet. She felt the solitude even as the animals in the pastures announced their presence. She imagined herself working in the Shaker community, without the tension of sexual relationships. The Shakers worked hard and produced fine farm products and furniture. At the end of the day, they probably had home-cooked meals followed by a good night's sleep. Plus they had their faith. Not a bad existence.

She must have napped because when she became aware, she remembered a man in old-style clothing. Much the same as Eileen wore. He didn't speak to her but he had paused and nodded before he walked into the house. She stood and looked around. The house wasn't exactly off limits but no one went in it. The fire several years ago had weakened the structure. Should she go in and warn him? She went to the door and called. No one answered, but she could swear someone was near by.

Maybe some re-enactors visited the farm from time to time.

* * *

Jake found the farm. He drove in and got out of the car. He noticed three signs. He read the one about Cracker Box Palace—and ignored the ones about Alasa Farms and the Genesee Land Trust. Could his Claire really be stuck out here with a bunch of animals? He knew she liked them, but he thought in terms of dogs and cats. He'd never ridden a horse, and cows were only good for eating. He heard some roosters and laughed. The perfect place for an uppity female—a farm ruled by roosters. Maybe Claire was here. He didn't see anyone so he wandered around. It must have been some farm in its day. All those huge barns and other buildings. He saw horses in the pastures, some sheep and goats, and he finally found the roosters.

Claire stepped out of the barn and stopped. Jake's old car was parked near the signs. Where was he? She looked around and saw him near the roosters. How did he know? She had to get out of here. She ran to the back of the barn and told Sara. "If a guy comes looking for me, please say you don't know me."

"What's wrong?"

"Just please. I have to hide."

"Sure. Where is he?"

"Down by the roosters. Thanks."

Claire slipped out the back of the barn and ran past the pastures. She hid behind an old piece of equipment. She could see Jake's car so she would know when he left. She wished she could get to her room, but it was too risky to try.

Sara kept a watchful eye on Jake. When he finally reached the barn, he stepped inside.

"Hello, anyone here?"

"Hi. Sorry I didn't see you." She stepped out from behind Diamond. "May I help you?"

"I'm looking for someone. You have a woman here named Claire?"

"Yes, we did. She's not here now though." After Claire's obvious fear, Sara hadn't expected the guy's clean-cut appearance. With wavy hair that reached his shirt collar, broad shoulders and deep blue eyes, he could be a model. He didn't look at all like anyone should be afraid of him. Only a determined frown seemed at odds with the rest of him. It gave her that something-out-of-place feeling.

"Where'd she go?"

"I don't know. I haven't heard anything except that she left."

"Are you sure?" Jake tamped down his impatience. He didn't trust her, but then he had learned the hard way not to trust any woman.

"Yes, I'm sure," Sara said. "She was assigned to me and now I have to do her work and mine."

Jake nodded. He walked out of the barn and looked around. He needed to ask someone else to make sure that woman wasn't lying. He got in the car and decided to drive down to that big barn near the road. He drove past the roosters, turned the corner and saw a guy outside the barn. He reached the barn and called out. The guy walked over to the car.

"Need some help?"

"Yes, I'm looking for someone who works here."

"And who might that be?" Elliott fought down panic. Was this one of Dominic's guys? He didn't recognize him but then he knew Dominic had a big organization.

"A woman named Claire. I was told she works here." Jake noticed a slight change in Elliott's eyes.

"Uh...yes, there's a Claire here."

"Where is she?" Jake fought to control the anger that surged through him. It had to be her.

"Don't know. Why?"

"I had a fight with my girlfriend. She left and I think she is working here."

"Your girlfriend?" Elliott didn't know what to do. If this guy was Claire's boyfriend, she would probably leave with him. Then his summer would be boring. He planned another opportunity to have Claire for himself.

"Yes, dude, my girlfriend. Where is she?"

"Not sure. I haven't seen her today." That much was true.

"Where does she stay?"

Elliott thought fast. "The women stay off the farm. There's only one building suitable for living and that houses all of us guys."

"And where is this place?" Jake wanted to shake it out of this guy.

"I don't know for sure. I think it's someplace in Sodus."

"Look," Jake said, "I need to talk to her. You ever been crazy about someone? I want her back, you know?"

"Yeah, I know." No way on earth would he help find her.

"I suggest you go into Sodus and ask around." Elliott realized he could use this to his advantage. If he saved Claire from a former boyfriend, maybe she'd be willing to show her gratitude.

After mumbling about people that don't know anything, Jake left.

Elliott waited to make sure he didn't turn around and come back. He wouldn't go to Claire yet. Sooner or later, she'd be back in the horse barn.

* * *

"I met your boyfriend today." Elliott found Claire as she was leaving the office.

"What?" The shock on her face answered any questions he had about their relationship.

"Claire, he was here looking for you."

"I knew it was him."

"Is there a problem with him?"

"Yes...no...well, I mean...not really. I left to work here this summer." She strove to control the panic.

"You're upset. I helped you though."

"What do you mean?"

"I told him you weren't here, that you lived in Sodus."

"But you admitted I work here?" Her voice rose.

"Yes, before he told me he was your boyfriend. Then I tried to protect you."

"Protect me? You can't. If he knows I work here, he'll find me." Claire needed to disappear. "Sorry, I need to go talk to Cheri."

"Calm down. I'll help. We can make sure he doesn't find you."

"Are you serious? This farm is open for anyone to drive in and walk around. He'll be back and he'll find me."

"You sound like you're afraid of him."

"I have to go." Claire ran out of the building and across the road. When she reached the privacy of her room, she tried to face her fear. Gulping sobs erupted. She lay across her bed and gave in to them. When the emotion ebbed, anger took its place. How dare he invade her life! She'd never go back to him. She'd never give him power over her again. She jumped off the bed and looked around the room. It wasn't much, but she'd made it hers. She'd hung her favorite artwork on the wall and brought in fresh flowers from the yard. It was home for now, but Jake's presence on the farm changed everything.

Fear seeped in, overriding the anger. He would find her and his revenge would land her in the hospital—or worse. She had to leave now. She got up and took out her suitcase. With no time for her usual neatness, she threw her things in and closed it. She had to find Cheri.

Elliott waited on the porch. He'd listened to the sobs and the frantic movements that followed. He could almost smell her fear. He cursed himself for giving her away. Maybe the guy wouldn't come back. In any case, he would be on the lookout. He had to convince Claire that she should stay. He admitted that she made the summer bearable. If he could make sure Jake never found her, she'd be grateful, and grateful women expressed that emotion. Maybe...

Claire found Elliott waiting. She walked past him.

"Claire, wait."

"I can't."

"I think I have a solution."

"There is none. I have to leave."

"Where are you going?"

"Right now, I'm going to find Cheri. After that, I don't know. Maybe Rochester. It might be easier to get lost in a city." She shrugged away his hand as he tried to draw her close. "Don't. Please don't make it worse than it is."

"Sorry," he pulled back his hand. "I'll walk you to Cheri's office, in case he comes back."

Claire walked away without acknowledging him. He kept pace with her, searching for a solution.

The fear on Claire's face forewarned Cheri. She looked at Elliott. "What's wrong?"

"I have to leave," Claire blurted. "Now."

"Her boyfriend came looking for her today. I admitted ..."

"Stay out of this, Elliott. It's not your fault and it's not your problem," Claire interrupted.

"But ..."

"Wait a minute, both of you." Cheri held up her hand. "One at a time. Claire, what happened?"

"He found me and I have to go. I can't go back with him."

"I told him she stayed in Sodus," Elliott said.

"I want to hear from Claire first. Why can't you see him?"

"I just can't."

"You're afraid of him, aren't you? Has he hurt you before?"

"Please, it doesn't matter. I'm sorry to leave you shorthanded but ..."

"Claire, take a deep breath and listen. He can't hurt you here. I think you're safest if you stay where people know the situation."

"You don't understand."

"Have you filed a restraining order?"

"No. Well yes, one time before but I don't know if it's still good."

"We'll file for one. In any case, it gives you a reason to contact the police."

"But he'll be back."

"And we'll be ready for him. I will give you some office work to keep you out of sight until he shows up again. If we contact the police now, I'm sure we can get a new restraining order. When he returns, we'll give it to him. Now, Elliott, what's your part in this?"

"This guy came in and asked if Claire worked here. I said yes before thinking. I saw his angry response and realized I shouldn't have said anything. I told him she wasn't here now and I didn't know when she'd be back—that she lived in Sodus." Elliott's voice pleaded for understanding. "I couldn't think of any other way out of it. Claire, I'm sorry."

Cheri watched Elliott's face. It was the first time she'd seen his concern for someone other than himself. Out of all this, that gave her hope. "You couldn't have known. Don't feel guilty. We need a solution, not remorse."

"Claire, call the police now. Whatever you do, we need that restraining order served. After that, you can look at your options. Okay?"

"I guess. It makes sense, but he won't stop because of a piece of paper. Especially if he's drinking." Claire stopped. She looked at Elliott. "Could you tell if he'd been drinking?"

"Not obviously, but I didn't think about it."

* * *

Jake knew that idiot had lied to him. He also saw something in his expression when he mentioned Claire. If he was her new boyfriend, he'd kill them both. No, he'd kill him in front of her, and bring her home where she belonged.

He didn't believe for a minute that Claire wasn't there. He hated liars and he had just met two of them. They didn't know whom they were dealing with.

He drove to Sodus and stopped at several places. No one had heard about Alasa Farm volunteers living in town. He bought a six-pack, headed back toward the farm and parked on the road. He walked into the farthest barn, the one that said cow barn. It was empty. Across the road, he checked out a small building. He found several rabbits, but no people. This might be easier than he thought.

He walked up the road passing the roosters and an old house that had been partially destroyed by fire. Two little girls played with some goats in the next pasture. He walked down to them.

"Hi," the taller girl said.

"Hi." He had no interest in casual conversation. "Do you come here often?"

"Yes, we love the animals. My aunt volunteers here one morning a week," she said.

"I was told that the women who volunteer here stay in Sodus. Do you know where?"

"No, sorry,"

"Are you sure?"

"She's sure," the blonde girl said. "All the full-time summer volunteers stay here."

"Are you looking for someone?" The taller girl was less trusting.
"None of ... no, not really."

Jake walked away. He needed to think. He walked back to the
car, opened and drank another can of beer. Those first two had likely
warned Claire that someone was looking for her. Claire may be too
independent for her own good, but she wasn't dumb. He'd bet money that she'd run. But then, maybe she knew that's what he'd expect.
No, she might try to hide. If she did, he'd find her. If she worked
here, she'd have to show her face, and he'd be ready.

RESIDENT OF CRACKER BOX PALACE

CHAPTER TWENTY

Remember the cries of those who are in need and trouble,
that when you are in trouble
God may hear your cries.

Mother Ann Lee, founder of the Shakers

A SCREAM OF TERROR THAT didn't stop. The animals reacted first, each adding their own sudden terror into the dawn. It took longer to penetrate the farm staffs' sleep-filled minds.

Sara jumped out of bed and ran to the window. Elena stood below screaming. She threw on some clothes and ran out of the house and across the road. Claire was right behind her. Jeff and Seth reached Elena first.

"What ...?" Jeff started.

Elena pointed. Her screams turned to sobs. "There ..."

Elliott lay in a pool of blood. Seth ran to him and checked for a pulse. Nothing.

"Don't go any closer," Jeff cautioned the others. "Sara, call 9-1-1."

"The blood ... Is he alive?" Elena asked between sobs. She fought to get herself under control.

"I can't find a pulse. Help will be here soon." Jeff looked at Elliott's face. Was that fear or pain that twisted his features? Hadn't he read that a person's face relaxed in death? Maybe Elliott was still alive. "Hold on. Help is on the way." He could find no other words. He checked again. Did he feel a faint pulse?

Was anything out of place? Jeff didn't move for fear of damaging a crime scene. He'd seen enough TV shows to know how easily people could destroy evidence.

Seth looked around. No one moved, a tableau frozen in time. It seemed an eternity before they heard sirens. The ambulance arrived first, followed by two first responders.

The EMTs took over and Jeff backed away. As one examined Elliott, he gave a slight nod to the other one who moved toward Elliott. No one spoke as a Sheriff's car pulled into the drive.

"I found a pulse, but it's faint and erratic," the EMT kept his voice low, but it raised hope in everyone.

"The sheriff will want to talk to everyone, but please give us room now."

"Most of us have an innate disability to erase a bloody scene from our minds." Seth spoke to himself more than the little group, stunned by the early morning horror. They had yet to register the distress of the animals, especially the horses and the nearby sheep and goats.

The first responder, not hindered by shock, suggested they go ahead and take care of morning chores. "As long as no one leaves the farm, there'll be no problem," he said.

Cheri and Burt arrived as the group dispersed. The deputy filled them in.

"Too many of our animals have known fear. We'll stay and help calm them. Let us know if you need anything from us." Cheri noticed the staff heading toward other barns.

Elena heard nothing. Seth put his arm around her shoulders and led her away from the barn. She looked back, amazed at how fast the paramedics worked. The one with Elliott checked his eyes, his skull and then his eyes again.

The other one went back to the ambulance and worked on IV bags. He had some kind of mask in his hand.

"Please let me watch," she begged Seth.

"Okay, from here. After they finish, we'll need to get back to work."

Elena barely heard his words. The paramedic with Elliott continued his examination, checking his eyes and his breathing. Elliott never moved. The other one brought supplies and a long board from the ambulance. They cut some of his clothes away, put a collar around his neck and rolled him over on his side. They checked his back, rolled him back over and strapped him to the board. Elena counted six straps. They then used some tape on his head. They checked Elliott's vitals many times as they worked. Finally, they carried him to the ambulance. The last thing she saw was the oxygen mask as they placed it on Elliott's face.

"I feel like that took hours. Will they get him to the hospital in time?"

"It only took a few minutes, probably seven or eight at the most. The EMTs know how critical each minute can be. They'll continue their work in the ambulance."

"Like the IV?" Elena asked.

"Yes, and they'll do an EKG, take his blood pressure and, of course, keep checking his heart rate. They'll keep an eye on his oxygen level, too. They'll notify the hospital before they arrive."

Elena stood rooted to the ground long after the ambulance left. Images of blood, the straps tying Elliott to the board, all the medical paraphernalia, played in her head like a looped reel. She shivered.

"Do you need to sit down, or go to your room?" The lack of color in her face worried Seth. "You've had a shock and I think you need to rest."

Elena didn't respond but let him lead her to a chair on the porch.

CHAPTER TWENTY-ONE

Many men go fishing all of their lives without knowing that it is not fish they are after.

Henry David Thoreau

HAP BAITED HIS HOOK AGAIN. This Canadian fishing trip was proving to be relaxing as well as challenging. It had been a last minute decision and he already knew he'd never regret it. One of his wife's friends had called and told him he had a last-minute opening. This'd been on his bucket list and he couldn't believe it was finally reality.

Two of the four other guys on the boat had reeled in some nice-sized salmon, but so far, all he'd accomplished was losing a couple of spoon lures. He'd tried the live bait first but that hadn't worked either. Both Bill and Ed caught their salmon on the spoon lures—a Chinook for Bill and a Coho for Ed.

He'd never claimed to be a first-class fisherman, but he'd met several that fit that title. Peg belonged to an outdoor writing group and he'd relished the time spent learning from the experts. This was his first Lake Ontario fishing trip. He'd fished Lake Michigan once. Spending time in Canada had appealed to him so he booked the trip. Peg tagged along to do some writing about the Canadian side of the lake.

Here he was, in the middle of the trip, waiting for a tug on his twenty-pound line that didn't end in lost lures. He tried to think like a fish. What would make him go for the spoon lure? It surely didn't catch the light on the bottom of the lake. He'd read that it reflected the light but he didn't know how far down in the water light reaches. He'd have to look that up.

The tug. He felt it. This was a little different than the snags. A come-and-go type of tug. Not the drag. He pulled up the rod, reeled in some line. The tug stayed. He jerked the rod and reeled in slow. Adrenaline surged through his veins. It felt like a big one. He stole a glance at Bill, who was busy setting his line.

"Keep your line tight," the captain walked up behind him. "Reel him in slow. From the looks of the rod, I'd say you might have a good-sized one."

Hap felt every muscle tense. He felt like he'd run a couple of miles but he knew that fish was nowhere near the boat yet. He reeled in the line, fighting the urge to speed up. Scenes from bygone fishing movies swam through his head. The fish tugged harder and suddenly ran with the line. Hap held tight.

"Keep control," the captain said.

His phone rang.

"Ignore it." Ed whispered.

The fish pulled and the phone rang. Seemed like both went on for hours. Then the phone quit, but the fish didn't. "You're doing fine," the captain said.

The phone chirped. Voicemail. Hap reeled in some more. The fish's response quieted. Had he lost him? He paused.

"Keep reeling," the captain said. "He's just tiring. Don't let the line lag."

Hours later, or at least it seemed like it, Hap looked at the Chinook salmon that lay on the deck. He didn't remember the final minutes of reeling or feel the tiredness in his arms. Once he saw that fish in the net, he grinned. Not the biggest catch of the day, but his first salmon in Canadian waters. Life was good!

His phone rang again as he watched the guide filet his catch. He ignored the distraction.

CHAPTER TWENTY-TWO

Always be in a state of becoming.
Walt Disney

ELENA TOOK HER PHONE OUT of her pocket. Hap would know what to do.

"Hap, I need you!"

"What happened?" Hap heard the panic.

"I ... I found Elliott in the barn this morning. There was blood everywhere and I thought he was dead. But the paramedic felt a pulse and they've taken him to the hospital. I couldn't reach you." Elena could hold the sobs no longer.

"I'm sorry. Elena, take a deep breath and tell me from the beginning. Are you at the farm?"

"Yes," she hiccupped.

"Okay. Are the police there?"

"Yes, the sheriff's department is here."

"Good. Is it someone you knew?"

"Yes." His questions began to calm her. "Elliott. He was another volunteer."

"Okay. Start at the beginning."

"I was going out to the barn. When I opened the door, I saw him lying there. There was blood everywhere. I screamed and couldn't stop. Then the rest came."

"Who? Do you remember?"

"Sara and Claire. No, Seth and Jeff came first."

"Tell me who each of them are."

"Sara is the horse barn manager and Claire is another volunteer. Seth works here and Jeff is the operations manager. Cheri and Burt are the owners but they didn't get here until after the EMTs and the sheriff."

"Good girl. Did you see anyone else?"

"No."

"Is there anyone else that works there?"

"There are some area people who volunteer part time. None of them were here."

"Has the sheriff talked to you yet?"

"No, he told us to do our work and he would talk to us later. Can you come?"

"It sounds like it's under control. When the sheriff talks to you, tell him exactly what you remember. I'm sure he'll handle everything just fine."

"Okay, but is it all right if I call you again after I talk to him?"

"Sure. You can call me anytime."

Hap relayed the conversation to Peg. "So much for an interesting but quiet summer job before college. I'm sorry she had to be the one to discover it."

"I know," Peg said. "I can't imagine how traumatic it would be. Especially someone you work with."

"I feel guilty for not answering her call earlier. She's been a big help in research a couple of times, but actually finding someone covered in blood is much more traumatic."

BARN AT ALASA FARM

CHAPTER TWENTY-THREE

Regret is a heavy burden.

MARY ANN FOUND IT DIFFICULT to rouse herself, but the restlessness was upon her again. She should visit the farm again and continue her search for her baby. She wanted to give up and beg God's forgiveness. Maybe He'd let her rest. It had been so long.

She always crossed over to the old house. It served as a reminder of her sin and disgrace. When the depression lifted a little, she remembered Ruth's kindness. Without that human touch, she might not have survived. She thought of Mollie's kindness, too— but that brought thoughts of Audrey's judgmental mutterings. She needed to focus on the positive. Horace. He always treated her kindly, but her own shame pushed him away. Even now, she felt he would forgive her if she had the courage to ask. It was easier to let things be.

God, Eaton, the Shakers and the world had abandoned her. Why didn't she accept her fate and let go? She hated that tiny grain of hope that ended with her holding her baby in her arms. Surely if she still walked the earth, her baby did, too. Would a baby be able to rest without knowing its mother?

She roamed the halls of the house, remembering days spent mending and refitting clothes. Ruth told the other women that Mary Ann had a special talent with a needle. She didn't know if it was true, but it made her feel accepted. She liked the women she'd lived with. The older ones seemed at peace with their faith and their lives here. If only she'd been able to find those same qualities. She'd done well until Eaton turned her head.

She recalled the first time she'd found herself alone with Eaton and Horace. She was feeding the chickens when they came around the corner of the hen house. They were laughing but stopped the minute they spotted her. Men and women had different duties and they seldom mixed, especially the young members. The guys said nothing, but didn't leave.

"Hi," she said.

"We're enjoying the beautiful weather today," the good-looking one said.

"Me too. The sunshine makes me happy." How could she have said something so foolish?

"You're right. It does make us all happy," the dark-haired one said.

"What's your name?"

"Mary Ann."

"Well, Sister Mary Ann, it's nice to make your acquaintance. I'm Eaton and this is my friend, Horace." Eaton bowed with a flare.

"We probably should not be talking," she said.

"On this gorgeous day, I think the Lord wants us to be friends." Eaton said. "What say you to that?"

"Maybe." Mary Ann felt the heat rise in her face. Whether it was embarrassment or the joy of youth, she didn't know, but she was enjoying herself. Eaton was so handsome and Horace was friendly.

"I'm feeding the chickens. What have you been doing?" She asked.

"Testing the cider, and it's good," Eaton laughed.

"I haven't tested as much as he has," Horace grinned.

"I think maybe it's the cider, not the weather." Mary Ann said. "Don't get me wrong, I envy you."

"Next time, we'll save some for you."

The two remained true to their word. The next day, they appeared at the hen house with a cup in hand. Eaton handed it to her. "Here, taste this."

Mary Ann took a sip and made a face. Eaton and Horace laughed.

After that, they found it easy to accidentally bump into each other. It became a joke between the three of them. Mary Ann looked forward to their meetings. Now, in hindsight, how she rued the day she met them.

* * *

The house was quiet. She paid little attention to the goings-on at the farm. If the present intruded into her misery, she focused on the animals. She loved the goats most of all. But then, it depressed her to think of Luke, her pet goat. She remembered how he followed her everywhere and seemed to know what she was thinking. She thought of the days of her confinement and how Millie had urged her to talk to Luke. She'd had a pet goat too, but Mary Ann could no longer remember its name. Now the farm's goats lived behind a wire fence and she felt no bond with any of them.

She felt a presence and stilled. She suspected Horace was here, but it didn't really feel like him. She slowly turned but nothing was there. Whatever or whoever it was, it had disappeared. Suddenly, she felt loneliness. If only Horace were here. The house seemed cold and damp. She could no longer imagine Ruth and the other ladies enjoying their work together. There was nothing here for her today.

CHAPTER TWENTY-FOUR

You can never enter the kingdom of God with hardness against any one,
for God is love
and if you love God you will love one another.
Mother Ann Lee, founder of the Shakers

"Will Elliott be okay?" Elena asked.

"I hope so. The doctors will do everything they can. Cheri and Burt followed the ambulance. They'll let us know," Jeff told the group that had assembled on the porch. The animals, fed and watered, had calmed down. The staff had failed to do likewise. Jeff looked around. "Most of us are still in shock. I think everyone needs to take an hour to do whatever will help you relax. I will keep you informed of any news from the hospital."

"In the meantime, we can all send prayers and good thoughts Elliott's way." Sara agreed that they were a sorry-looking bunch. The first shock had given way to exhaustion. It surprised her that no one had yet thought to ask any questions. At least, not out loud.

They all looked at Elena. "I'm better now," she assured them. "I just want to know if he's going to make it."

"We all do," Seth said, "and I'm sure we'll know as soon as the doctors can tell us anything."

"Where are they taking him?"

"Newark-Wayne Community Hospital. It's about twenty miles from here," Seth answered.

Sara and Jeff left. Claire looked from Elena to Seth. He nodded and she left.

"Do you want me to help you to your room?"

"No, I'll wait here," Elena answered.

"Will you be all right by yourself?"

"Yes, please don't worry about me. I just know I can't go back to my room now. I need to be in the open. It's like if I stay close to the barn, it will help Elliott. I know that sounds crazy."

"Not really. I understand. Do you want me to wait with you?"

"No, I'd rather be alone."

"How about if I come back and check on you in half an hour?"

"Okay." Elena nodded.

Once she was alone, she prayed, begging God to take care of Elliott. Violence had never personally touched her before. She thought of the research she'd done when Hap had asked for her help. She'd known about violence, and ached for those that experienced it. But this was different. Seeing the reality was a slap in her face. She realized this morning changed something in her, allowed malice into her consciousness, awakened her to a darker side of life. She prayed some more.

* * *

Time crawled. Finally, Cheri called Jeff. He gathered the group on the porch. "Elliott is alive. He's lost a lot of blood, has several broken ribs, a concussion and numerous contusions. The doctors have stopped the bleeding and cleaned him up. They can't do anything for the broken ribs. Fortunately, they didn't penetrate his lungs. He regained consciousness but they will keep him heavily sedated with pain meds. They will keep him for at least a day or two to watch his concussion and treat his wounds to avoid infections."

"Will we be able to visit him?"

"Not now. They'll let us know."

Elena cried. After the relief of knowing Elliott would survive, the next concern raised its ugly head. Who did this? Why would anyone hurt Elliott? And the unspoken question, were they safe?

CHAPTER TWENTY-FIVE

He who broods upon his unhappiness only increases it, and makes himself more unhappy.

Shaker saying

I did not harm Elliott. Did I wish him pain and suffering for his actions? Yes. Did I wish him beat nearly to death? I don't know. I never really thought in those terms. But I know I'm not free from all guilt. I wandered into the old house and imagined I could still smell burnt wood. Maybe I did, but it didn't matter either way. The only thing I wanted now was to find Mary Ann again. I cursed God. If He were truly in charge of all things, then why didn't He let our paths cross? After all these years, the spirit world still confounded me. I had more control when I was alive.

For years, I thought He was giving both of us time to come to terms with our changed existence. But as the frustration grows, I realize I know even less now. I've spent over two centuries trying to understand Him. I've raged at Him for allowing violence and selfishness to rule the world. Then I think of my years with the Shakers. I never found the peace or acceptance that the religion offered.

* * *

Mary Ann felt strong today. She had an urge to find Horace. This time she would try to talk to him. Maybe he would help her find her baby. She made her presence known in the house. She wished she had a way to contact him so they would come over at the same time.

Maybe he no longer resided in the spirit realm. She hadn't seen him for a few weeks. She had watched spirits come and go, never understanding the process. How could some people die in peace and others were cursed to live on until they found resolution or redemption? Did all sinners suffer the same fate? What was Horace's big sin? He had always been nice to her.

Funny, she had never seen any of the other Shakers on the spirit side. Maybe they had found the answer to peace with God. But then again, she had never encountered Eaton among the lost souls. It was all beyond her grasp. She ran her hands across the old piano and remembered her favorite hymn, "Tis a gift to be simple, tis a gift to be free." Her heart sang, filled with a long-forgotten joy, "Tis a gift to come down where I ought to be. And when we find ourselves in the place just right, 'Twill be in the valley of love and delight."

"I love to hear you sing with joy." Horace smiled as he appeared next to her.

"Horace, I'm afraid I got carried away remembering the song."

"It's a beautiful song, and I loved hearing you sing. You seem happy."

"I am, today. Not often. I ... I want to thank you for coming. I haven't been kind to you."

"I know you're hurting. I'm here for you, whenever you need me."

"Please don't say anymore. I'm not sure how much kindness I can handle. I have to go."

Horace held his tongue to keep from lashing out. Didn't she know he was so tired of waiting? By some miracle, they had actually communicated. Maybe it was the joy in the old Shaker hymn. Maybe God rewarded those who loved the hymn. He had never pondered God's rewards in this light. Maybe singing was a higher form of prayer and therefore more pleasing to Him.

Mary Ann cursed her own cowardice. She had longed for kindness in the months before the baby, and ever since. Now, when Horace offered it, fear seized her. Back on the other side, she acknowledged her angst was of her own making. Horace had extended compassion but she had refused it. Maybe she'd try again but not now. She gave in to the sadness that haunted her every minute. If only it would smother her, and end her misery.

* * *

Rage has possessed my soul through several generations of human history. Why did it take me so long to learn? Mary Ann didn't need my rage. It solved nothing. She didn't need my protection either. It was far too late for that. She needed my understanding. I needed to open my heart. Hopefully, it's not too late for either of us to find redemption and the answers we seek.

Her singing today has replayed in my mind since I heard her. I love the Shaker hymns, the way they made me realize that life is really simple if I choose to love and praise God with everything I do. 'Tis a Gift to be Simple is my favorite call to live in His love. I wish it had been sung at every meeting, but I did like other hymns, too.

My second favorite was called The Rolling Deep. I wish I had known Eldress Polly Lawrence. She was one of the original group who came here from New Lebanon in 1826. I've read some of her journal entries, but her song is my reason for thinking of her now.

The rolling deep may overturn

The allies sink and mountains burn

But thou my soul shall firmly stand

Supported by God's righteous hand.

There's another verse but I don't remember it, except the last line was 'to bear the cross and wear the crown.'

Although I no longer sing, the words run through my mind. They calm me, and make me thankful for my Shaker faith. Unworthy as I was, I believed in Mother Ann's pathway to perfection and redemption.

CHAPTER TWENTY-SIX

An animal's eyes have the power to speak a great language.
Martin Buber (www.brainyquotes.com)

"I CAN'T ERASE THE SIGHT of Elliott in that pool of blood," Elena texted Hap. "Please come."

Hap punched in Elena's number. She answered on the first ring.

"We will be leaving Canada tomorrow. If we come by, what town would we stay in?"

"I'll get back to you."

"Call me. It's easier than texting," Hap said.

"For you, maybe." Elena laughed. He could be so old-fashioned but he knew more about human nature than she would ever know.

Elena texted Cheri. "I have a friend coming into town. Where should he stay?"

"Sodus Point. One of the B&Bs. Try Maxwell's."

"He has a dog. Does that matter?"

"They don't take dogs. Try the Carriage House Inn B&B. Jerry and Claudine own the place."

"Thanks."

She called Hap. "Try the Carriage House Inn in Sodus Point. It's a B&B. You'll talk to Jerry or Claudine, the owners. They'll take Luke. Let me know."

"Will do."

Elena felt better just knowing that she'd see Hap soon. She had always appreciated his straightforward, common sense approach to problems.

* * *

Peg called and made the arrangements. They would arrive in Sodus Point tomorrow night. Luckily, Jerry said he had a room on the first floor that would be perfect for Luke. She looked forward to exploring Sodus Bay. After looking it up online, she knew she had to find the old lighthouse. Fortunately, it was just up the street from the Carriage House Inn. Hap made arrangements to see Elena after breakfast the next morning.

They arrived in Sodus Point mid-afternoon, in time to visit the lighthouse museum and learn some of the history of the area. Jerry laughed when he told them of the pride New Yorkers have in their home.

"People hear New York and think of New York City, but you're in the heart of New York here. We love our orchards and farms.

FARMHOUSE AT ALASA FARM

Produce the best apples in the world. You'll miss apple season but you're just in time for strawberries."

"It's beautiful here and we're looking forward to exploring." Hap knew Peg was already plotting some time for touring the countryside.

"Then there's the lake. We're proud of Lake Ontario and our bay. Sodus Point sets right where Sodus Bay meets the lake. And, of course, we love our lighthouse and all the history connected with it."

"We want to take it all in, but first, I have to visit Cracker Box Palace and find out what's going on there."

"I hope everything's okay. For now I'll give you some literature and a list of restaurants. You'll need that."

They decided to try the Steger Haus in nearby Sodus where they enjoyed a delicious pork chop dinner, managing to save a few bites for Luke. He liked it every bit as much as they did.

They ended the evening walking out on the pier to the current lighthouse. Hap stopped to visit with a couple of the fishermen who said they have good luck fishing the bay.

The next morning, they ate a leisurely breakfast while enjoying Jerry's stories about the community. He gave them directions to Alasa Farms and suggested they visit Burnap's Farm Market and Garden Cafe sometime before they left town. Peg had made reservations for three nights, so they assured Jerry that would try it.

When they arrived at Alasa Farms, they marveled at its size and the many buildings. Luke immediately reacted to a couple of cats in the driveway, letting them know he was there. They ignored him and he soon lost interest.

Elena had been waiting and ran to the car. "I'm so happy to see you," she nearly knocked Hap over with her enthusiastic hug. She gave Peg a less boisterous greeting and then picked up an excited Luke. Hap gave Peg his "he's so spoiled" look and she agreed. Nothing like a happy dog, though.

All serious talk seemed to be put on hold. Elena wanted them to see the horses and goats. She led them from one pasture to another, patiently giving Luke time to become familiar with all the new smells. "I'll bet he thinks he's in a cat farm," Hap said as they noticed several more around the barns. "Are these rescues too?"

"Some of them are, but some have been born here." Elena's love of the farm lit her face.

"Plenty for them to eat. They look fat and sassy."

As they walked down the road toward the roosters, Luke stopped. Hap tugged on his leash but Luke refused to move. He stared at the house and his fur began to stand on end. "Come on, little man," Hap urged.

Luke remained frozen.

"He senses the ghosts," Elena said. "They're in the old house."

Hap looked at the house on the left side of the road. The roof and third floor had been caved in, obviously by a fire. The rest of the house looked abandoned but not burnt. It'd been a grand old home in its heyday. Was Luke reacting to the burnt smell or was there something else?

"The place has two resident ghosts they know, although a psychic said there are many more."

"Are they friendly?" Peg asked.

"They don't seem to bother anything. The two they know were Shakers a couple hundred years ago."

"What do they know about them?"

"Mary Ann was kicked out of the Shakers when she became pregnant. Horace is the other one, but I've not heard any stories about him, except for Griff's. He thinks Horace caused the fire that burned the house."

Luke hadn't moved. Hap picked him up and walked away from the house. By the time they reached the car, he had returned to his normal doggy self.

Elena saw Cheri and waved her over. "I want you to meet good friends of mine and of Griff's. This is Hap and Peg Lynch and Luke. They live near South Padre Island. Peg is a writer and she loves spending time at Griff and Joni's store. Hap is a retired cop, and he's done consulting work with the Port Isabel Police Department."

"Welcome. I'm Cheri. Griff is a special friend of ours too. He's the one who wanted us to have Alasa Farms."

Luke's wagging tail slowed all conversation as she greeted him.

"He senses ghosts," Elena said. "You should have seen him near the house. He froze on the spot. He knows they're in there."

"I'm sure he does. Animals have a far greater sense of the unexplained than we do."

"I think he needs a break," Hap said. "I was just going to invite Elena for lunch. Would you join us?"

"I'd love to, if we can go someplace close. I have a lot of paperwork to finish this afternoon."

"Fine. Any place you suggest."

"Then let's go to the Alton Coffee Cup. It was one of Griff's old hangouts, it's close and the food is good. I'll drive my car and you can follow."

"Sounds good."

"Isn't she wonderful?" Elena settled into the back seat with Luke on her lap.

"She has to be smart and caring to run a venture like this. She sounds like an excellent role model. So you're enjoying your summer?"

"I've already learned so much, but I never suspected that violence would reach us here."

"My guess is it came from the outside. We can't control that."

"I know." Elena played with Luke's front paws. He leaned his head against her.

Once seated in the restaurant, Cheri told the waitress that her visitors knew Griff from South Padre Island. After a few good stories, they ordered their food.

Cheri regaled them with stories of some of the animal rescues. Hap liked her genuineness. She truly loved the animals she rescued. He felt that Elena was in good hands for the summer.

After lunch, Cheri left and said she'd see them back at the farm.

"Shall we see if Luke can walk the farm this time?" Hap asked Elena as they pulled up in front of the horse barn. He wanted to give Luke more space.

After watching the horses, they visited the goats and Elena introduced each one by name. "They are so much fun. I love their curiosity," she told them.

"Obviously, they love you too."

Luke's attention turned to the smallest of the goats. They stared at each other.

"Look at them," Elena said. "It's like they know each other."

Hap watched. Luke stood planted, but he sensed no fear in him. No, it was more as if he and the goat had met before. "Wouldn't you like to read their minds?"

"Yes," Peg answered. "One would think they recognize each other."

Their attention turned to the alpaca that came to the fence hoping for a treat. Elena pulled a piece of carrot out of her pocket and handed it over. The alpaca readily chewed up his treat and wanted seconds.

Hap turned to check on Luke, who was no longer at his side. He looked along the fence, but no Luke.

"Luke," he called. He checked all around, thinking Luke would come bouncing back through the grass.

"Where is he?" Peg asked.

"I don't know. He was right here beside me a minute ago." Hap walked back up to the road.

"Luke," he called again. When Luke didn't show on the second call, he started walking back toward the horse barn. "Come on, buddy!"

"I'll check the barn," Elena walked through the partially open door. Luke stood motionless and alert at the last stall. She called his name as she walked back to him. As she got closer, she saw his fur standing on end.

"Hap, in here."

Hap walked into the barn. When he spotted Luke, he knew the signs. The dog was rooted to the ground and wouldn't take another step. Hap looked in the stall.

Elena gasped.

"What's wrong?"

"Did you see anything?"

"No, but apparently Luke did."

"I saw movement, something that looked like gossamer wings. Then it disappeared."

"Maybe you're being fanciful, tuning in to Luke's wavelength," Hap chuckled. He saw nothing but in no way would he dismiss the possibility that something was there. Not after Luke's reaction. "Or maybe the farm is haunted and I don't have the ability to make that connection. In either case, I'm taking Luke outside. He's still rigid as a statue."

Luke began to relax when they were out in the open air. "I think we need to go," Hap told Peg. "If we come out here again, I don't want to bring him."

"Let's go back to our room for awhile. Luke will relax there," Peggy suggested.

"I'll come into town this evening if you want to have dinner together," Elena said.

"Sounds like a plan. Call us, or texting will work too."

Elena shook her head in mock despair. "When will you join the tech revolution?"

* * *

Shock gripped me. Luke, the name that man called the dog. Could it really be? For a minute, I was taken back in time. I thought of Mary Ann's Luke, her special goat. I remembered how he had followed me around after she left the farm. Even while I was alive, I was aware he had some sort of sixth sense. Now this little white dog named Luke, responded to me. Not just sensed me there, but his eyes acknowledged me. Only one other animal had ever done so, a hackney pony that Alvah Strong raised on the farm. I remember thinking of him as Luke, because he reminded me of the goat. Decades have flown by, and now, Luke the dog. I wanted to break down and cry. It was a touch, not a human touch, but a touch from another creature, a recognition in someone's eyes that I still exist.

I mean the poor little guy no harm. We simply acknowledged each other's existence. I hope his awareness doesn't include fear. I sense more fear in the man who picked him up and took him away. I hope I get to see him again. Anything to break the overwhelming loneliness.

Then there's the young woman who sensed my presence. I've watched her before. I believe she is called Elena. Can I hope that she has an awareness? I know she saw a fragmented shadow as Luke and I connected. I will watch her. If she remains bewildered, I will make an effort to connect with her.

My step is lighter than it's been in days. I want to do something kind to repay the joy Luke gave me. I wandered the farm, looking for opportunities. Invisibility has both an upside and a downside. On the one hand, I can go anywhere and do anything undetected. On the other hand, loneliness haunts any soul that never makes contact with another. For me, I don't care if it's a living soul, an animal soul or another spirit. Sometimes I think I'll die without that connection. Crazy me. I'm already dead. Can a spirit die too?

How will it end for me? A disease or an accident poses no threat. It's one other thing I ponder as I wander the farm. I like to think it's about redemption. That at some point, God will decide I've atoned for my sins, and take me into His heavenly kingdom. But what if God turns out to be merciless rather than merciful? Is atoning for sin a process? As a Shaker, I lived life with that belief. Everything I did, from working hard and accepting all people as equal to my striving toward simplicity and a peaceful spirit, I did to prepare myself for eternal life with Him. I pray he hasn't cast me aside forever.

* * *

"I know you're going to realize it's just the old cop in me, but we need to help piece together information," Hap told Elena as they sat down to dinner at the Franklin House Tavern.

"I know but first, let's talk food, okay?"

"Stomach before brain, huh?"

"Sorry, but I want to suggest a couple of things. Cheri and Burt love the fried fish special they have tonight. I like the chicken tenders and the pizza. Their burgers are great too."

"Pizza sounds good. Does that work for everyone?" Peg asked.

"Sure. Do you like sausage and pepperoni?"

"Sound great."

After they received their drinks and ordered the pizza, Elena turned her attention to Hap. "Okay, what do you need to know?"

"I realize you probably don't know Elliott well, but start with the facts you know."

"His dad sent him here. Not sure why but we all assume he had gotten into some kind of trouble at home. His family owns a business and they expect him to follow in their footsteps. That's all I know. None of that came from Elliott but from conversations around the farm."

"Can you describe his behavior since he's been here?"

"He was here when I came. Elliott's always courteous, but he never appears happy. He smiles whenever he's around people but if you watch, it's like unhappiness drapes over him when he's not with others. Sometimes he can be edgy, more so the last few days."

"How does he get along with everyone here?"

"Friendly, I think, but I don't think any of us would call him a friend. Tomorrow we can talk to Seth. A couple of times when we've all been together, I've sensed some tension between him and Elliott."

"Good. Anything else?"

"No. Oh, I think he's attracted to Claire, but it seems like she avoids him. I'm not sure that means anything because she likes her alone time." Elena took the last sip of her Coke.

"You've been a big help. Do you think Cheri would be willing to talk to me?"

"Sure, I'll vouch for you."

"Okay, you two. That pizza was delicious but I shouldn't have taken that last slice. Let's go for a walk before we call it a night."

"Let's go to the pier. It's really nice in the evenings," Elena suggested.

As they strolled along the pier, Elena pointed out the Chimney Bluffs. "I want to go the state park there. Those bluffs were formed by the glaciers."

* * *

"I'm going to gain ten pounds on this trip," Peg complained as she finished breakfast the next morning.

"We hear that frequently." Jerry refilled Hap's coffee cup. "Do you need anything else?"

"Not really. We're headed back out to Alasa Farms this morning."

"I'd like to visit a winery today. Any suggestions?" Peg asked.

"Sure. There's Young-Sommer and Thorpe. You'd enjoy both of those. Any interest in sampling some local hard ciders at our orchards?"

"I think Hap would like those."

"Then I suggest Rootstock Ciderworks or Embark Craft Cider-works. Both are close by."

"We'll try to hit at least one of those today," Hap said. "Thanks again for a delicious breakfast."

"Let's go to the farm first," he suggested after they buckled themselves in the car. "Looks like we could get some rain today. Maybe it will hold off 'til afternoon."

"I've been reading about the Shakers," Peg said. "I find it fascinating that people would take up such an organized and regimented religion."

"What do you mean?" Hap admired the sailboats as they passed the bay. "Look at those."

"Beautiful, aren't they? I'd love to go out on one."

"Me, too. What were you saying about the Shakers?"

"Their lives were so structured. They woke up at 4:30 every morning to pray and do morning chores before breakfast. When they went to their meetinghouse, they lined up at a door according to sex, men on one side and women on the other. Everyone worked and they rotated jobs every month." Peg made a face at the thought of all the rules.

"Sounds practical, at least."

"Yes, but our lives are so unstructured. Since you've retired, you get up when you want. You work when you want. I've done that longer than you, and I don't think I could change."

"We did it for years when we were younger."

"Work schedules maybe, but they even use their right foot first when they walk into church. Another thing, they believed so strongly in simplicity that they didn't decorate their walls. They didn't have anything setting around for decoration. That would be impossible for me."

"Yeah, their faith had to be strong. Aren't they the ones who practiced celibacy?"

"Yes, and more than that, they separated families. If a man with a wife and children joined, the whole family would become brothers and sisters and live separately. The parents no longer had control or responsibility for their children. In fact, the children were raised in a different house."

"That's tough. A person would have to really feel the call to the faith."

"Yes, I guess that's the good part. They believed in God's love and mercy. Everything they did glorified Him."

"I suppose you have to admire someone who would accept the lifestyle for the love of God."

They arrived at the farm to find that Cheri wasn't due for an hour. Hap asked Elena if she could find Seth. Peg took Luke to watch the two donkeys. Hap watched Sara working with a horse while she waited for Elena and Seth.

"Found him," Elena called as they walked toward Hap.

"Great. Seth, my name is Hap Lynch. Nice to meet you."

"Hi. Any friend of Elena's is welcome, for sure. I'm Seth Green, by the way."

"Seth Green? Any relation to the Seth Green of fishing fame?"

"Yes, you've heard of him? He's my great-great-grandfather."

"He's a legend in the fishing world. I suppose he spent many hours fishing around here."

"He sure did. I think of him every time I pick up my pole. I'm impressed you know about him."

"I had an uncle who tied flies and sold them around the country. He's the one who told me about Seth Green. What a small world. I've just come from a fishing trip on the Canadian side of Lake Ontario."

"Any luck?"

"I caught a couple of Coho Salmon and a Chinook. My first Canadian fishing trip and the Chinook was my first catch. It's definitely one for my memory bank."

"Awesome! Elena said you wanted to talk to me about Elliott?"

"It's the former cop in me, always asking questions. Sorry."

"Forget it. I'll do anything I can to help find out who did this to Elliott."

"First off, tell me about him."

"I don't know much. He's only been here this summer. I do know he's never done this kind of work and he doesn't like it. He has made a couple of references to his dad forcing him to work here. He's pretty cynical about it. A couple of days before it happened, he said something about being in trouble, but I didn't ask any questions."

"Anything else?"

"Not really. I don't like the guy. He thinks he's too good for this work and has no interest in the animals. He fancies himself a ladies man. A couple of times he asked me to help him get alone time with Claire. You might want to ask her."

"Do you have any idea who might have done this?"

"No, but I'm sure it wasn't one of us."

"Okay, thanks." Hap liked Seth. Bet the original Seth would be proud.

"If you want to go fishing while you're here, let me know. I'll share my favorite spots."

"You're on. Can't wait to tell everyone I went fishing with Seth Green's grandson."

"Or you can tell them that you fished some of the finest waters in the country. When one of the Shakers visited the community here, Elder Benjamin somebody, he wrote back home that he'd seen some huge catfish and Sheepshead in Sodus Bay. If you think about it, back in the day, this property had plenty of bay shoreline. Can you imagine the fish they caught?"

* * *

"Elena, shall we try to find Claire?"

"She's usually in the horse barn. Let's walk over and check."

Hap checked the donkeys to see if Peg and Luke were still there. She was taking pictures and he was sniffing everything in sight.

They found Claire walking out of Diamond's stall.

"Claire, this is my friend, Hap Lynch. He's a retired cop and I've done research for him on a couple of cases. He's interested in helping find out who attacked Elliott."

"Hi, I'm Claire." She moved the dandy brush from one hand to the other and shook hands with Hap.

"Is now a good time for a few questions?"

"Sure. Let me put the brush back and we can talk while I check out the pasture."

"That works." They walked out to the fence and Hap was struck by the serenity of the scene. Beautiful horses of all colors and green fields. "Peg has to see this."

"Peaceful, isn't it? When I'm out here, all my problems seem smaller. It helps me keep life in perspective."

"I know what you mean. Tell me your impressions of Elliott."

"He came here about the same time I did. I really don't know much about him."

"Did you and he talk much?"

"Not really. Casual stuff when we were all together." She kept her eyes on the horses.

Classic signs of lying — or fear, Hap thought. Maybe both. "Claire, it would help if you're honest with me."

"I am. Almost."

"Can you go the distance?"

"Can we talk in private?"

Elena nodded, "I'll be with Peg when you're finished."

"Now, what do you know?"

"I don't like him. I didn't want him to get hurt but I'm happy he's not here. Is he coming back?"

"I don't think that's been decided yet. Why don't you like him?"

"He's arrogant and he thinks every girl will fall all over him."

"Ah, I know the type. Anything else?"

"I don't know. He makes me uncomfortable. I avoid him whenever I can. I feel a little guilty now but I know deep down it's not my fault."

"I'm sure you don't have any reason to feel guilty. But there's more, isn't there?"

"Yes."

"Can you talk about it?"

"Yes. He wouldn't leave me alone. He tried to force himself on me once in Diamond's stall but she took care of that. I think she really frightened him."

Hap waited, knowing she had more to tell.

"Then a couple of days before the attack, he tried to rape me. He'd been drinking. Then the strangest thing saved me."

"What was that?"

"A brush flew through the air and hit him in the head. I saw the blood, but couldn't see anyone else in the barn. I was scared and I ran outside. It was all so spooky. Someone had to throw that brush. It didn't drop, it literally flew at a target."

"I understand. Not that I understand what happened, but that I realize how difficult it can be when something is unexplainable. Did you ask the others if any of them had thrown it?'

"No. I didn't want anyone to know. I should be able to handle a guy making a pass at me."

"I think it was more than a pass."

She nodded. "Is that all? I need to get back to work."

"Yes, thank you. And, Claire, I'm happy that brush flew through the air and hit the right target at the right time."

"Me, too." A faint smile crossed her face.

"One other thing. Tell me about Seth."

"He's a nice guy. Everyone likes him. I don't know him well but I feel comfortable with him."

"Thanks again."

Jeff found them. "I've been looking for you. Cheri called to say she wouldn't be back today. Said to tell you she'll see you tomorrow."

"We might as well go back to our room. I could use a nap before dinnertime," Hap suggested.

"Sounds good to me and I think Luke approves." If a wagging tail signaled approval, he was definitely in on the plan.

"Will I see you tonight?" Elena asked.

"We have to have dinner, so you pick and we'll be there."

"Captain Jack's. I love the outside patio. It's right on the water."

"Want to meet us there about 6:30?"

"Sure. See you then."

"Let's visit the wineries and cideries today," Peg suggested. She looked through the literature Jerry had given her and found that Thorpe Vineyard was close to the Chimney Bluffs State Park. "Let's start with Thorpe Winery and maybe I'll get some better photographs of the bluffs where we're close by."

"Sounds good."

"Fumie, the owner, usually runs the store but she isn't here today," the sales clerk said when they arrived. "Would you like to sample some of our wines?"

"Sure," Peg said. "I have a sweet tooth, so let's start with the semi-sweet and go from there."

"I'll go for the dry," Hap said.

"Fumie is an artist and she designs her own labels." The clerk handed each of them a sample.

"I love them and the names she gives them. The Evening Glow is my favorite." They enjoyed the tasting and Peg purchased a couple of bottles of Evening Glow semi-dry rose before they left. They then stopped at the state park, where she put her camera to good use. The bluffs looked more imposing from the shoreline.

On the way to the cideries, they sidetracked to Burnap's Garden Cafe.

"This strawberry shortcake is to die for." Peg practically swooned after each bite. They had split an order and still both left comfortably full and well satisfied.

"New York has more vibrant colors than I expected." Hap looked across the fields as they drove toward their next stop. "I've never imagined so many acres of orchards."

"I know and have you noticed how big the trees are compared to Missouri and Kansas? I'm happy we're spending a day exploring."

"Me, too, and here we go." Hap pulled into a parking lot.

The cideries introduced them to multiple flavors. Peg admitted she preferred the wine but they decided to take home a bottle of Apple Jack to share with their friends.

That evening, they shared one of the wines with Jerry and Claudine, and filled them in on happenings at the farm.

CHAPTER TWENTY-SEVEN

If we really want to love, we must learn how to forgive.
Mother Teresa

I often wonder if the spirit world is the same as the Catholic's view of purgatory. If my soul cannot rest because I cannot turn loose of my anger, is my spirit life in the same cleansing process? If I can let go of my rage and desire for revenge, will I move on? I ponder these things frequently, but I have never found any proof. I hear the anguish of souls around me, some of them Shakers but others too. A sad part of the spirit world is that we live our pain alone, in a solitary existence. We do not communicate with each other. I'm not saying we can't. We just don't. That's my frustration with Mary Ann's spirit. I want to apologize, to offer her friendship, but I can't. On the few occasions I've tried to communicate with her, I think she has heard me, but there's a wall I can't break through. And the last time, she turned me away.

Maybe she holds no grudge against me; that is my hope. If time cleanses our souls, will we achieve the ability to communicate? Or maybe purgatory is simply an unendurable loneliness.

CHAPTER TWENTY-EIGHT

Adversity introduces a man to himself.
Albert Einstein

ELLIOTT OPENED HIS EYES. WHERE was he? He tried to raise his arm but discovered an IV held it down. He heard voices that drew closer.

"Well, young man, you're awake," a middle-aged man in a white coat said as he looked at the monitor by the bed. "It's about time."

"What do you mean?"

"You've been sleeping your life away." The man grinned.

"Where am I?"

"You're in a hospital in Newark."

"Why?"

"Well, you got yourself pretty banged up." The man busied himself with Elliott's IV, checking the port and the amount of solution.

"I did?"

"Yep, 'fraid so."

"How long have I been here?"

"This is the fourth day."

"My God, what happened?"

"We're waiting for you to tell us that. You've had some visitors. Your parents and your uncle. Your mother is still here, but your father and your uncle had to go home for an important meeting."

"Oh." Should he feel something?

The doctor, a young woman who looked like she should still be in school, walked in the room. "Hello. We're so happy you're finally awake. How do you feel?"

"Sore all over. Who are you?"

"I'm Doctor Mallory. Joseph and I are taking care of you today." She pointed toward the man. "I need to ask you a few questions."

Elliott didn't respond. He didn't think he'd seen either of them before.

"Can you tell me your name and your date of birth?"

"I'm ... I'm ... I can't think of my name."

"Do you remember your date of birth?"

Elliott's wrinkled brow told Dr. Mallory what she suspected. "Do you remember what happened to you?"

"No, is that why I'm here?"

"Yes, you were beaten and arrived here in an ambulance."

Elliott stared at the ceiling.

"Your name is Elliott Werner. You were working at the Cracker Box Palace Farm Animal Rescue. Do you remember that?"

"No, I've never heard of it. Elliott Werner, that's my name."

"Yes, does it sound familiar?"

"No. My head hurts." He felt the pounding grow stronger. He could almost picture somebody hammering his skull. "I feel sick."

Joseph gave him a shot but it wasn't in time to prevent his stomach from heaving. The pounding in his head grew stronger for a few seconds and then it was gone.

The next time he woke up, he saw an older woman sitting next to his bed.

"Oh, Elliott darling, I'm so glad you're awake. I've been so worried."

Elliott looked at the strands of gray in her otherwise dark hair. In spite of her casual dress and the tired look in her eyes, she was an attractive woman.

"Talk to me, Elliott, please."

"Who are you?"

"Oh my God, it's true. The doctor said you might have amnesia. I've been so worried. This is all my fault."

"How can this be your fault?"

"I let your dad send you to that farm to work. I knew it was too hard for you."

"Who *are* you?"

"I'm your *mother*. Virginia Werner. How can you not remember me?"

Elliott felt sorry for her, but he couldn't remember ever seeing her before. "I'm sorry. My headache is starting again. Can you call someone?"

The next time Elliott awoke he was alone. He checked the IV in his arm and noticed the bruises. He looked at his other arm and found cuts and bruises. He lifted the sheet and looked at his legs. Again, he saw dark bruises and cuts that were beginning to heal. What had happened to him? His head began to throb but he didn't want another shot just yet. It gave instant relief, but he felt no better when he awoke each time.

Why couldn't he remember? Had he been in an accident? What was the place the doctor said he worked? Some kind of farm. The more he strained to remember, the worse the pounding in his head. He pushed the call button.

"Headache again?" Joseph said as he answered the call.

"Yes. I need something."

"I'll be right there."

* * *

I felt the difference in the farm. The violent attack on Elliott had sobered everyone. I watched them as they continued taking care of their chores but conversations had become infrequent and muted. How I wish I could tell them what I had seen, but I had no way to communicate with them.

Claire remained out of sight most of the time. The others came and went throughout the day. I hadn't seen Mary Ann since the attack. The spirit world at the old Shaker house grew even more depressing. I sensed the crankiness of some of the noisier souls and felt the melancholy clouds that smothered the others. I had never seen or communicated with most of them. Had Elliott's attack frightened even those who were past the violence of the human world?

I wondered if I could have stopped it. I had prevented Elliott from completing his attack against Claire. Could I have stopped the attack against him? I had watched the car drive in and the man get out. He had looked around and walked the road. The night sky hid him from view, but I doubted if anyone was watching. It was a time of sleep for the animals and those who cared for them. I'll never know why Elliott came out of the bunkhouse, but that turned out to be a nearly fatal mistake.

The man noticed him immediately and followed him as he walked toward the horse barn. I should have paid more attention but I am easily bored. I wandered around the house and tried to transition back but it was not to happen. Why didn't I hear Elliott? I'm sure he pleaded for his life. No one can sustain that kind of beating silently.

I didn't hear the man leave, but by the time I heard Elena's scream the next morning, his car was long gone.

* * *

"Elliott has amnesia."

Claire listened as Cheri updated them. "He's getting much better physically but this adds a new complication. The doctors suspect the beating caused a traumatic brain injury. Emerging from the coma was a step in the right direction, but now the amnesia is a cause for concern."

"Is his brain injury permanent?" Like an electric current, tendrils of distress arced through Elena.

"The doctors don't believe so. Much of the problem was the swelling caused by the blow to his head. He did not have severe internal bleeding. In fact it was mild. They'd warned that Elliott would most likely need rehabilitation therapy, but the prognosis was good. The amnesia is a new problem for Elliott, but not for his doctors. I understand it's not unusual for some form of memory loss."

"Will he recover his memory?" Claire wished him well, but maybe he'd never remember their encounters.

"As with a brain injury, there are many levels of amnesia. If it's mild, he could recall everything all at once. The more severe, the longer it will take. He may recover in stages."

"But he will get well?" Elena found it impossible to imagine anyone losing his identity.

"They are hopeful he will have a full recovery. But it may take time. He may start to remember in bits and pieces. Right now, he remembers nothing. He doesn't recall the beating and didn't recognize his mother."

"How horrible for her," Claire said.

"Yes. There's another thing. The doctors said the amnesia may lead to some changes in his personality. When he's well enough to return to work, and the doctors suggest he do just that, we may see that he is different in some ways. They think we can start visiting him in a couple of days. Short visits and no more than two of us at a time. I suggest we set an informal schedule so everyone gets a chance."

Everyone agreed. Cheri offered to set up the schedule.

"Oh, and one other thing, it's okay to talk about our work here on the farm. The only advice from the doctors was that we are positive at all times, about his recovery and his return to work. They don't want us to talk about the beating or his injuries. Only positive energy."

"Will the police try to question him?" Seth asked.

"I'm sure they will. They may not find out much until he recovers his memory."

Seth and Claire found themselves first on the visit schedule. When they arrived at the hospital two days later, they learned that while Elliott was fully conscious and feeling much better, he still had no recall. He proved this to be true when he saw them. Neither could believe the lack of recognition in his eyes.

"I thought I was prepared for this," Claire whispered to Seth.

"Me, too," Seth answered.

Elliott listened as they talked about the farm and their daily activities, but he might as well have been watching a movie. None of it touched him his emotions or his memory. He responded to their questions and comments, but wanted them to leave. Within a few minutes, his headache had returned. Not the severe headache, but a dull aching that grew as the minutes passed.

"Your fifteen minutes are up," the nurse walked into the room.

Elliott's tired smile spoke volumes. He wanted them to leave.

Elena and Sara visited the next day and came home with similar results.

Two police officers visited him, but he could tell them nothing. He not only couldn't remember who beat him, but he had no memory of the beating. They told him he'd been found in the horse barn at Alasa Farms. He'd never heard of the place and even though he knew nothing about his past, he suspected he'd never want to be in a horse barn.

For the present, he wanted to get out of the hospital. The woman who claimed to be his mother wanted to take him to her home. The owner of the farm wanted him to come back there. It didn't really matter. The doctor encouraged him to resume his old life, but he had no idea what that was. His frustration grew, causing his headache to return. He rang for the nurse and asked for more meds.

As he waited for the meds to work, he felt something hit him in the back of the head. He reached back but felt nothing. It hurt but it wasn't bleeding. He called Roger, the nurse on duty.

"Something just hit me in the back of the head."

"Here, let me check." Roger gently probed Elliott's head. At one place, Elliott flinched.

"That's it, right there. Can you see anything?"

"No, it's your old wound and it's healed. Maybe you are having ghost pains."

"I don't believe in ghosts. Something hit me."

"How do you know you don't believe in them?"

"Huh ... what are you talking about?"

"Elliott, if you don't remember anything, then how would you know whether or not you believed in ghosts?"

"Oh. I don't know how but I do know that I don't believe in them. I'm tired." The pain meds did their job and soon he slipped into a painless sleep.

When he awoke, the doctor stood at the side of his bed. He couldn't read her name tag. "Hey, sleepyhead. Nice to see you're awake."

"I'm hungry and thirsty. Good signs, huh?"

"They sure are. Take a drink from your water. I'll have it refreshed and order a meal for you in a minute. First I want to talk a minute."

"Okay, but I don't remember your name."

"Doctor Mallory. Do you remember seeing me before?"

"Sure, you've been in here several times."

"Earlier, you told Roger that something hit you in the back of the head. Do you remember that conversation?"

"Of course, I'm not stupid." He let his irritability show.

"I know you're not. You have amnesia and I simply wanted to know if it's affecting your short-term memory, too."

"Sorry," he mumbled, even though he wasn't.

"Back to something hitting you on the head. Can you describe it to me?"

"Something hit me, hard. What is there to describe?"

"My, we are cranky today. It's important that you help me, Elliott. With a brain injury, it is possible to have simulated pain occur days or weeks after the trauma. Roger assures me there was nothing to fall on you and no one else in the room. I suspect your brain was reliving its injury. That could be a very good sign."

Elliott stared at her. "At least that sounded more plausible than whatever Roger said about ghosts."

"He wasn't referring to 'ghost,' but rather what we call 'ghost' pains. They're not really happening but your nervous system is reliving them. It's not uncommon in an injury such as yours. You had multiple contusions and lots of bruising on your head as well as the rest of you. The spot you identified for Roger was the exact spot where some object made contact with your head."

"What was it?"

"That I don't know. Maybe the police do."

"So you really don't know anything."

"Not true. I know that ghost pains can be a positive sign in a situation like yours. And I know that you are getting crankier every minute." She picked up her chart and walked to the door. "I'll have Roger check on you in a few minutes. Hopefully, you'll be awake for a while. We need to evaluate your headache and ask you more of these stupid questions you love."

Elliott hated his own bad humor. It wasn't like him, or he didn't think it was. Well, truthfully, he had no idea what he was like. Even if he had no memory, would he have the same personality? Would he feel the same emotions? He still didn't buy the 'ghost' business, but whenever he thought about it, his head began to ache. He reached for the TV control. Maybe he'd find something to take his mind off his troubles. No such luck. The first channel had a soap opera and they were loading someone into an ambulance. He clicked to another channel, where a hospital scene filled the screen. He tossed the control down and lowered the bed. Maybe if he stared into space, a memory would come to him. Anything, no matter how small, would be better than what he had accomplished thus far.

His mother walked into the room and took his hand. "You're looking so much better today, dear."

Elliott felt nothing, no recognition nor emotion. "Please tell me about myself. I need to remember something, anything."

"Sure. Where do I start? You were such a darling little boy. I loved being your mother and we spent hours together everyday. Your dad was working hard to build the company and was seldom home. I didn't mind because I had you."

"What else?"

"You were a good student, always getting good grades. You didn't like to study and you hated homework but you were so bright that you achieved anyway. And you were always charming. Your teachers loved you."

"Did I play any sports or have any hobbies?"

"You played baseball when you were young, and took up golf in junior high. You were a Cub Scout but never went on to the Boy Scouts. Let's see, you played the drums in your junior high band, but you gave that up in senior high."

"I sure sound like a quitter."

"Well, that sounds like your dad. He says you're smart but lack perseverance, which is essential for success in the work world." She twisted her pearls. "Elliott, he wants you to take over the company someday!"

"What company?"

"Werner Enterprises, of course."

"Anything else?" He yawned. "Did I have a girlfriend? Go to college?"

"No current girlfriend. I'm afraid your inability to stick to anything carried over into relationships. You finished college, but your grades were mediocre. You have so much ability but you just haven't found yourself yet."

"Quit making excuses." His uncle walked into the room. "How are you feeling, son?"

"Okay, but I still can't remember anything. Mother was trying to help me."

"Mollycoddling you is more like it."

"Stop it, Gavin. He needs kindness, not criticism."

"He needs reality, and the reality is that you, young man, were on your way to messing up your life."

"What do you mean?"

"Gavin, please ..."

Roger entered the room and conversation ceased. "Is everything okay in here? Elliott, your heart rate is accelerating. I think maybe he needs a break," he told the visitors. "But most of all, he needs your emotional and moral support."

"See, I told you," his mother said as she stepped past Gavin.

"Maybe it's not all bad to lose your family memories," Roger chuckled. "I think we've all wished that at one time or another."

"I'd like to remember what I want to forget, if that makes sense."

"Yes. It makes perfect sense."

"The funny thing is, I don't remember anything, but I feel like this is normal in our family. It's like they were playing the role I might have assigned to them."

"A good sign. While not a memory, it's an emotional awareness. I'll let Doctor Mallory know."

CHAPTER TWENTY-NINE

Little strokes fell great oaks.
Benjamin Franklin

AFTER ANOTHER OF JERRY AND Claudine's excellent break-fasts, Hap, Peg and Luke headed back to Alasa Farms.

"You're not even working with the police here," Peg said. "You don't need to get involved."

"I do, for Elena's sake. Besides, this didn't turn into a murder case and the police seldom have much time to spend on assault cases, unless it's racially, ethnically or sexually motivated. None of that seems the case here."

"You're incurable."

"I afraid you're right."

They found Cheri updating the group when they arrived. Elliott was improving everyday. Little signs gave the doctors hope for a speedy recovery, but as of yet, he remembered nothing.

"He's grumpy," Seth said. "Jeff and I visited him last night. We didn't stay long because it was obvious he wanted us to leave."

As the meeting broke up, Hap asked Cheri if she had time for questions.

"Sure, here on the porch okay?"

"Yes, have you talked to the police recently?"

"Not in the last couple of days. Now that Elliott is getting better, they don't seem as interested."

"I'm afraid that's par for the course. When I was with the Kansas City force, we were always so far behind in major cases, that assaults and burglaries got lost in the system. Do you think they'd be willing to talk to me? I'd like to help."

"The Wayne County Sheriff's department answered the call. Their office is in Lyons, a few miles down Hwy 14. The sheriff is a nice guy, and I think he'd be happy to talk with you. Whether or not he'd want your help, I don't know. One of his deputies, Susan Mondel, is prickly and I never know how she will respond in a situation."

"Thanks. What's the sheriff's name?"

"Joe Briggs."

"I'll check with him and avoid Susan." Hap's smile belied the seriousness of his intention.

When he returned a couple of hours later, he learned that Cheri was out for the rest of the day. He caught up with Elena as she was feeding celery to one of the goats.

"Hey, watch her eat this. She loves almost any vegetable I've given her."

"She should be a healthy goat."

"Are Peg and Luke with you?"

"No, I dropped Peg off at the Sodus Library. She's developed quite an interest in the Shakers and hopes to find some research materials. I went to the sheriff's department in Lyons. Joe Briggs, the sheriff, told me they have no leads and have no one actively working the case now. After we told a few war stories about upholding the law, he said he'd be happy to look at anything I discover."

"So, we'll be working another case together," Elena grinned. "I should have known that it would happen sooner or later. Think we'll be able to get Luke's help?"

"I don't know. He's a little squeamish about the place. He senses something we don't. Reminds me of the time we took him to a cemetery in Arkansas. We had wandered around but when he came to this one family plot, he froze, fur on end. I couldn't budge him. When I told him we'd go back to the car, he took off like a racehorse."

"He's made a believer out of me. Who else do you want to talk to?"

"Cheri, but she's out the rest of the day. Maybe I'll talk to the others, too."

"Cheri will be the most help, but Jeff may know more about Elliott than the rest of us. Since he's the operations manager, Cheri probably shares more with him. Let's go find him." Elena gave the last of the celery to some happy goats, and they walked toward the boardinghouse.

When they saw Jeff getting off a tractor, Elena called, "Hey, wait up."

"What do you need," he asked.

"This is my friend, Hap Lynch. He's my friend who ..."

"The investigator. Elena has talked about you." Jeff reached out to shake Hap's hand.

"Don't believe everything you hear," Hap joked.

"Well, we know Elena can tell some tall tales," Jeff answered.

"Be serious, you two. Those cases I told you about are true. He's worked as a consultant with the police department in Texas, and before that, with the Kansas City Police Department."

"Calm down, Elena. I believe you," Jeff said and turned to Hap. "Are you here because of Elliott?"

"Yes and no. I came at Elena's request. Since I'm here, I'm willing to help any way I can. I visited Sheriff Briggs and he said he'd follow up on anything I find."

"How can I help?"

"Do you have any information on Elliott's background? Anything that might be useful?"

"I know his dad and uncle came over from Syracuse and visited with Cheri. Elliott had gotten himself in some trouble, and they wanted to get him out of town, and teach him about physical work. They made a major donation to the farm when Cheri said she'd take him in."

"Do you have any idea what kind of trouble he was in?"

"No, but Cheri probably does."

"Has he learned much about physical work?"

"As little as he can get away with. I suspect he's just a spoiled-rotten rich kid. His family owns a successful business in Syracuse. He doesn't know anything about work, and he's not at all self-motivated. At least not to learn about the farm."

"How does he treat the other employees and volunteers?"

"Okay, I guess. Haven't heard any complaints. He can be arrogant on occasion, but he is also charming enough to get away with it."

"Anything else?"

"Not really. One of our volunteers, Claire, has a problem with an ex-boyfriend. He showed up here. Elliott gave her away before he realized he shouldn't have. He tried to cover up his error and sent the guy on his way. Actually, Elliott apologized to Claire and seemed sincerely sorry for what he did."

"Okay, thanks. If you think of anything else, let me know."

"Sure. Guess I better get back to work," Jeff climbed up on the tractor.

CHAPTER THIRTY

*The more I think it over, the more I feel that there is nothing
more truly artistic than to love people.*

Vincent van Gogh

"EILEEN, HI!" CLAIRE SMILED. "I'VE missed you. What days
are you here?"

"It varies."

"Oh, are you here to help today?"

"Maybe, but I'd like to just talk."

"About what?"

"Do you have a mother?"

"Silly girl," Claire smothered her laughter. "Everyone has
a mother."

"I mean a real one."

"What are you asking, Eileen?"

"Did your mother love you?"

"Very much. She's a wonderful lady and I've always wanted to
be like her."

"Why?" Eileen asked her questions with a natural sincerity that
only children can express.

"Because she's kind, loving, generous and has a beautiful heart."

Eileen brushed her hand across her eyes.

"Is there something you'd like to tell me?" Claire's heart ached
for her.

"No. It's just that my real mother gave me away." Eileen's tears
flowed. She lifted her skirt to wipe her eyes.

Claire noticed the old-fashioned petticoat underneath. *I don't
know who her mother is, but she could definitely use some fashion
lessons,* she thought.

"Why don't you tell me about it?"

"I don't know much. I know my mother didn't want me, and gave me away. My pretend parents didn't tell me. They always said they loved me, but I don't think you can love someone and lie to them at the same time."

"Hey, Eileen. Let's start with your mother. You said you don't know much. I'm sure your mother loved you and if she gave you away, she did it because of that love."

"That doesn't make any sense."

"You're a little girl, and sometimes it's hard to understand adult emotions. But one thing I feel sure about, your mother loved you. Maybe she thought you'd have a better life with adoptive parents. Maybe she was alone and had no way to support you. Or maybe she was too sick to keep you."

"You think it could be one of those things?" Hope seeped into Eileen's eyes and disappeared almost immediately. "I don't even know her name."

* * *

Claire thought of Eileen as she finished her chores. She hated seeing the pain in her eyes and wanted to help her. Remembering that she had never asked Cheri about her, she walked over to the office. Cheri hung up the phone as she entered.

"How's it going?" Cheri asked.

"Fine. Diamond is more open every day. She's such a sweet girl. I guess I've fallen in love with her."

"I know the feeling. I did that with Melvin, the first horse I rehabilitated from start to finish. Took forever but it was worth it. Diamond is much like him. Did you need to see me for something? You look like you have something on your mind."

"Eileen."

"Who?"

"Eileen, the funny little girl. I gather she's a volunteer, but she's not here that often."

"We have no volunteer named Eileen."

"Are you sure?"

"Yes. I guess she could come with one of our adult volunteers but no one has mentioned her to me. Is she a problem?"

"No, not at all. She's a lonely little thing. She wears old-fashioned dresses. At first I thought she was a re-enactor. And she is heartbroken since she found out that she was adopted."

"She wears old-fashioned clothes. What do they look like?"

"Like you see in pioneer movies. A long, cotton dress with an apron pinned to it. Kind of a flowery print. Come to think of it, she's been wearing the same dress every time I've seen her."

"Does she talk to you?"

"Yes, I think she really needs someone to listen to her."

"And she talks about her mother?"

"Yes."

"Wow!" Cheri's rubbed her hand through her hair. "And you've never seen her with anyone?"

"No."

"It can't be." Cheri gave a half-laugh before she turned serious. "What is it?"

"I need to check with people. See if I can find someone she belongs to. Otherwise, ..."

Claire waited but Cheri seemed distracted. "I didn't mean to bother you."

You didn't," Cheri said. "I'm just thinking."

CHAPTER THIRTY-ONE

Be the change that you wish to see in the world."
Mahatma Gandhi

*I don't do change well. After nearly two centuries, I
am pretty 'set in my ways' as my mother used to say. The
little girl's spirit is strengthening. I watched her actually
correspond with Claire. She appears in human form and
calls herself Eileen. I believe it's a special gift from God.
Neither I nor the other spirits here at the farm have ever
manifested ourselves. On rare occasions, some of us have
been able to assume enough form to allow people to sense
us or even see us as a shadow. But this child spirit actually
appears as a normal, living girl. How do I know she isn't?
Because I've watched her fade back into the spirit world.
I've sensed her crossing over to the other side, and I've
sensed her returning.*

*What does she have that the rest of us don't? If indeed,
we're here to atone for past sins, maybe it's her child-
like innocence that transforms her. She seems taken with
Claire, which is a good thing because Claire has a kind
spirit that flows from her. She may be frightened by life's
circumstances but she exudes a positive energy.*

*Meanwhile, some of the souls in the cellar grow more
restless and Mary Ann more vague. I fear the restless souls
can grow angry and mean. Thus far, I'm the only one who
has ever caused problems for the living. Mary Ann, I worry about even more. The more she fades away, the less
chance of her finding her own redemption.*

*I can feel myself changing, and I am resisting. Why?
Who knows if I am growing or regressing? Sometimes I*

think I've pondered the mysteries of my being so long that I exacerbate my situation. I pray that God knows that I am making progress in controlling my bitterness and that I am actively seeking my own salvation and that of my spirit community. Before it's too late for all of us.

* * *

"You're healed physically," Doctor Mallory's cheery voice did nothing to change Elliott's mood. "I think it's time for you to leave the hospital."

"Where will I go?"

"Your mother wants you to return home with her, but your dad seems less supportive. He says he's paid for you to work at the farm the rest of the summer. Cheri is open to your return to the farm."

"She's the owner, right?"

"Yes, she's been here to see you several times. I've talked to a social worker and a psychologist who both feel you should assume the life you were living before the attack. How do you feel about returning to the farm?"

"I guess it's okay. I'm a little apprehensive. I don't want to go home with my parents. Even though I don't remember them, what I've seen here at the hospital is stressful."

"I agree. You're blood pressure shoots up every time they visit. Our medical team has a suggestion."

"Yeah?"

"We can keep you here a couple more days. We suggest that your co-workers visit you today and tomorrow, knowing that you are returning to the farm. Hopefully, that will improve your comfort level with all of them beforehand. They've all been here but you weren't fully awake for some of their visits."

"That's okay with me. Have you talked to them?"

"Cheri has, and they all agree. They'll reintroduce you to themselves and farm life. Hopefully, going back into the same environment will prompt some memories. You'll still need some physical therapy. We can set up a schedule for you with the rehab center."

"What about my memory?"

"Elliott, I'll be honest with you. I think you'll regain your full memory, but I can't state that with one-hundred-percent certainty. You are young and have no long-term physical damage. You may have small triggers that bring the past into focus or it may be like a lightning strike, where your memory comes washing over you all at once."

"What can I do?"

"Try to keep your mind open — to people and places. Don't resist yourself. Relax and let it happen. I really do believe it will, and reasonably soon. I want to see you once a week when you return for therapy. I only ask that you be completely truthful with me when we meet."

"I can do that."

"Good. I much prefer the friendly Elliott to the grouchy one!" She smiled. "I'll call Cheri and get the visits started. I'll see you tomorrow."

* * *

"I think we have another ghost," Cheri told Burt as he came through the door.

"Whoa! Who? And what makes you think that?"

"Claire told me a story today, about a little girl dressed in what sounds like Shaker-era clothing. She is lonely and talks to Claire about her mother. She is adopted and is apparently searching for her birth mother."

"How little?"

"I didn't ask. I will. She said her name is Eileen."

"We've never heard of anyone actually seeing one of our ghosts before."

"I know," Cheri agreed. "That's what's so strange. Do you think she can be real?"

"As in real ghost?"

"Of course. Stop making fun of me," Cheri laughed. "I know it sounds crazy."

"We have Horace and Mary Ann for sure. We might as well have another one living with us."

"Do you suppose there's a connection?"

"I suppose there's some kind of connection. Whether it's to the others or the farm, I have no idea." Burt never even thought about ghosts before they came to Alasa Farms. However, he readily admitted there was a lot more to this world than he understood.

"I'll find out how old she is, but that won't tell us anything."

"Interesting thought, is a ghost always at the age the person died? I wonder if they can be younger."

"I don't know. It would make sense that they couldn't be any older. We really don't know much, do we?" Cheri thought she should call Kris Faso, the psychic who had already visited the farm, and fill him in on the latest development. He had sensed many spirits living in the old house.

* * *

All the farm crew visited Elliott over the next couple of days. Much to his dismay, Elliott could not recall one memory of any of them. He left the hospital, caught between hope and despair. He hoped the farm and his co-workers would jog his memory. They had all been friendly and apparently happy that he would be returning. However, the despair was a heavy blanket that he couldn't throw off. At times he saw his life stretching out for years, never remembering anything about who he was.

He had voiced this concern to Seth.

"Even if that's the case, Elliott, you can become whoever you want to be, starting today. Lots of people would love to swap places with you for that ability." Seth believed that might be a blessing for Elliott. But what if he became a better person and then remembered what he had been before? Would he be able to handle that? Maybe he wasn't really bad before, but he sure could have used a change in attitude.

"You know the scary part?" Elliott asked.

"No, what?"

"What if I remember and then find out I don't like the person I was?"

"I'm sure that won't happen." Seth wanted to encourage him but couldn't believe they were thinking about the same possible outcome.

Claire hated being caught in the quagmire of conflicting thoughts. Although she hoped for Elliott's full recovery, she dreaded the possibility that his unwanted advances would resume.

The crew planned a celebration for Elliott's return. When he arrived, the smell of barbecue wafted through the air and for the first time in his memory, he craved food. A cake decorated with 'Welcome home, Elliott,' brought unfamiliar emotion. He was wanted. Maybe, just maybe, he had been an integral part of the farm before. His spirits lifted.

Elliott enjoyed the party and the attention. Conversation and food kept the anxiety at bay. He loved it all and never wanted it to end.

"Now that you've returned, we'll have to get you back in the routine. I've asked Seth to work closely with you." Cheri had watched him interact with the others. Hopefully, he would adapt better the second time around. Second chances, she thought. Many times they worked for the best.

* * *

I watched the gaiety as everyone talked and ate. It brought back so many memories. After I joined with the Shakers, I never experienced that type of relaxed enjoyment and fellowship. True, we had communal dinners and meetings where we danced with joy in the Lord. We had interesting conversations and listened to the voices of those filled with the Spirit, but we never simply celebrated a person. I suspect some of the partiers, like Claire and Seth, joined in the merriment more out of hope for a better future than for memories of who Elliott had been. I wondered if Elliott's attraction to Claire would re-ignite.

I've watched people for generations. Change occurs. Usually it is a gradual process, but sometimes, an event triggers an immediate metamorphosis in personality or attitude. Elliott has suffered a major trauma. Hopefully good will result. However, I remember the day he threw away his phone and I fear his problems may have survived with him.

I wait for change in my existence. Sometimes with patience, but more often with a degree of anxiety and irritability. I believe that Mary Ann holds the key to my ability to move forward. I'm tired. Tired of hoping and trying. Tired of anger. I feel exhausted even as I watch the energy of the partiers.

The spirit world is quiet for now. Mary Ann must be back on the other side. The little girl has kept to herself and the spirits in the cellar have calmed.

I need to cross over for a while, to remember the good things in my life before Eaton and Mary Ann. Roaming the farm always leads to melancholy and pain. Once when I crossed over, I recalled a childhood memory. My mother had baked an apple pie and the aroma, mixed with that of beef stew, filled the house. My dad had called us to the table, led the prayer, and looked at Mother. "I don't know which I enjoy more," he said. "Sitting across from my beautiful wife, surrounded by our children, or enjoying her cooking talents."

Mother had blushed and encouraged us to fill our plates. As we ate our fill, Dad talked about the year's apple crop. Although I hadn't noticed or understood, it rained at all the right times, and he predicted the best crop we'd ever had. I can still taste the pie and the joy.

Yes, I need to leave here for a time.

* * *

Hap had grown accustomed to the niggling that accompanied every investigation. Today, it centered on the lack of motivation in Elliott's assault. There had to be more. He needed to talk to Cheri. He dropped Peg off at the library again and headed to the farm. He found Cheri in her office.

"Do you have a few minutes for questions?"

"Sure. I need a break from paperwork anyway."

"I'm trying to find a motive for Elliott's attack and I'm hoping you can help."

"I've heard you've already talked to several others. I'll help in anyway I can."

"Why did Elliott's dad send him here?"

"Elliott got into some trouble, repeatedly I think, although his dad didn't tell me that."

"Do you know what kind of trouble?"

"Gambling. He owed money and his dad refused to bail him out this time."

"Tell me about his dad."

"Harsh. That would be my short description. I certainly didn't catch any signs of a relationship between father and son. He's a successful businessman and he expects Elliott to follow in his footsteps. He sent him here to straighten him out. Those are his words, not mine."

"Did he give you any details about who Elliott owes the money to?"

"No, and I didn't ask. Do you think that has something to do with the attack?" Cheri hadn't made that connection, but the thought frightened her. "I've heard stories about such things but I never thought about it happening here."

"I hope that's not it. Do you know anyone else who may have wanted to harm Elliott?"

"No. There was an incident with Claire's ex-boyfriend but it was pretty casual."

"Tell me about it."

"Apparently Claire came here to escape her abusive boyfriend. His name is Jake. A couple of days before the attack, he came to the farm, wanting to know if she was here. Sara told him that Claire used to work here, but left. Then he cornered Elliott, who told him she worked here. When he realized he shouldn't have given her away, he tried to backtrack. He told Jake that she did work here but she lived in Sodus. Jake left and that's the last I've heard of him. I can't see him as the attacker."

"Probably not. I think I'll ask Claire about him though."

When he left Cheri, he went in search of Claire. As he walked toward the horse barn, a cool breeze tickled his skin. He looked around and the leaves on the trees were perfectly still. Better not tell Luke, he thought. He'll think it was a ghost.

Claire was carrying on a conversation with Diamond as she combed her. Hap smiled and thought, if Peg were here, she'd grab her camera. The two presented a serene pastoral scene.

"Sorry to interrupt, but I just talked to Cheri and she brought up something I'd like to talk to you about." Hap leaned against the railing.

"Sure. Give me a minute to put my brushes away. See you later, beautiful," she planted a kiss on Diamond's nose before she left the stall.

"Now, ask your questions," she told Hap as she walked back from the tack room.

"Jake, your ex-boyfriend. Cheri said he was here."

"Yes."

"Tell me why you left him."

Hap gave her a minute.

"When we first met, he was charming and supportive. I was displaying my artwork at a show and he stopped and admired it. We talked for quite a while. He ended up buying one of my canvases and asking me out. Things progressed from there and I finally moved in with him. Then he began to change. He became possessive and jealous of the time I spent painting. He got mad and verbally abusive, and then he apologized and promised to change. As time went by, the mad times became worse and more frequent."

"What do you mean by worse?"

"One time he shoved me and smashed one of my paintings. Of course, he apologized. The verbal abuse worsened. He didn't want me to have anything or do anything that didn't involve him. The final straw came when he knocked me down. That night I packed my clothes and left."

"How did he find you?"

"I have no idea."

"So what happened when he came here?"

"Sara was sharp enough to recognize trouble. She told him I no longer worked here. Elliott was clueless and admitted I did. Then he tried to undo the damage. Told him I lived in town. Jake was upset when he left. I haven't seen or heard from him since."

Hap remained quiet.

"But one thing I do know," Claire said. "He doesn't forget and he doesn't give up. He will hunt me down. Cheri advised me to stay here and get an attorney. I did that and he filed a restraining order. But that won't do any good when Jake is angry."

"I'm sorry you have to experience this. Can you remember anything else that may be useful?"

"Not really. He doesn't give up. After every incident, he begged, cried and charmed me until I gave in and forgave him. He told me that I belong to him and he'll never let me go. He means it. I want to leave but the attorney agrees with Cheri that I should stay here."

"I'm sure they told you to never leave here alone. I assume you keep your phone with you at all times."

"Yes to both. I try to be on full alert all the time."

* * *

As Hap walked to the car, he noticed Cheri waving to him.

"I just thought of something," she called.

He walked over to her.

"Elliott went home to visit his mother shortly before the attack. He came back with a $4,000 donation she made to the farm. I don't know if she can shed any more light on the situation, but I can give you her number. And his dad's too."

Hap put the numbers in his phone and planned to call them as soon as he arrived back in Sodus Point. However, after a quick lunch, Peg wanted to shop. By the time they arrived back at the Carriage House Inn, he was ready for a nap. He and Luke curled up on the bed while Peg took a walk up to the old lighthouse. Luke woke him up an hour later, ready to go outside. After a short walk, he sat in the gazebo, called Elliott's mother and identified himself and the reason for his call.

"My poor baby," she said when Hap mentioned Elliott's name.

"Mrs. Werner, Elliott visited you shortly before his attack. Was he worried about something?"

"I don't think so. He was so concerned about the farm that he wanted to take back a donation to help feed the animals. He's such a sweet boy."

"Did he talk about himself?"

"Only his work at the farm. Oh, and how happy he was to see me. He's always been my special boy. Anyway, we had a lovely visit but he had to leave so soon."

"Was your husband home at the time?"

"No, he's never home. He works so hard."

"Is he home now?"

"No, he's on a business trip. I don't expect him back until some-time next week. How is Elliott?"

"He's back at the farm and doing fine."

"I wanted him to come home. He needs his mother. But the doctor thought he'd regain his memory faster at the farm. It's the hardest thing I've ever done. Well, that and putting Elliott at that farm in the first place. He's a good boy, really."

"Yes, I'm sure he is. Thank you so much." Hap couldn't wait to get off the phone. He understood why the doctor didn't want Elliott to recuperate at home.

That call wore him out and he decided to wait until tomorrow to call Mr. Werner.

* * *

Elliott couldn't say he enjoyed the work, especially mucking out the stalls in the cow barn, but he liked the people. The friendly smiles and offers to help. In just a couple of days, he felt like part of a team. He wondered if he'd ever felt that way before.

Seth and Jeff joked with him as they re-taught him his duties. Elena stopped to talk whenever she saw him. He enjoyed her enthusiasm. Sara was usually busy but she was friendly. Claire was the only one who seemed reserved. She was polite, but kept to herself.

If only he could remember anything. He looked around the farm and couldn't imagine he'd ever wanted to volunteer here for the summer. His mother said he'd been born and raised in Syracuse, but couldn't remember it. Maybe he needed to see his home, but he didn't want to see his mother. The hospital visits had assured him that he couldn't handle her cloying sympathy.

He finished his chores just as a slight breeze filled the air with the pungent smells of the farm. Every muscle in his body ached but his mind was fresh with anticipation. He found himself looking forward to the workdays and the evenings. He noticed Claire leaning against the horse pasture fence. He walked down to join her.

"This breeze sure feels good, doesn't it?"

Claire looked up. "Yes, just what we need at the end of the day. It should be a beautiful evening." She still hesitated to accept the 'new' Elliott, even though he'd been a perfect gentleman since he returned.

"Is it always like this? It seems we've had perfect weather since I got back."

"Count yourself fortunate," she laughed. "We had a week of rain while you were in the hospital."

"Oh, glad I missed that."

"Truthfully, it's been a great summer thus far. I really enjoy working with the animals. Do you remember Diamond?"

"No."

"Diamond is the horse that came to us at the beginning of the summer. She'd been severely beaten by her owner. She nearly died and probably would have if an anonymous donor hadn't paid for her care at Cornell. We're still working to rehabilitate her. Want to see her?"

"Sure, is she one of these?" He pointed out in the pasture.

"No, she's in the barn. Come on. I'll show you. She is still cautious around men, so you need to stay out of the stall." Claire hoped she was doing the right thing. It was a test and she admitted it.

They walked into the barn.

"Do you remember anything?" Claire asked.

"No. Is this where Diamond is?"

"Yes, right here on the left. I'll go in the stall and talk to her. You watch. We still give her a treat on the rail when we leave. Here's one for you to leave." Claire handed him a piece of carrot.

Diamond whinnied and tossed her head. Claire's heart swelled at her happy response.

"I think she likes you," Elliott said.

"I hope so because I certainly like her."

Claire wondered if Diamond noticed the change in Elliott. She wondered if the horse puzzled over the change in his personality. She certainly did. She found herself liking him. Too bad it took such pain and suffering to make that happen. She looked back at Elliott.

Elliott was staring at Diamond. Was he remembering something? Claire wasn't sure she'd want Diamond's earlier rejection to be his first memory.

"Are you remembering something?" she asked.

"What? No, I thought I was, but my mind is still a blank. I am developing a headache though so I suppose that means my brain is trying."

"Sorry. Let's go." Claire told Diamond good night and they left her with a couple of treats.

Elliott stretched out on his bed, hoping to get rid of the headache before it cranked into high gear. He couldn't remember a thing but he somehow knew he had changed. Caught in a never-ending circle, he vacillated between wanting to remember and fear of remembering. He knew someone attacked him and that there had to be a reason. Had he done something to earn the attack or had he simply been in the wrong place at the wrong time? When he strained to remember, his headache always stopped him. He reached for his pills on the nightstand and swallowed one without water.

A shadow floated through the room, of a man pulling a woman behind him. He held onto her arm as he tried to bend her to his will. His grip tightened as she fought against him. He grabbed her other arm. Neither spoke, but the scene needed no dialogue. The man was forcing the woman against her will. The more she resisted, the more the man insisted. He kissed her, backing her body against the wall. He pressed against her as she struggled, pulling both arms above her head. He gripped both wrists in one hand and let the other travel down her body.

Elliott awoke in a sweat. Was a man raping one of the volunteers? Did someone need his help? He jumped off the bed, ready to help. Then it hit him. Maybe that was him — before. Maybe he was reliving a memory. Oh, God, I hope not, he thought. The thought sickened him.

He left his room and walked the farm. No one else was out and he didn't want to create a disturbance so he walked the roads. It was three-thirty before he returned to his room and tried to sleep.

He awoke to a gentle rain, the kind that washes clean the mind and the land. Both were needed.

* * *

Hap contacted Claire for Jake's phone number and address. Then he called Elena and left a message.

"I'm going to Syracuse today. I hope to talk to Jake, Claire's ex-boyfriend. I'll let you know when I get back. Peg wants to go along and visit the Erie Canal Museum."

He hoped to find Jake at home. He lived in the Irish part of town, Tipperary Hill. Hap was anxious to explore. Luck held, and Jake answered his door.

"Yeah?" Jake wore a pair of jeans and a dirty Syracuse t-shirt, and he held a can of beer in his left hand.

"My name is Hap Lynch and I'd like to ask you some questions about your visit to Alasa Farms."

Jake shoved the door shut, but not before he heard Hap. "I can get a warrant if I need to."

Jake opened the door partway.

"May I come in?" Hap pushed the door all the way open and walked in. He had lied about the warrant, but it had gotten the results he wanted. "I just need to ask you some questions."

Jake remained silent.

"You talked to two people at the farm. Sara, a manager, and Elliott, one of the farm hands."

"So? I don't know their names. I didn't do anything to them."

"You were looking for your ex-girlfriend, Claire."

"Nothing ex about her. She's my girlfriend and she needs to come home."

"That's another issue. I'm only interested in the visit."

Again Jake didn't respond.

"Where were you on the night of July 23?"

"How do I know? That was weeks ago."

"Sixteen days to be exact."

"Look, I have no idea where I was and what business is it of yours?"

"Someone took a ton of vengeance out on a young man named Elliott Werner that night. Someone with a lot of anger inside. From what I've learned, that pretty well describes you."

"Yeah, lots of luck. I don't know who you talked to but they're crazy. If it was Claire, don't believe a word she says."

"Why is that, Jake?"

"She lies. That's why. After all I've done for her, she leaves."

"What have you done for her?"

"Everything. I treat her like gold. I try to give her everything she wants and she has no gratitude. When she gets home, things will change."

Hap didn't like Jake and he feared for Claire if Jake ever found her. "You haven't answered my question. Where were you the night of July 23?"

"If you're a cop, show me your badge. Otherwise, get out of my house."

"I'm not a local cop, but I will certainly relay our conversation to them."

"Yeah, yeah, yeah. Get out."

Hap knew he'd get nothing more from Jake. He left with no more information than when he came, but saw enough to know that Claire had been lucky to get away. He also knew that Jake wouldn't hesitate to ignore the restraining order. Whether or not he had attacked Elliott, he had no idea.

When he returned to the farm, he told Cheri about his conversation with Jake and his concern for Claire's safety.

* * *

Mary Ann made a decision to communicate with Horace. This time, she would not let cowardice stand in her way. She would wait in the house until he returned from the other side. Giving up became more of an option everyday but she didn't know if she had that choice to make. She had never been one to think deeply about her faith. It had been easy to live in a community where decisions were made for her. Her only obligation had been to follow the rules. That should have been easy, but she had failed miserably. Since then, she'd spent more time wallowing in self-pity than contemplating God and the meaning of her life.

If she gave up her search for her child, would He be more accepting of her? Is that why she hadn't been able to enter the gates of Heaven? These questions weighed more heavily today than the thought of her lost child.

She'd waited for days and Horace hadn't appeared. She wandered down to the goats and sheep. Oh, how she wished her Luke still waited with the rest of the herd. But he'd been gone for so long. She went back to the house, remembering the little goat that'd always listened to her problems.

Out of boredom and despair, she decided to transition to the other side. If Horace had been spending time there, maybe she'd have a better chance of reaching him. Before she could act on that decision, she felt his presence. He had returned and was with her. She felt their energy connect. How she wished she could hug him, feel the touch of another, but she knew that kind words were the most she could hope for.

"Last time we met, you were singing," he said. "Your lovely voice soothed me."

"I remember. You were so kind and it made me uncomfortable. My response frightened me and I ran away."

"Yes, you did. I only wanted to help."

"I know, but my emotions get in the way."

"What do you want of me? I felt your spirit tugging at me."

"I ... I wanted to talk to someone. I need a friend."

"Mary Ann, I have tried to be your friend ever since ..."

"I know. I know. And I've rebuffed you at every turn. Please be patient with me," she pleaded.

"Patience is not one of my virtues."

"I'm sorry. I try, I really do. I need you but then when you're here, I think of my great sin and I can't face you."

"You didn't sin against me. Why should it be difficult to face me?"

"I don't know, Horace. I ... it's because you represented the good part of our friendship. Eaton and I destroyed that. For all three of us. I wanted to contact you before I left, but I didn't get the chance. You weren't there to say good-bye."

"I'm sorry, but I was so angry with Eaton for not supporting you, that I failed to do so. Can you forgive me?"

"There's nothing to forgive. Can we be friends again, as if nothing ever happened?"

"No, not as if nothing happened. We can be friends but only if it's to help each other find resolution and forgiveness. Otherwise we'll live in the netherworld for all eternity." Horace felt he couldn't survive much longer.

"Okay, then. As long as we're friends. I am so lonely and I get depressed too easily."

"I understand. Mary Ann, have you come to terms with losing your child?"

"Some days. But then other days, I go crazy looking for my baby, trying to figure out what happened to him ... or to her. Do you realize I don't even know if I had a boy or girl? Do you know how much that hurts?"

"I think so, but I know I can't feel the pain as deeply as you."

"Do you ever wonder about him?" Mary Ann asked.

"Him? Eaton? No, I don't. I've never forgiven him for what he did to you. I don't think I ever can."

"Please do. It wasn't all his fault. I fell under his spell and didn't have the strength to stop him. It was my sin, too. I know that now."

"No, it was never your sin. He raped you, Mary Ann. Do you understand?" Horace felt his anger building.

"I know that I enjoyed his kisses at first. That makes it my fault, too."

"Did you tell him to stop?"

"Yes, but ..."

"Then it was rape. Don't shoulder a sin that isn't yours. I know God wouldn't want you to."

"If that's true, why did I get shut out of Heaven? Why am I here, not a part of any existence at all?"

"It was not the rape. You have to know that."

"I guess I do. I think it was my refusal to accept the death of my baby. I was so sure he survived."

"Did God turn you away?" Horace refused to believe that.

"I saw the light, but as I walked toward it, it disappeared. I know God left me here."

"Did He leave you or did you choose to stay?"

"I don't know," Mary Ann cried. "I can't think about it anymore."

"I'll leave you alone, but let's be friends. Okay?"

Mary Ann nodded.

* * *

"And who are you?" Mr. Werner's voice rang in Hap's ear.

"My name is Hap Lynch and I'm helping to investigate your son's attack."

"Are you a cop?"

"More of a consultant now. I retired from the Kansas City Police Department."

"Then what in the world are you doing here?"

"Good question. Let's just say I'm doing some of the work that the police don't have time for. I'm sure you want to find out who perpetrated the attack on your son."

"Of course, I do."

"I've learned that Elliott was in some kind of trouble, a gambling debt."

"Has that Cheri woman been blabbing? I told her about Elliott in privacy. She'll not get one more cent from me. In fact, I'll have my attorney contact her."

"Wait a minute. You say you want to find your son, but you're more worried about Cheri helping with an investigation. Seems to me you'd be thanking the woman for caring enough to take him in and try to help him."

"Well ... I do, but she didn't have any right ..."

"She did what the police asked. For Elliott's own good. Now can you do likewise?"

"What do you want to know?"

Hap could almost see Werner deflate. Between him and his wife, he was beginning to understand the burden of Elliott's childhood.

"I want to know who Elliott owed money to."

"How should I know?"

"I know you paid his debts in the past. So who did you pay?"

'I don't know. His name is Dominic. He's with a local private club. More exclusive than the casinos. I told Elliott he'd come to no good if he kept in with that crowd, but you can't tell a hard-headed kid anything."

"Do you have a phone number?" Hap couldn't wait to get off the phone with this egotistical jerk.

"Yes, let me look it up. But don't expect any help. Dominic is nothing but a cheap hood who preys on kids and gambling addicts. He's a hard-nosed bastard."

After Hap had the phone number, he ended the call. Now, he needed to talk to the sheriff before he contacted Dominic. Or maybe Sheriff Briggs would take it from here.

He placed the call.

"Briggs here."

"Good afternoon, Sheriff. This is Hap Lynch. Do you have a few minutes to talk?"

"Sure. I'm sitting in the Alton Coffee Cup enjoying a piece of pie."

"How about I join you in a few minutes?"

"Not a problem unless you want lemon pie. I am devouring the last piece."

"No, I'll survive," Hap laughed.

By the time he arrived, Briggs sported a well-satisfied look.

"You missed it, Hap. Good stuff. Best lemon pie I've ever tasted."

"Guess I'll have to get here earlier than you next time."

"You're right there. What did you want to see me about?"

"I've been busy. Talked with Jake Clements. Claire O'Malley's ex-boyfriend. He had a small run-in with Elliott when he came looking for Claire. Nothing big, but Jake is an angry guy. Capable of taking that anger out on anyone. If he suspected Elliott had an interest in Claire, he'd definitely be capable of beating him to a pulp."

"Sounds like a possibility," the sheriff nodded.

"Yes, and then there's Dominic, the guy that Elliott owes money to. He runs a private gambling club in Syracuse. I haven't talked to him. I figured you might want to make that call."

"Well, sounds like you're doing just fine without our help. Why don't you make the call and report back?"

"I can do that, but you know if this guy collects gambling debts frequently, he's not going to scare easily."

"You just get us information, that's all. If you think he's a likely suspect, we'll take over."

"Okay. I'll give him a call." Hap said with a lot more confidence than he felt. He had absolutely no authority for any action he took here. He'd never felt quite so helpless at the thought of an interrogation.

* * *

"I don't have to talk to you," Dominic began after Hap introduced himself and the reason for his call.

"If not me, then the Wayne County Sheriff. Your choice," Hap bluffed, not sure if Briggs would have the time to follow up.

"Who did you say you are?"

"Hap Lynch. I'm a consultant with the Wayne County Sheriff's Office." Another white lie, but Hap didn't think he was likely to call and check him out.

"Okay. I know Elliott. He's a gambler and a loser. He played here frequently as long as Daddy was paying the bill. Daddy puts a stranglehold on the money, and son comes whining to me."

"As I told you, someone attacked and seriously injured him. From where I stand, it looks like you had the best reason to do that."

"Look, I don't care how it looks to you. Sure, I threatened him, and he ignored me."

"You threatened him? How?"

"You mean he didn't come whining to you?"

"Never mind that. What was your threat?" Hap was sure he knew, but wanted to hear Dominic admit it.

"Only that it'd be better for his health if he paid up."

"Sounds to me like that's a serious threat."

"Look, I didn't rough him up, but whoever did, I'm sure he deserved it. When did this attack occur?"

"The night of July 23. Where were you?"

"The same place I am every night. Right here at the club. Any of my staff can verify that."

"And what about your collection staff? Where were they?"

"I don't know what you're talking about. I'm a busy man, so this conversation is over." Dominic hung up the phone.

Hap had nothing concrete to report to Briggs. He felt that violence would certainly fit into Dominic's mode of operation, but proving it was another thing.

* * *

Elliott awoke to the sound of rain. Not the gentle rain of a couple of days ago, but a strong peppering pouring from angry clouds. The wind roared intermittently, offering a small reprieve now and then. He pulled the covers over his head and wished he could ignore the alarm. He was learning that they had to tend to the livestock regardless of weather or personal issues. He threw off the covers and pulled on his jeans. He looked through his drawers for a clean t-shirt and socks. Something in the sound of the wind whistling through his room tugged at a memory. He wanted to dig in and pull it out but the incessant throbbing in his head brought all thought to a halt. He lay down, breathed deeply and cleared his mind until his pain lessened. By the time he made his appearance in the barn, only a dull ache remained.

"You're looking a little green this morning," Seth greeted him.

"I probably look better than I feel."

"Another headache?"

"Yeah. Every time I think I might remember something, the throbbing throws a major punch."

"Give it time, buddy." Seth wished he had better advice. He liked Elliott more everyday.

They worked in silence until their morning chores were finished.

"Was I in some kind of trouble?" Elliott asked as they left the barn. The rain had stopped and the wind had died down. Rivulets of water ran down the gravel road and puddles filled the spots where the grass was sparse.

"What do you mean?"

"Someone beat me up, and every time a memory lurks beneath the surface, my head reacts. Maybe it's telling me it's better not to remember."

"I don't know. That's a question for your doctor, but maybe you're afraid to remember. Seems that would be a reasonable response to a violent attack."

"How bad did I look?"

"Bad. Lots of blood. You probably looked better when they cleaned you up. Apparently, most of your injuries were superficial, except for your amnesia."

"It gets really tiresome, you know. Every person I meet and everything I do makes me wonder how I reacted before the attack. Did I know all of you? Did I like you? Was I a good worker? Questions like that."

"I think I understand. We rely on our memories in most of our everyday encounters. It would be exhausting to constantly face new situations with no idea whether or not you knew something or someone."

"Yeah, that's pretty much it."

"Hang in there! Oh, there's Jeff. I need to catch him. See you later."

Elliott watched Seth until he reached Jeff. He was beginning to hate this mid-morning lull in his duties. He had nothing to fill the time, and he didn't want to bring on another headache.

Hey, Elliott!" He turned to see Elena jogging toward him. "One of the goats is missing. Want to help me look for it?"

"Where could he go?"

"If he got out of the pasture, he could be down at the tree line. I'm going to take the four-wheeler."

"Sure, I'll help."

"Do you want to drive? That'll give me a better chance to look."

"Hey, I'm a guy. We like to drive."

They found the lost goat nibbling at the brush near the tree line. Elliott picked him up and they carried him back to his pasture. They then found the hole in the fence and texted Jeff. By noon the fence had been repaired and everyone was ready for lunch.

"We've got an adoption today," Cheri told them. "Two of our bunnies will leave for their forever homes. It's a family in Sodus and the daughter is diabetic. When they visited last week, she begged for a bunny. Her dad said two would be better than one, so he built a pen and they are picking them up today."

"That's awesome," Claire said as she finished her sandwich.

"The best part of our work is to see our animals find homes," Cheri said.

"Don't you hate to see them go?" Elena asked.

"Yes and no. We do get attached to them, but we can never give each one the attention they get in a home."

Gray clouds rolled in again and everyone headed back to work before the sky opened up.

* * *

There are few advantages to the spirit life, the purgatory I abide in. Immunity to weather is one of the few. Neither rain nor snow, heat nor cold can bother me. I watched the crew today as they slopped through the rain and mud to finish their chores before dark. I am heartened by Elliott's change in personality. He has found himself at home and seems at peace until he tries to remember the past. I wish I could tell him that he is lucky. The past is not always worth remembering.

If I could have one wish for him, it would be to continue building a better life, and forget the old. I think if I had that power, I might be able to move forward.

CHAPTER THIRTY-TWO

In three words I can sum up everything I've learned about life: It goes on.
Robert Frost

HAP MET JOE BRIGGS AT the Alton Coffee Cup again. This time, he arrived early and ordered the lemon pie. He had already taken a bite before Joe walked through the door.

"I had a feeling you'd beat me to that pie today." Joe's hearty laugh brought a smile to everyone's face. It's difficult to ignore such an infectious emotion.

"I think she has a piece saved just for you," Hap said.

As they enjoyed their pie, Hap filled him in on his conversations with Jake, Mr. Werner and Dominic. "If I want to be cynical, I can easily picture Werner as the attacker. He's a hard man, and, most likely, a poor excuse for a father. I can see him turning to violence, what he'd call 'discipline.' But the sad truth is, I don't think he cares enough to drive down here and deal with his son."

"Sad state of affairs," Joe mused. "The older I get, the less I understand human nature."

"Fair warning, it never gets easier."

"So what's your gut feeling on the perpetrator? Jake or Dominic?"

"I wish I knew. Jake is certainly capable of violence. Angry, impulsive violence. Dominic, on the other hand, would mete out punishment without a thought for the victim."

"In other words, given the right situation, either could be guilty." Joe scraped to get the last taste of his pie.

"You gonna eat the plate, too?" Hap laughed.

"Nope, I think I've scraped it clean. I think it's time I get involved. If only Elliott would regain his memory, I think we could get this cleared up."

"You just gave me an idea. I haven't tried to question him. I wonder if a little pressure might help him remember."

"Worth a try. In the meantime, I'll run some checks on Dominic. I have some friends on the Syracuse force that might be able to help."

A loud clap of thunder warned of impending rain. "Guess we better get out of here while it's still dry." Hap pulled out some cash and left it on the table.

* * *

The rain-soaked, grayish world fit Hap's mood as he pondered the best way to approach Elliott. He didn't want to create any more anxiety than the poor guy already felt. It was be difficult to imagine anything more anxiety-ridden than losing your memory.

When he drove in the farm driveway, he saw Elena walking away from the old house, ignoring the rain that had lightened to a steady patter. He called to her and she ran to the car.

"Can I get in?" she asked.

"Sure. What are you doing out in the rain?"

"I had nothing to do so I decided to walk through the old house. I felt as if someone was pulling me toward it." She used her jacket sleeve to wipe the water from her face.

"There's a cloth in the glove compartment," he told her.

"I'm okay. I'm so glad you're here. I had a weird experience."

"Why am I not surprised?" Hap couldn't wait to hear this.

"I saw a spirit. Well, not really. Have you been in the house?"

"No, I figured it isn't safe after that fire."

"I don't know about that. I just felt this pull. When I walked in what I think was a closed-in porch, I saw the rocking chair moving back and forth in a slow rhythm. I felt someone." Elena paused. "He was there."

"Who?"

"I don't know. I smelled pipe smoke. The chair came forward suddenly, as if he stood up. Then it rocked back and slowly grew still. I looked around and saw a shadow go into the other room. I wanted to follow it, but I felt like my feet were glued to the floor."

"Is the pipe smoke what made you think it was a man?"

"Maybe. I just sensed that he was. I don't know if I disturbed him or if he was even aware of my presence. It made me sad."

"Why would it make you sad?"

"I don't know. I think he was sad, and I felt it. It's weird, isn't it?"

* * *

I had been sitting in the rocker, remembering. For once, I concentrated on the good times. I rarely saw past the bad, but today I thought of my mother. I remember sitting beside her in a rocker much like this one. My baby sister sat on her lap and we listened as Mother read to us. I don't remember the story but I remember her voice. When she read, she made the stories come alive. It became my favorite time of day. We had her to ourselves before our father came home for the evening. Then she fixed dinner and cleaned up the kitchen before she tucked us in bed. Father made an appearance to say goodnight, always with his pipe in hand. I love the smell of tobacco to this day. It reminds me of happy days.

By the time I joined the Shakers, my mother had died and my father had remarried. I've often wondered how Mother would have felt about my conversion. She raised all of us in the Episcopal Church, but I never once heard her disparage those of other faiths. I like to think she would have approved of my decision. But maybe not, if she could have foreseen the outcome. I never once saw bitterness in her. Oh, I sometimes made her angry, but she was quick to forgive and forget. Her love was constant.

My spirits plummeted as I thought of her pain if she'd lived to see me filled with rage and bitterness. I wish she were here with me now. Would she be able to soothe away my anguish?

Then the girl wandered into the house and sensed me. Or maybe the movement of the rocker unnerved her. I wanted to reach out and touch her. She looked forlorn standing there, like I had spilled my despondency onto her. I didn't want her to suffer my moodiness so I left. Elena is an open heart. She knew I was there and I think she would have liked to reach out to me. Good Lord, I am trying.

* * *

Elliott followed Claire down to the horse pasture. "Where are you going?"

"Sara asked me to bring one of the horses back to the barn. Want to help?"

"Sure. I'm lost once I've finished my chores. Especially on rainy days like today."

"Well, as least it's slowed down for a little while. It's that black one there," she pointed to one of the two horses grazing along the fence."

"I have a question. Do you have any memories of me before ... you know, before the attack?"

"Nothing special," Claire hedged. She didn't think honesty would be the best policy in this situation. Elliott had treated her with kindness and friendliness since his return. In no way was she going to do anything to change that.

"Did we spend much time together?"

"We went into Sodus Bay as a group several times. You enjoyed the sunset as much as the rest of us."

"Did we have conversations? You know, about where I came from or what I wanted to do with my life?"

"No," she answered honestly. "We never talked about anything important. Just casual stuff."

They reached the horse. Claire petted her and put a rope halter around her neck. Elliott followed as she led the horse back to the barn. Every time he tried to discover anything about his past, he reached a brick wall. Had he never said anything important, anything that people might remember? What had he valued? What did he want to do with his life?

He watched as Sara took the horse into the stall and checked its legs and hooves. Claire went to the tack room and came back with two brushes.

Elliott leaned against a post and wished he had even one memory.

By the time he left the barn, the rain had settled into a light drizzle. He saw Elena and her friend get out of his car. He couldn't remember his name.

"Elliott," Hap called. "Do you have a minute or two?"

"Sure."

"I'd like to talk to you, but we need to get out of this weather. How about my car?"

"That'll work."

"I have to check on something so I'll see you both later." Elena walked toward the boarding house.

After they settled in the car, Hap began, "I have a few questions. I've been talking with Sheriff Briggs about your attacker. At his suggestion, I've followed up on a couple of leads and I'd like to know if either of the incidents I'm going to mention spark a memory."

"You know I can't remember anything."

"Yes, but I'm hoping hearing about the people I've talked to might help both of us."

"Okay."

"First of all, I talked with your father. He gave me the name of a man who runs a private club in Syracuse. You've gambled there often, and your father has paid the debts you accumulated. The last time he refused and sent you here to the farm. Does any of that jog your memory?"

"No. I must not have been much of a gambler if my father had to keep paying my debts."

"Apparently not. Dominic is the name of the man who owns the club. According to your father, he's not a nice guy. When he refused to pay your current debt, I suspect Dominic made some ugly threats."

Elliott not only couldn't remember, he couldn't imagine he'd ever be wracking up gambling debts. If that were true, he must have been a total jerk. "No, but I sure don't like the picture I'm getting of my past life."

"You're young, Elliott. Forgive yourself if you made some foolish mistakes."

"I sometimes wonder what I'll do if I remember who I was and I don't like that person."

"Then you'll change." Hap's heart went out to Elliott. It was hard to imagine having no past. Even harder if you found a past that filled you with shame.

"There's another person I talked to. His name is Jake Clements. He came here looking for Claire. You told him she worked here before something about him made you want to hide her from him. Then you told him she lived in Sodus. Do you remember any of that?"

"No." The conversation brought on the usual headache and Elliott went to his room after he assured Hap that he recalled nothing.

* * *

I watched Elliott leave the car. He went to his room. Time is forcing me to change my opinion of him. He is in no way the same person as before. I feel the need to pray, that if and when his memory returns, he will not hate himself. I learned the hard way that self-hate is death to hope.

I have no idea if God hears the prayers of spirits, but I have begun to talk to God as I ask for His forgiveness. The Shaker way encourages us to invoke His forgiveness. There was a song that advised us not to dwell on the sins of our youth, something about the 'sting of misspent days.' I wish I could recall the rest of it. I no longer sing, and I now realize how much I missed it. Maybe that's why I felt so overjoyed when I heard Mary Ann singing, "'Tis the Gift to be Simple." Its melody is one of hope and its message of delight in our faith. I realize I retain a healthy respect for the wisdom of Mother Ann and our leaders.

But I digress. Should I intervene in Elliott's life? If I choose to do so, do I have the power? I ponder this as I watch him sleep. His medication works quickly and I am thankful he has it. At first I hoped that he would never recover his memory, but now I think he must to develop into a good man.

* * *

Hap and Peg spent the next couple days sightseeing. Peg especially loved the Hotchkiss Peppermint Museum in Lyons. Hap accepted that he'd long remember the smell since she bought peppermint oil, peppermint soap and peppermint candy. Peppermint had invaded his life.

They drove down to the Montezuma Wildlife Refuge and savored their good fortune. Even though they had enjoyed watching the eagles, Hap's thoughts had returned again and again to the farm. He was eager to visit tomorrow. After hundreds of pictures, they returned to the Carriage House Inn, exhausted but happy.

CHAPTER THIRTY-THREE

Life is mostly what we make it,
Filled with sunshine or with storm;...

Anonymous

EILEEN TOOK A STEP THROUGH the door of the old house. Emotion filled the room. She could sense it although she saw no one. Were there living people here or were they like her? She didn't understand the spirit world but she accepted that she lived on a different plane than Claire and her friends. This had been happening to her for generations. She'd find someone she bonded with, but it never lasted. Time moved forward for everyone but her. The friends left or grew old and died. She remained the lonely child who couldn't understand her world. Would Claire leave too? Could she make other friends? There was a girl here, not that much older than she. Why hadn't she been able to talk to her?

She walked into the next room and noticed an old rocking chair. A memory formed. She sat with her pretend father as she told him about her day. She chattered on and on about her tea party with her dolls, and he listened to every word. He smiled and hugged her when she finished her story. Her heart hurt.

She sat in the old chair and slowly rocked back and forth. She closed her eyes, remembering, until she felt a presence. A shadow of a man stood in the doorway. Was it her father? She jumped up and ran toward the door. The shadow faded and she was alone. If she called to him, would he return? If she admitted to her pretend father that she was no longer angry with him, would he listen? He'd been her daddy all her life. How had she ever convinced herself that he was simply pretending? She cried, but felt no tears on her cheek.

"Daddy, if it's you, please come back."

She waited. "I'm sorry." She cried harder. She walked back to the chair and rocked until she felt nothing but lethargy.

* * *

I watched her cry. I had no idea who she was or where she was from, but her despair reached my heart. She called for her daddy. I wished I could answer her, but a barrier stood between us. Caught partway in a different dimension, she could neither see nor hear me. I watched helplessly.

* * *

The next morning after breakfast, they decided to return to the farm. Luke ran to the car ahead of Hap and Peg. He wasn't about to be left behind.

"Do you think he'll do all right at the farm today?" Peg asked.

"We'll soon find out. I'm afraid I've done all I can do in this investigation. Briggs says he'll take it over, but I'm afraid it'll be dropped."

"Something will happen. It always does."

"Positive thinking today, huh?" Hap grinned. "You think I need that?"

Peg's laughter was the only reply.

Luke danced around in anticipation of a fun day. He totally ignored their conversation. As soon as they reached the farm, Luke shot out of the open door before Hap had a chance to stop him.

"Looks like he's on a mission," Peg said.

"Probably looking for the nearest tree."

They found Elena in the barn with Claire and Diamond.

"Sara said we're getting two more horses today," Elena announced.

"I hope they're not abuse cases," Peg said.

"No, the man who owns them has to move into town and can't take them along. I can't wait to see them."

"Diamond is a beauty," Peg said as she watched Claire brush her.

"Inside and out. She's such a gentle soul."

They talked for a few minutes before Elena asked if they brought Luke.

"Oh, I almost forgot about him." Hap looked around and walked out of the barn. "I don't see him."

"Where do you suppose he went?" Peg sounded worried.

"He's around here somewhere. He'll find us when he's ready."

"But remember his encounter the last time," Elena said. "I'm going to look for him."

She checked around the goats while Hap went one way down the road and Peg the other. They all called Luke, but he neither barked nor came running. Since that wasn't his usual response when he was called, Hap became concerned.

"He wouldn't go out in the road, would he?" Elena asked when they were together again.

"No, I don't think so." Hap said.

"You never know what he'll do." Peg remembered all the times they'd searched for him.

"Would he go inside one of the buildings?"

"I don't think so."

"I'll check the boarding house. He might find Elliott or Seth in there." Elena searched each room. The building was empty and Luke was nowhere in sight.

"He liked the donkeys the other day. I'll check there," Peg offered.

Hap walked toward the old office building. It was locked. He walked around by the old gas pump, thinking that was a prime spot for Luke to visit. He thought he heard a growl. He stopped and listened. Yes, he was sure it was Luke's growl. Where was it coming from?

"Hear that?" Hap asked Elena when she joined him.

"That's him, isn't it?"

"I think so. Sounds like it's coming from around the house."

"Or inside," Elena added. "If you'll walk around the house, I'll check inside."

"Okay, but be careful. I'm not sure it's safe in there."

"It's safe."

"There's probably mold and heaven only knows how many critters," Hap protested.

"I won't be in there long." Elena walked toward the back porch. The screen door stood open just enough to let something of Luke's size through. She opened the creaky door and Luke's growl grew stronger.

She looked around the room and walked through to the old porch. Luke stood in front of the rocking chair, obviously sensing something she didn't see. With his fur up, he stood his ground, a low growl that didn't get any louder or more threatening. *Whatever it is, he isn't afraid of it*, she thought.

"Luke, are you okay?"

He ignored her. His growl softened, but he stood his ground. Elena looked around. She too sensed something, but saw no earthly signs of movement. Then the rocker creaked and began rocking.

"Hap," she called. She didn't think the presence was unfriendly, but she wanted Hap to sense it, too.

By the time he came in the door, the rocker had stilled and Luke began to relax. She explained what she'd seen. They watched Luke sniff around the wall. Nothing else interested him, so he was content to follow Hap and Elena outside.

"Wow, can you believe that?" Elena rubbed her arms as she thought about Luke's response.

"It's amazing. I do think he senses a spirit here. I wish I did so I could understand him better. If I h ad his senses, I might more easily discern if a person is lying or telling the truth."

"Do you think he can tell?"

"More easily than I do." Hap explained that Sheriff Briggs was ready to take over the investigation.

"Does that mean you'll be leaving?"

"Soon, we need to get home and I think I've done as much as I can. I believe we have two people who could have attacked Elliott. Totally different motives, but both capable. Jake, Claire's boyfriend, is a hothead and I can see him reacting to what he considered lies to keep Claire away from him. Dominic, the guy Elliott owed money to, is capable of cold, hard decisions to protect his assets. I don't think he'd dirty his hands, but I'm sure he has people who clean up situations for him."

"Do you think Sheriff Briggs will follow up or will he drop it? After all, Elliott is back at work."

"I hope he does, but I'm afraid more pressing matters will get in the way." Hap knew from his police experience that assault cases often fell by the wayside once the victim began to recover and there were no clear cut suspects.

"You didn't know Elliott before, but he's been great since he returned. We all like him, but we wonder what will happen when his memory returns."

"What do you mean?"

"If he finds out he was a jerk before, how will it affect him now?" Elena paused. "I mean, will it help or hurt him? I think I'd be in some major depression if I found out something like that."

"Maybe not. Maybe it will strengthen his resolve to be a better person."

"I hope so."

* * *

I will never understand the plane in which I exist, but today I heard every word of their conversation. Sometimes I can see people but not hear them; other times I pass by them and don't even know of their presence. But today I listened to Elena and Hap's conversation.

Luke knew I was there, even after I grew quiet and still. I was ready to leave but he accepted my presence and went on about his way. I am thankful I followed them out of the house. They helped me make a decision to act. I will help Elliott, if I can. I have been pondering an incident that occurred on the farm soon after I united with the Shakers.

A horse had kicked Brother William in the head. He lay unconscious for days and when he awoke, he had lost his memory. Much like Elliott. When he recovered, he resumed his duties. However, there was a difference. I don't remember any changes in his personality, except a little more impatience whenever his head ached. Then one day, he fell off a ladder. He lay unconscious for a few minutes, but when he woke up this time, it was if his memory had never left him. We all considered it a miracle, and to this day, I still do. Sometimes it is difficult to understand God's ways, but He watches over us. I believe that everything happens for a reason. I say that with great questioning though, because I still do not fully understand why He has left me in this spirit existence for so long. But I believe He knows, and He expects me to figure it out. I feel I am doing so in bits and pieces.

Enough about my self-contemplation. My question now, would a similar recovery happen to Elliott? If so, he should be able to tell us the identity of his attacker. I will ponder this. Could I contrive an accident that would restore his memory, or would I simply injure him? No one but God had planned Brother William's fall. Will He be angry with me if I intervene with Elliott? Do I have the right to harm another, even if I think the outcome will be beneficial? I must pray.

* * *

Hap found Claire in the barn. He needed to have a conversation with her before he left.

"Do you have a few minutes to talk?

"Sure. I'm finished with my chores for now, but one thing I've learned with farm work, it's never finished. One just learns to enjoy the lulls in between."

"How about taking a walk?"

"After yesterday's rain, it will be nice to enjoy the sunshine. Lead the way."

Fresh air and a cool breeze enticed them to walk to the woods.

"I plan to leave soon," Hap said. "I talked to Jake. Actually I questioned him regarding the attack on Elliott. I don't know if he's guilty, but I know that he is capable of violent behavior."

"Yes, I know that, too."

"That's why we're having this talk. Claire, it's not over for him."

"I know."

"It may never be. A restraining order may work in a public way, but at some point in time, he will try to see you. He will wait until you're alone. Although his temper is volatile, I believe he has the ability to rein it in until he thinks the situation is favorable."

"You're scaring me."

"I mean to. If you stay here, you should never be alone. Even in the barn, like you were. Make sure Sara or someone knows where you are at all times."

"That sounds horrible. I don't want others to have to protect me all the time."

"You may want to leave here. There are organizations that deal with domestic abuse. They can help you move on and form a new life."

"I've grown to love it here. I would hate to leave." Claire thought of Diamond, who had become her confidante.

"I know, but take it seriously. Jake is a violent, angry man. He sees you as the reason for all his problems. It's imperative in his mind that he get you back and keep you in line."

Tears streamed down Claire's face. "I'm so tired. I wake up dozens of time every night, sure that he's here. Will there ever be an end?"

"I wish I could tell you that he will forget, but he won't. If he's the one who attacked Elliott, and it can be proven in a court of law, then he will go to prison. That will give you a reprieve, but not a permanent solution." He pulled Claire close to him, and pulled a tissue out of his pocket.

"Thanks," she took the tissue, wiped her eyes and blew her nose.

"I don't mean to frighten or depress you, but I want you to understand the seriousness."

"Believe me, I do."

* * *

Hap texted Cheri that he was planning on leaving in a day or two. He and Peg sat in the Carriage House Inn living room when she called him. He gave her a rundown of his meeting with Briggs and his talk with Claire.

"I think we'll stop in Rochester for a day. Peg wants to visit the Strong Museum of Play and the Eastman House."

"Be sure to visit Nick Tahou's while you're there. It's downtown and is a hole-in-the-wall kind of place. You have to order the garbage plate. It's a Rochester tradition. Better split one because it's a lot of food."

"What in the world is a garbage plate?"

"Just what the name says. Lots of garbage food that we all love. He starts with fries and macaroni, topped with two hamburger patties covered with cheese and a bunch of different sauces mixed in. It's served with bread."

"Sounds like heartburn waiting to happen."

"Gotta try it though!" Cheri didn't need to tell him it was definitely a young person's item.

"Will do. Unfortunately, a garbage plate sounds like a lot of human relationships. Keep piling too much stuff on and it can cause heartburn or worse. If you need me, call. I'm hoping that Briggs follows through."

CHAPTER THIRTY-FOUR

Let there be no purpose in friendship save the deepening of the spirit.
Kahlil Gibran

"WANT TO EXPLORE THE OLD house with us?" Elena had finally convinced Claire that it was safe.

"I'm hoping the ceiling doesn't fall in while we're there," Claire said.

"I've been in it and it's safe. The ghosts live there."

"Maybe so, but they don't have to worry about falling ceilings and other accidents."

"How can you know what they have to worry about?" Elliott laughed. "Elena, do you promise I'll see a ghost if I go with you?"

"Can't promise anything, but I think they stay in the house. I forgot. You don't remember their story, do you?"

"Afraid not."

"The two we know are Mary Ann and Horace. They both lived here when the Shakers owned the farm, and built the house."

"How do you know their names?"

"That I don't know. You'll have to ask Cheri."

"I'll do that. Have you seen them?"

"No, but I've sensed them. I know that one of them was sitting in the rocking chair while I was there. Luke sensed them too."

"Maybe so," Claire said, "but we can't ask him to tell us about it."

"Come see for yourself. Besides, it's fun to explore. There's an old piano in there. I would love to know who played it. Think how many generations have lived in the house. It is full of stories."

"Maybe you should be a novelist and write ghost stories," Elliott said.

"Or maybe my stories would be non-fiction."

The banter brought out the explorer spirit in Elliott. "Shall I lead the way?"

"Why don't I? I've been in here before. Watch for cobwebs around the door." Elena led them into the room where the rocking chair stood empty. No rocking today and no sense of anyone sitting quietly.

"Where are the ghosts?" Elliott circled the rocker. "I think it's empty." He pushed the back, making the rocker move back and forth a couple of times.

"You want to see the ghosts, don't you?" His lightheartedness made Claire smile.

"Sure, don't you?"

"Not really."

"Let's look through the other rooms. I'll show you the piano. It's almost one-hundred-years old. Mr. Strong had it custom made after he bought the place back in the 1920s."

"He's the one that named it Alasa Farms, right?" Elliott asked.

Elena looked at him. "Where did you hear that?"

"I don't know. Why?"

"Has anyone talked about it?"

"I don't know. What's the big deal?"

"I get it. She's wondering if it's a memory," Claire said.

"I don't remember where I heard it or why I know that. I must have read it somewhere."

"That's possible," Elena said. "It's just that, for a minute, I thought you remembered something. Sorry I made a big deal out of it."

"No problem," Elliott said. "I know you are trying to help. I'll think about this, but I don't think it's a memory from before."

They continued exploring every room on the main floor. "It smells old, doesn't it?" Claire asked.

"Yes, but it doesn't smell burnt. That's what I expected the first time I was in here," Elena said.

"What's upstairs?" Elliott put his hand on the wood bannister.

"I haven't been up there. The fire was on the third floor and I heard that the second floor had damage, too. I don't think we should chance it."

* * *

Elliott's hand on the banister brought back a memory. I had been told how unusual it was for a dwelling house to have a single staircase. Usually, men and women had

separate doors and staircases. However, we were a small community here and the elders and eldresses decided on efficiency. We would use the same staircase, but women would sleep in the retiring rooms on the second floor and men on the third.

* * *

"Come on, I'm going upstairs," Elliott stood on the first step.

"I don't think you should," Elena answered.

Elliott's laughter as he took the second step almost concealed the sound. It wasn't a loud crack, it was more a mushy sound. Then, as if in slow motion, he began to fall. He yelled, catching himself on the banister and stopping the momentum before he hit the floor.

"Are you all right?" Elena and Claire both cried and leaned over him.

"Oh, my God. Look at his foot. It's still twisted in the step." Claire stood up. "We have to get help. Don't let him move."

Elliott moaned and tried to move.

"Stay still," Elena urged. "Your foot is caught. Claire went to get help." The pain etched on his face calmed her rising panic. I can't let him see my fear, she thought.

Seth arrived first. He immediately scoped out the problem and started working on the stair. Without touching Elliott's foot, he managed to move the board that held him down. He grabbed Elliott's leg, and slowly pulled his foot free. "It may be broken. I don't know if we can get him up without hurting it more. Let me think a minute."

Elena kept talking to Elliott, not sure if she was trying to soothe his anxiety or her own. Jeff and Claire ran into the room. After assessing the situation, Jeff looked at Seth.

"Do you think we can get him up without him putting any weight on that foot?."

"Let's try."

"Claire, get the car ready. We need to lay him across the back seat and keep his foot free."

Claire ran to the car and drove it up to the door.

Elliott moaned when they moved him. He concentrated so hard on Jeff's diagnosis that the pain dimmed. Another stupid move on his part. No one else could mess up a summer the way he was doing. What else could go wrong?

By the time they loaded him in the car, his foot throbbed in wave after wave of pain. Elliott swore to himself he wouldn't pass out. No way would he add insult to injury!

Jeff looked at him. "Keep that determination going strong," he told Elliott. "We'll have you to the doctor in no time. I wish we had a vet on staff. He could have looked at it."

"If only you were a horse or cow," Seth joked.

Elliott's attempted smile turned into a grimace.

"You're doing fine," Jeff assured him. "We'll be there soon. I grabbed some Tylenol. Take a couple and be thankful that Seth didn't bring his cow liniment."

At the doctor's office, Jeff and Seth waited while a nurse took Elliott for x-rays. When the doctor appeared, he confirmed that the foot was broken. "The good news is that it's a clean break. We can cast it and let you take him home in the next hour. He will need crutches and some pain meds. I'll prescribe them."

Seth texted Cheri and Claire. By the time they arrived home, they had moved a bed and his belongings into the room closest to the door. Cheri had cleaned up an old wheelchair that she found in the corner of the old museum building. Burt and Sara were putting the finishing touches to a makeshift ramp.

"This is one of those 'it takes a village' moments," Elena said.

"For sure, and we'll need help getting him inside now. He's full of pain meds and he's pretty much out of it."

Once they had made him comfortable in bed, the meds did their job and Elliott slept for several hours. Cheri and Jeff divided up Elliott's duties among the others.

"Man, he's had the bad luck," Seth said. "Do we have any black cats that keep crossing his path?"

* * *

I watched in horror. Did thinking a thought make it come true? For a minute, I wished I had pushed him. He would have had a much better chance of hitting his head. The plight of Job in the Old Testament came to mind. Had God allowed Satan to put a curse on him? But Job had been an upright and honorable man. Elliott was an ordinary, flawed but decent human being. I find myself understanding less and less of God's ways.

I try to remember if my Shaker training included any way of helping others. I can't remember anything in particular but I know that we always focused on the common good. That would include helping others in need. I'm not sure how to apply that to Elliott but, for the first time in years, I find myself concentrating on someone besides Mary Ann and myself.

For now, I will find the wood and tools.

* * *

The pain medication kept Elliott groggy for the first couple of days. By the time, he started on the reduced dosage, the pain in his foot had lessened. Adapting to crutches became his immediate problem.

He had plenty of visitors who urged him to stay in bed and rest for a few days. No way would he tell them that brought out the demons. Despair and self-hatred were their names. They arrived the minute he awoke and left only when visitors came.

On the third morning, Cheri suggested he spend the day outside. "Sunshine, a blue sky and a gentle breeze will do wonders for your spirit."

He sat up and reached for the hated crutches.

"No, let's use the wheelchair to get you outside. We still have the ramp. You carry the crutches and once you're outside, you can use them to move around as you wish."

Cheri wheeled him outside and parked him in the shade of a tree. From his vantage point, he could see the road, the barns and some of the pastures.

"It's a great place to lift your spirits," Cheri assured him.

He assumed everyone was busy because he saw no one. He heard the tractor somewhere but it was out of his range of vision. Cheri had brought him a bottle of water before she left him alone. Elliott tried to clear his mind, wanting the breeze to blow in pleasant thoughts. Instead, gusts of anxiety engulfed him. Would he ever return to whatever his life had been before this summer?

One of the cats came to his chair, curled up beside him and settled in to keep him company. He laughed at the inordinate amount of joy he felt with the companionship of a scrawny cat. The cat looked up and he could swear it smiled at him.

The tractor drove into sight. Seth waved and yelled, "Be back in a minute." He stopped the tractor and disappeared behind the chicken run. A few minutes later, he reappeared, jumped on the tractor, drove up and slid off a few yards from Elliott.

"Run you a race," Seth grinned as he pointed at the crutches. "How you liking your new transportation?"

"I think I'd rather have your fancy-dancy wheels."

Seth caught Elliott up on the farm activities. Two rabbit adoptions and one horse possibility. No new animals had arrived.

"How's Diamond?"

"Improving everyday. Wanna grab those crutches and walk over there?"

"Not today. I don't think I'd make it that far."

"Then let's take a short walk. You need the exercise and I need someone to make fun of."

"You're a laugh a minute. Too bad we're not hiring comedians," Elliott shot back.

With encouragement, Elliott walked to the barn and back. He knew he'd have blisters on his hands, but it felt good to navigate on his own.

Elena came out of the barn and saw them. "Hey, it's great to see you outside. How's it going?"

"Pretty good. At least I don't feel as groggy as I did."

"Yeah, that's the meds. You'll be off those soon."

"I hope so. I hate the feeling."

"Seth, let's go check out that step. We need to fix it," Elena suggested.

"Okay. We'll walk Elliott back to his wheelchair and then we'll go."

Elliott felt alone again when they walked away. He realized he enjoyed their company more each day. In fact, he felt part of something important. Everyone here worked hard for a good cause. He liked that.

Elena ran ahead when they entered the house. "Oh, look," she called to Seth. "Someone has already fixed it"

They looked at the newly repaired step. The new wood looked out of place in the dusty old staircase, but the workmanship was good.

"Whoever did it, knew exactly what he was doing," Seth said.

"What do you mean?"

"See the way the board is cut. It's a perfect fit." He stepped on it. "And it's solid. It should hold for another couple hundred years. That is, unless Elliott decides to go upstairs again."

"You're mean," Elena laughed.

"Just joking. He seems a little down, so we need to keep it all lighthearted."

"I know. I really like him more everyday. He's not had an easy summer here."

"For sure."

They left in time to see Cheri wheel Elliott back into the house.

"Let's go ask if she had Burt fix the step," Elena said.

Elliott was settled back in bed by the time they walked in. Cheri was leaving.

"Cheri, did you or Burt fix that step?"

"The one I broke?" Elliott asked.

Seth nodded.

"No, we haven't even had time to think about it. We should probably close the building so no one goes in until it is fixed."

"It is."

"Is what?" Cheri asked.

"Fixed."

"Who fixed it?"

"I don't know. I thought you probably did."

"I'll ask Jeff. Maybe he did it. At least we won't have to board the place up."

"Whoever did it, did a good job," Seth said. "I don't have the carpenter skills to make a board fit that snug."

"Good deal. I need to meet Burt so I better get out of here."

* * *

Elena found Jeff walking back across the road. "Hey, are you the one who fixed the step in the old house?"

"No, hadn't gotten around to thinking about it yet."

"Well, it's fixed but so far, I don't know who did it."

"Maybe Seth."

"No. Not Cheri or Burt either. Cheri thought maybe you did it."

"I doubt if Sara or Claire did. Guess that would leave one of the volunteers."

After their conversation, Elena went to her room. The repaired step intrigued her. She needed to talk to Hap.

* * *

Elena's call came just as Hap and Peg were packing their suitcases.

"Elliott broke his foot. He fell through a step in the old house."

"Please tell him I'm sorry to hear that."

"I know you're getting ready to leave, but I want you to stay. There are too many strange things happening around here."

"What do you mean? A broken foot is unfortunate, but not strange."

"No, it's more than that. Somebody repaired the step, but nobody did."

"Whoa, run that by me again."

"What I mean is the step is repaired, but no one here did it. I've checked. No one knows anything about it."

"So where are you going with this?"

"Don't laugh at me, but do you think the ghost ..."

"No," Hap said, "I can't imagine a ghost working with carpenter tools and wood. There are plenty of things I don't understand, but this one is a stretch."

"I believe it." Elena had hoped for validation of her theory, but maybe Hap was right. "Please don't leave yet. I don't think it's over yet."

"What's not over? The danger? I'm willing to stay longer, but I'm not seeing how I can help. Don't let emotion rule you. Step back, and look at the whole picture."

"Can I come meet you, and talk to you?"

"Sure, how about we meet at Burnap's Garden Cafe in an hour? That will give me time to talk to Jerry about extending our visit."

"Super. See you there."

* * *

Elliott improved physically everyday, but his disposition soured. He complained about his foot and leg itching inside the cast, the heat bothered him and the enforced idleness was driving him insane. No one wanted to tell him that he was driving everyone insane even faster. It only took a few days for Cheri to find some computer work for him. She needed some research done for a grant she was writing. That seemed to quiet Elliott's restlessness and soon no one tried to avoid him.

"I was a jerk for a few days, wasn't I?" he asked Claire.

"No more than any of us would be if we traded places with you."

"Thanks. I needed to hear that. I'm okay now, and I only have six more weeks before I get a boot instead of this thing," he tapped on the cast.

"At least then you can get rid of the crutches. Have you thought about getting a knee scooter?"

"No, I've never seen one."

"It's much better than crutches, but I don't know if it would work on a farm. It's great on floors so you could use it in the house. Check it out online."

Elliott turned on the computer and found a used all-terrain scooter online. He couldn't afford to buy one and from what he'd seen of his parents at the hospital, he didn't want to ask them.

That evening, he reported his findings to Claire and the group. Seth suggested they look into renting one.

Within the week, Elliott was learning to navigate gravel roads and grass with his newly rented scooter.

* * *

Jake wandered around the house. In a fit of rage a couple of weeks ago, he had destroyed Claire's art studio. Torn it to pieces, shredded her work and thrown away her paints. When she came back, he would show her the price she paid for her defiance. He took another drink. Getting drunk and passing out was the only respite from his anger. He had to go to the farm again.

She had gotten that worthless restraining order. The law had no right to stop him from taking what was his. He would make another attempt at the farm. The last one failed miserably.

He had gone to Coleman's a couple of nights ago and flirted with a pretty, preppy waitress. A couple of his buddies asked about Claire, and his thoughts darkened. As he drank his Guinness, he fantasized about a night with the waitress. By the time he finished his dinner and a couple more beers, he decided to ask her out. But when he looked at her, Claire's face got in the way. A crude remark and angry look replaced the tip she had worked for.

* * *

I feel happy. For the first time in my spirit life. No, for the first time since the Shakers turned off Mary Ann and kicked her off the farm. I had forgotten how if feels to do something good.

No, my anger isn't gone, nor is my depression. I know that, but for right here, right now, I feel happy. Poor Elena is the only one who seems baffled by the repaired step. I heard her ask one of the volunteers today. She is the one most in tune with the spirit world, so I shouldn't be surprised.

Mary Ann has not been back since the day we finally communicated. I doubt she has crossed over for the final time, but I will have to wait and see. Sometimes the change in me is frightening. There are days I almost wish I had my rage back. It was a comfortable cloak that I had worn for many decades. It's difficult to replace comfort with new things that can be scratchy, stiff and vulnerable.

I have seen the young girl several times but she is as ethereal as a fleeting dream. As far as I know, she has not shown her earthly form to Claire for weeks now.

As I become involved with the living world, I find my spirit world receding. I can't lose it until I have resolved all issues with Mary Ann. I know my redemption is intertwined with hers. I worry.

* * *

"Hey, wait up. You're moving way too fast for me," Seth jogged toward Elliott.

"This thing can fly." Elliott patted the handles of his scooter.

"If you're not careful, you'll find yourself flying right through the air."

"So, what's up, besides me endangering my life?"

"Well, just a suggestion. One evening, before your amnesia, we all went into Sodus Bay. We went to the beach, walked out on the pier to the lighthouse. Then you and Claire went to take pictures. Anyway, I've been thinking. That pier is a good fishing spot. I don't know about you, but I'm craving a good old fish dinner."

"So, are you going fishing?"

"The beach has some deep sand, the walk to the pier is solid. Would you like to go fishing with me? I've got several poles, so we'd be all set."

"Maybe. When do you want to go?"

"I don't know. Some evening soon when you get tired of looking at the farm all day."

"Maybe so. Right now, I'm happy just to be moving around here."

* * *

Luckily for Elliott, the warm, dry weather held. Within a few days, he felt like he'd been riding his scooter for years. The pain was little more than a memory, and he grew restless. He wanted to do something outside. Elena had invited him to feed the goats and sheep. With a bag full of treats, he rode his scooter to the fence. In a matter of seconds, several hungry goats were nuzzling against his hands. He petted them and laughed at their silly expressions. "I can tell by your eyes that you guys are mighty smart. Have you figured out that I have a bag full of treats?" They didn't need words. He reached for a handful of treats and looked up to see a comical grin on the alpaca that had suddenly appeared. He reached across the goats

185

and petted him, before he started handing out treats. All manners went by the wayside as the goats, alpaca and newly arrived sheep all nosed their way toward his hand.

He had found a new chore and loved it. Maybe Cheri would let him feed the horses too.

* * *

"It's time to take care of Elliott." Dominic straightened his tie and the cuffs of his pinstriped shirt. "We've given him more time than most."

"I'll take care of it. How and when?"

"That's your expertise. Just make it happen."

After Dominic cut off the call, he poured himself a finger of bourbon. Careful never to over pour, he considered himself a man in charge of all facets of life. He hated dealing with the Elliotts of this world. Not only did they cost him money, they also infringed upon his well-ordered life.

RESIDENT OF CRACKER BOX PALACE

CHAPTER THIRTY-FIVE

*The Shakers fished in the Bay, with seines
and fish was smoked and salted for sale
Barrels of salted fish were shipped east by the canal.*

From Shaker historical records, Sodus Public Library

"HEY, YOU MENTIONED FISHING AT the pier the other day."
Elliott found Seth straightening a fence post.

"Yeah, my favorite pastime."

"Do you have good luck there?"

"Usually. Have your remembered going fishing? If so, you know
it's up to the fish, not us."

"I think it sounds like fun. I'd like to go if you think I can navigate the pier."

"Sure you can. When would you like to go?"

"Maybe tomorrow. Everyday makes me a little more secure on
my new wheels."

"Sounds good. Let's do it."

* * *

"Elliott caught two walleye tonight, so who's cooking tomorrow?" Seth nudged Elliott to show his catch as they all gathered on
the boarding house porch.

"I'll do it if you'll help me. How should we cook them?"
Claire asked.

"We can fry them, bake them or grill them. These are big enough
for grilling, but it's your choice."

"Can you get them ready?" Claire was unsure of what she'd
agreed to.

"Sure. If you decide on grilled, I do that too. You can take care
of everything else. Does that work?"

"That's a relief. I don't have any experience with grilling. What should we have to go with it?"

"Baked potatoes and a salad," Sara said.

"How about some garlic bread?" Elena asked.

"Looks like we have our menu planned. If that's okay with you, Claire."

"Sounds good. I can handle my part."

"I'll help," Elena offered.

"Then I better go take care of these babies. Elliott, want to learn more about fishing?"

* * *

I smelled the fish cooking. Elliott and Seth had brought home a good catch and thrown me into memories of the packinghouse. Like most of the men, I enjoyed fishing the bay. Although it was our work assignment, we would engage in good-natured competition for the biggest or the most fish caught. However, the jocularity ended on the days when we salted the fish and prepared them for packing. It was hard work and the salt always irritated my eyes and my skin. Even though I wore gloves, the salty brine would seep through. And the smell! Summertime was the worst. Salted fish stink in the heat of the day.

Although I soon moved on to a new assignment, the irritation and the odor stayed with me for days.

Mary Ann would tell us about the wonderful smells she loved when she worked in packaging the herbs. I envied that the days I stank of salty brine and fish.

We had many other jobs, but few more unpleasant. Mucking out the stables wasn't high on the list of enjoyable occupations but I'd rather do that than the salting.

CHAPTER THIRTY-SIX

A mother's arms are made of tenderness and children sleep soundly in them.
Victor Hugo

"I LOVE LOOKING AT THE Main House," Cheri told Elliott. "Even with the fire damage, it still speaks of order and simplicity. I would have loved to see it back in the day."

"It's growing on me. I never thought about design before I came here. I like the clean lines. I grew up in an old Victorian home that I never liked."

"Elliott!"

"What?"

"You remembered something?"

"The house I grew up in." Amazement shone in his eyes. "I did, didn't I?"

"Do you remember anything else? Your mom or your dad?"

Elliott's eyes clouded. He strained to remember, but even his mental image of his home had disappeared. "No, I don't. What is happening to me?"

"I don't know, but I'll call Doctor Mallory and let her know. Do you have any other memories at all?"

"No. I think maybe I made that up about my house. I can't picture it at all."

Cheri called Dr. Mallory's office and left a message. Within the half hour, the doctor returned the call. After Cheri explained the brief appearance, and then disappearance of Elliott's memory, she waited for a response.

"This is not unusual," Dr. Mallory said. "Remember how little we know about the brain. In an injury such as Elliott's, it's possible for it to slowly recover."

"I remember you said it may happen all at once or slowly."

"Yes. Don't push him to remember. If a memory surfaces, take note of it and let his brain heal at its own pace. He has an appointment next week, so we'll see what happens between now and then."

"It's a good sign though, right?"

"Yes, it is. It tells us that healing is occurring. Please tell Elliott to let his memory return naturally. I don't want him to become anxious and try to force it."

"Thank you for returning my call. I'll let Elliott know about our conversation."

* * *

Mary Ann came back to the house. She had stayed on the other side, hoping that God would shine his light on her and invite her into eternity. She'd found only emptiness and darkness. The longer she dallied, the more despondent she became. She wanted to end it all, but almost laughed at the thought that only the living could make that choice.

Her attempts at praying were as rusty as the hinges on the old cellar. She had shrunk away from Him and had no idea how to recover. As a Shaker, she had loved prayer. Singing, most of all. After all, singing was an advanced form of prayer. She thought about the day that Horace had heard her singing her favorite hymn. "Tis a gift to be simple," she murmured. She tried to sing, but once again, rusty was the word that came to mind. She chanted the hymn's title. Surely it was a prayer of some sort.

The more she said the words, the more they penetrated into her thoughts. 'Tis a gift to be simple.' Maybe that was the key to her salvation. Had she cluttered her mind with self-pity for so long that there was no room for a simple prayer, or for the virtue of simplicity in her current situation? Is that what she must acquire to start her journey back to faith and redemption? Did simplicity include, or exclude, her need to find her baby?

She sat down in the rocker and looked out at the old locust tree that had stood the test of time. It had been small when she first arrived. But it had grown and survived. It had withstood the worst that nature could throw at it. She suspected she could learn a lot from that old tree.

Laughter filled the air. She rose from the chair and looked out at the group gathered there. They were happy, all gathered around a young man in a wheelchair. Not like the chairs she remembered. The Mt Lebanon community had sent a wheelchair to the Sodus community when one of the men, Brother Cyrus, developed such severe pain in his hip that he could no longer walk. It had been constructed of such fine wood that he didn't want to mar the wheels. The chair had rockers, too. Brother Cyrus could rock and then wheel himself around the house. She remembered that he learned to make the paper dolls that the girls played with. He didn't know much about the clothing pieces for them, but he liked to make the dolls. Then he started carving wood into toys for the children. They especially loved the animals he carved.

Children. The Shakers offered homes to orphans of every age. From babies to nearly adult, they brought them in, fed and educated them, and at the age of eighteen, gave them the opportunity to unite in the faith or go out into the world. Mary Ann wondered if her baby may have found a home in a Shaker village. It would be simple justice if that happened. Her baby at home in a place that kicked her out. She liked the thought of that. It was definitely preferable to living with the fear that her baby may have died.

She wandered around the house, hoping that Horace was nearby. If so, would he manifest himself so that they could continue a conversation. She would not leave this time. She felt not only prepared, but also filled with expectation.

* * *

Elliott opened the letter. It might be the first he ever received. He had no memory of others.

My dear son,

I would like to visit you at the farm this weekend. I hope you are recovering and enjoying a good summer. I called Dr. Mallory yesterday and she said you had experienced a small memory. I am praying that before too much longer, you will remember everything.

It is unbelievably painful as a mother to know that you remember nothing of the precious years of your youth. You were always my darling boy, and I miss you beyond words.

Maybe together we can elicit a few of those memories. I want you to come home where you belong.

I love you forever,

Mother

Syrupy. Sticky and sweet. The image of his mother at the hospital fit the letter and the words. Had his childhood been filled with this cloying sweetness? The letter elicited neither familiarity nor affection, although it spoke of emotional need.

He couldn't stop her from coming, but he had no desire to see her.

* * *

The wheels crunched on the gravel drive and dust rose behind the white Lexus. Elliott sat in his wheelchair at the foot of the boarding house steps. He watched as she straightened her hair and applied lipstick before opening the car door. She stood and looked around, her slim skirt and silk blouse out of place amid the gravel and dust. He waited until she saw him.

"Elliott, darling," she called. "I'm so happy to see you." She ran toward him, but slowed down when a rock almost caused her ankle to twist. He sensed a vulnerability in her that he hadn't seen at the hospital.

He wheeled his chair toward her. "You came on a perfect day. I've been sitting outside enjoying the feel of the sun on my face."

"You look wonderful. Have you remembered anything yet?"

"No, but I do remember things that happened since the attack."

"What do you mean?"

"I remember you at the hospital, and Uncle Gavin saying you were mollycoddling me. That means my brain still works, right?"

"Well, yes, I guess it does. You just don't remember anything from before?"

"Dr. Mallory says I have to give it time. I'm trying to avoid stress. Whenever I work to remember, I get a headache. She says it's due to anxiety. Come on over here," he motioned toward a bench and wheeled himself toward it.

"Are you able to do any work here?"

"Yes, Cheri's been good to me. She's given me some computer work. I also enjoy giving treats to the animals everyday. Would you like to do that with me?"

"Oh, no, I don't think so. Maybe we can just sit here and talk."

"Sure. At the hospital, you talked about some of the activities I enjoyed as a child. What about books? If I liked to read, what kind of books interested me? What did I watch on TV?"

"You always liked to read, but your interests changed as you grew up. You went through several different kids' series before you started reading biographies of your favorite baseball players. You started doing research on your computer for school projects and you loved that."

"Did I like history?"

"Stories about people, yes. Issues between countries, not so much. Except for the Civil War. When you were first learning about it, we watched an old Jimmy Stewart movie, "Shenandoah." It upset you that brothers would choose different sides. You watched that movie over and over, trying to figure out why."

"I don't remember that."

"No, but someday you will."

Elliott enjoyed his mother's company and that surprised him. In the hospital, he had hated her visits. She didn't push him to remember, but she shared his likes and dislikes, the restaurants he enjoyed, his fascination with the Erie Canal, and his love of water sports. He was sorry to see her leave.

* * *

There was something about Elliott's mother that held my attention. In spite of her beautiful clothes, perfect hair and expensive car, she seemed lost and alone. You could almost see her heart falter when Elliott still didn't remember her. I have to hand it to her, she tried. She shared memories for hours, but never once shed a tear. My guess is that as soon as she is away from the farm, she'll stop and have a motherly cry.

I had once watched my mother cry. She and my dad had argued over something that I no longer remember. What has stuck in my memory is the scene of her walking away from the house and breaking into tears. I followed her. I ran to her and put my arms around her hips because that was as far up as I could reach at the time. She tried to turn away but I wouldn't let go.

"Don't cry, mommy," I repeated again and again. "I love you."

"I love you, too," she smiled as she dabbed at the tears with the sleeve of her blouse. She finally quit crying, and burst into laughter. "You give my heart such joy," she said as she gave me a fierce hug.

I had never loved her more. To this day, I remember
the emotional low and high. A mother's love is a special
gift from God. I saw that again today in Elliott's mother.

* * *

Eileen watched Elliott and his mother for a while, but it made
her heart hurt so bad she had to leave. She hurt for Elliott because he
couldn't remember his mother and she hurt for herself because she
had no mother to remember. She even hurt for her pretend mother,
because she had given her a home and loved her. If only she could
tell her she was sorry!

* * *

Jake took another drink, slammed the bottle down on the table,
grabbed his keys and headed out the door. He'd waited too long,
and it was going to end today. Claire would be coming home with
him. He hated weekends alone, and it was her fault. He had cooked
for her, watched her favorite movies, bought her flowers — all the
things a guy can do for his woman. In return, he'd been humiliated
and deserted. And she'd actually filed a complaint against him. The
local cops weren't fools. He had some drinking buddies on the force
and they'd take care of him. No, he had the right to bring her home
and it was time.

It took less than an hour to reach the farm. If things worked out
the way he planned, he'd find her, apologize, declare his love, and
have her back in Syracuse in time for dinner out. He'd even let her
pick the restaurant.

When he drove in the farm, some idiot on a scooter ran right
in front of him. He braked in time, but the guy fell and hit the dirt.
Who did he think he was? Jake jumped out of the car, yelling one
obscenity after another.

Elliott lay on the ground, winded but not hurt. He hadn't
seen the guy at all. He must have been doing seventy when he hit
the driveway.

Jake rounded the front fender. Elliott saw his face and froze.
He'd never remember his first thought because a lifetime of memories flooded him. He knew that face. Jake. He had to warn Claire. He
tried to get up but realized he couldn't do it without putting weight
on his foot. He reached for his cell phone.

Jake knocked the phone out of Elliott's hand. "What do you
think you're doing?" He stomped off toward the horse barn. He noticed a girl and older man down by a bunch of goats. A little white

dog turned and growled at him. "Come any closer and try," Jake muttered. Even a stupid dog was against him.

Elliott scooted himself to the phone and stretched to reach it. He punched on Claire's name. It was quicker than a text. No answer. He punched in Cheri. She answered on the second ring.

"Jake's here!"

Running out the door, Cheri called to Jeff to call 9-1-1. She saw Jake headed toward the barn. She knew that Claire was in her room, so she was safe for the moment. By the time she reached the barn door, Jake was inside.

"Damn dark," he mumbled. He looked in each stall, all empty except for one horse that pawed the ground when he stopped at the stall.

"Jake!" Cheri called.

"Where's Claire?"

"She's not here."

"I know she is."

Cheri felt Jeff and Seth behind her. "You are not allowed on this property. Claire filed a restraining order."

"That doesn't mean anything. Besides, if she's not here as you say, then the order doesn't apply. I'm going to look around."

"No, you're not." Seth stepped forward.

Jake lunged for him, throwing a punch that hit Seth in the shoulder.

Elena, Hap and Luke entered the barn as Seth spoke, "You better go."

Jake ignored him and swung again. Seth tackled Jake and threw him to the floor. Cheri watched in horror as Jake swung at Seth again. Luke ran closer, barking and howling at Jake.

Seth sat on Jake's thighs and tried to restrain his arms as he threw punch after punch. Seth grabbed Jake's left arm, pinning it down. Suddenly, Jake's right arm twisted and slammed down on the ground. It felt like he had a weight on it and couldn't move. He screamed.

Luke stepped back and stopped barking, his attention focused on Jake's arm.

Seth and Cheri watched as Jake writhed. They stared at the arm that wouldn't move. Seth released his hold on Jake's left arm and still the right arm stayed glued to the floor. Jake squirmed and cursed. No one moved to help him.

"What's wrong? Why isn't he moving now?" Cheri had expected him to take another swing at Seth, but he stayed still, as if glued to the floor.

After what seemed like hours, but was little more than a couple of minutes, Jake rubbed his right arm and tried to sit up. He stared at his arm and shook his head, frightened by who knew what. He only wanted to escape.

Luke turned and walked out of the barn. "I think he's following someone," Elena whispered to Hap.

* * *

I pray God was watching as I protected another innocent person. I twisted his arm with all my might and sat my spirit self down on top of his injured arm. I don't know if I have any weight, but he couldn't move his arm and that was my goal. I wanted to do more, but at least I hurt him enough to keep him away for a while. If he ever comes back, I will think of something.

Then there's Luke. He knew I was there. The second he quit barking I knew he recognized me. I'm so happy he followed me out of the barn. I think he'll be my friend, the kind of friend the first Luke proved to be. For the first time, I find out that a ghost can smile.

* * *

Sheriff Briggs arrived and escorted Jake off the property, after charging him with assault and failure to heed a restraining order. Jake turned and glared at Seth as the sheriff read him his rights and helped him into back seat of his car.

"He won't be bothering anyone for awhile," Briggs told Cheri. "Adding assault to a restraining order violation should put him away for at least a year."

When Seth found Claire and told her about his encounter with Jake, she couldn't control her shaking. "I knew he'd be back. I'll never be safe from him."

"Yes, you will. He'll be going to jail."

"But he'll get out and then he'll be back."

CHAPTER THIRTY-SEVEN

Let not the sting of misspent days
Be treasur'd in your store,
For Lo, how quick you've run your race,
And time appears no more.

A Manual of Good Manners, 1844
(from Simple Wisdom by Kathleen Mahoney)

MICK HATED CARRYING OUT DOMINIC'S orders. Sure, he'd been a brawler all his life, and had spent the last five years as a bouncer for Dominic. But kicking someone out because he caused a disturbance is totally different than beating someone to within an inch of his life. From his orders, Mick knew that Dominic would be happy if he went that extra inch. All over a few thousand dollars.

This wasn't the first time he'd had such an assignment, but it's the first time since his son had been born. The first time since he held that precious baby in his arms and marveled at the miracle of life. It changed his perspective. Mick knew it was time to find another job, but for now he needed to money to pay this month's bills. He'd look for other opportunities as soon as he finished with this.

He knew Elliott from the casino. A total idiot, but he'd done nothing to earn what Dominic expected him to mete out. He looked up the farm on the Internet, and drove over there the next morning. The place looked fairly deserted so he drove in the driveway. He spotted a guy on a tractor, a woman working with a horse, and a couple of people feeding some goats. Otherwise the place looked deserted, a bunch of mostly run-down buildings and a big house that showed signs of extensive fire damage. He left with no one noticing him.

He did the same the next day, at a different time. A sheriff's car stood in the driveway. Mick drove on by, but in the rearview mirror, he saw the sheriff walk out with his hand on some guy's arm. Mick kept driving.

The next day, he drove by again and spotted a young man on a knee scooter. He drove on, turned around and came back, parking his car along the road. He got out of the car, quietly closed the door, and walked toward a pasture with a couple of donkeys. He watched them for a few minutes, keeping an eye on the scooter.

"Elliott," Elena called.

"Hey, what's happening?" He wheeled toward her.

Mick had seen all he needed to see. Elliott had some kind of foot or leg injury. He certainly wouldn't be able to fight back. Mick's challenge would be to find him alone. He walked back to the car, sat there most of the afternoon, watching. Elliott wheeled back to a wheelchair and spent a couple of hours outside. Several different people stopped to talk to him, then went about their business. Mick waited until Elliott wheeled himself up the ramp in one of the buildings. That was most likely where he stayed.

Mick drove into Sodus for dinner, made some phone calls, and headed back to the farm shortly before sunset. He would plan the attack at night and he needed to move quickly. Dominic was already impatient. Through the evening, people wandered around the farm, in and out of the barns. Some fed the animals in the pasture. He didn't see Elliott again. By eleven, all was quiet. He made the decision for tomorrow night.

* * *

Elliott's newly recovered memory brought far more stress than the amnesia.

Who had attacked him? If only he had seen the guy, but he had come from behind. He had grunted an obscenity, but Elliott couldn't identify his voice. Had it been one of Dominic's thugs? Or as Hap suggested, Jake? If it was Jake, he was safe now, but if it was Dominic, he would come again.

He avoided Claire and Seth, wishing he could undo the damage he had done. He wore his shame hidden beneath the cloak of good humor, but it scratched at him like coarse wool. How could he ever apologize to Claire for his behavior? She had shown him kindness and concern. In the past, he had shown a crude disrespect for her as an individual and as a woman. Someday he would have to talk with her, but he couldn't face her yet. Seth had offered friendship, even after he'd brushed him aside with indifference. They were his friends. Although he had no recollection of ever mistreating Elena, he had never extended any courtesy or offer of friendship to her.

He received a call from his mother who wanted to visit again.

"Elliot, honey, I'm so happy you've recovered your memory. Dr. Mallory filled me in on the frightful way it happened but if that's what it took, so be it. Do you think that crazy man is the person who beat you up? I heard you had an encounter with him shortly before."

"I'm fine. I have no idea if Jake was the one, but he easily could have been. He's a hothead and he'll do whatever it takes to get Claire back. I'm happy he's in jail. Please come. I need to talk to you."

After the conversation ended, Elliott made the decision to come clean with his mother. She had always taken his side and protected him, but she didn't realize that he caused most of his problems. He would confess it all.

* * *

Virginia Werner vacillated between worry and pride after her visit with Elliott. He had changed and she'd gotten a glimpse of the man he was capable of becoming. For the first time in her memory, he expressed more concern about others than about himself. In fact, other than telling her about his gambling and his current debt, he hadn't focused on his problems. How would she convince Charles that Elliott had changed and that they should pay his debt? The sooner Dominic was out of their lives, the better. Elliott had shown no interest in his former lifestyle or the people he drank and partied with. He talked about people and animals. He told her all about Cracker Box Palace's success with abused animals. He hoped to stay there and finish his education through online classes.

He was the person she always thought he could be.

Elliott felt close to his mother. He had shed the heavy burden of lies and guilt. For the first time since childhood, he saw her as the person who would always love him unconditionally.

By the time she arrived home, Virginia had made a decision. She would visit Dominic tomorrow, pay Elliott's debt and then have the dreaded conversation with Charles. But plans often go awry, and it took two days before she obtained the money and went to the casino. She wanted to slap the smirk off Dominic's face when she told him that Elliott wouldn't be back.

"The leopard can't change his spots," Dominic said.

"Elliott is no leopard and people do change." Virginia couldn't wait to leave the casino.

Dominic was sure that Elliott wouldn't change, but his mother had paid his debt. He was, after all, a man of honor, so he would call Mick and tell him to stand down.

* * *

I polished the staircase banister again this morning. Deep in thought, I heard voices coming from the back porch and my curiosity prodded me to listen. It turned out to be a private conversation but I admit to having no shame.

"I need to talk to you." I recognized Elliott's voice. I looked out the door and saw Claire sitting on the porch. She looked up from her phone as he sat down beside her. I didn't have time to reflect on the many changes since my day before she responded with a simple greeting. Anxiety played across Elliott's face and I sensed that this would be a difficult conversation for him.

"Since my memory returned, I've had to face many unpleasant things about myself."

Claire said nothing, and my thoughts returned to the day he tried to force himself on her. I looked at her guarded expression as she picked a blade of grass from her jeans and flicked it away.

"I know I was a total jerk and ... what I want to say ... oh, hell ... I don't know ..."

Claire did nothing to make it easier for him. I liked that. Make him pay.

"What I mean ... I'm sorry ... I'm so sorry!"

Claire looked up and searched his face. I wondered if his obvious sincerity touched her, as she remained silent.

"Please say something ... anything," he pleaded.

Still, she remained silent. Her face had turned to stone and I wondered at the emotions that she must be feeling. Although her expression gave nothing away, I sensed the disquiet in her heart. I don't think Elliott did though, because he was too deep in his own misery. "I hope you can forgive me."

After a few minutes that dragged like hours, he stood up.

Claire reached out, "Please don't leave."

He looked into her eyes and slowly sat back down. This time he seemed to accept the silence.

"I just left a boyfriend who abused me ... and tried to force me to his will ... too many times to count ... I can't live like that ..."

Elliott remained silent as he gazed off into a distance he probably didn't see.

"You frightened me beyond words ... but I was determined to never be a victim again ..."

"I'm sorry. I don't know why I did what I did. I had never really forced myself on a girl before. I always found girls who were willing ... I was mad because my dad and uncle had sent me here and I took it out on you. I needed a victim, because I was feeling like one."

Claire nodded slightly and silence returned.

If only Eaton'd had the courage and character to have this same conversation with Mary Ann, how different might our lives and afterlives have been. I became lost in my own thoughts and resentment reared its ugly head. I was so wrapped up in it that I only heard part of Claire's words.

"...I can forgive you, but please don't ask me to forget."

"I understand. Can we at least be friends?"

"I think so, if you can learn to accept my right to be wary of you ... to avoid being alone with you ... to want my privacy."

Elliott nodded. "Thank you. I never want to be that person again. You have every right to not trust me, but I am going to try to earn it from now on."

I left then. My mind couldn't get around Eaton's arrogance and righteousness that had caused such a different ending for him and Mary Ann.

* * *

Mick drove to Alasa Farms with the radio off. He could never listen to his favorite oldies station when he was on one of Dominic's jobs. Beautiful music with hopeful lyrics didn't fit with the violence he needed to inflict. He didn't get angry or think of revenge. It might have been easier if he did. He thought of the paycheck and the bills it would pay.

It was almost midnight when he parked the car down the road from the farm. He picked up his phone to check for messages. The damn thing was dead. He'd forgotten to charge it. He plugged it in so it would charge on the drive home.

The place was quiet and deserted. A dog barked and Mick stopped. He waited until the barking ceased and walked slowly toward the building Elliott had entered the other afternoon. As a bouncer, he had learned that quiet and patience usually paid off. He employed both this evening.

He opened the door to a dark hallway. Although there were several doors, only one had a light shining through. He would save that room for last. He opened the first door and thanked the gods of chance that he found Elliott with so little effort. His breathing revealed his light sleep. Mick paused and waited. He felt the gun in his pocket. He fingered the silencer. A fatal shooting would please Dominic. Mick needed money, but he couldn't pull the gun from his pocket. His son's face flashed in front of him. No, he would not make him grow up knowing his father was a murderer. He would beat the guy and collect his money. Then he was finished.

* * *

I often roam the farm during the night. I don't know why, except for the restlessness that drives me. I usually check the animals and the barns because they were our livelihood when I was alive. Tonight I had wandered through all the barns and was on my way back to the old house when I sensed a disturbance. I waited and watched. At first I could see nothing, but then I heard a slight creak as the boarding house door opened. No one came out of the door, so I could only assume someone entered. I hadn't seen anyone outside.

I followed. A man stood in the doorway to Elliott's room. I sensed indecision warring within him. But most of all, I sensed danger. Whatever this man's intentions, Elliott was clearly the target and the man meant him harm. I reacted quickly. I went to Elliott's side and blew in his face. His nose twitched and I blew again. Same result. I blew in his ear. He reached his hand up and rubbed it. I blew again, searching for another idea that would silently wake him.

The man walked forward. I passed through him, making my way to the next room where Seth slept soundly. I patted his cheek. I needed him to awaken quickly without making his presence known to the intruder. Seth turned his head. I patted his other cheek harder. He shot up and started to speak. I covered his mouth and waited. I don't know if he sensed me, or if God intervened. I released his mouth. He moved quietly. He crept to the door and looked out in the hallway. His bare feet made no sound as he walked toward Elliott's open doorway.

We heard it at the same time. The sound of flesh and bone hitting flesh, and Elliott's resulting cry. By the time we reached the room, we found the man pounding on Elliott as he tried to get out of the bed and fight back. Seth grabbed the man and yelled for Jeff. I flew across the road and banged on the window to wake Claire and Elena. I picked up rocks and threw them against the old bell that hung on the porch.

Then I sped back across the road to help Seth. He didn't need me. He had the man on the floor. Elliott was calling 9-1-1. I had done my work, so I backed away.

* * *

Elena called Hap and he said he would be there as soon as possible. Thank goodness, he didn't have to fight off sleep. He'd become engrossed in a good novel that was destined to keep him awake through much of the night.

When he arrived, he almost laughed at the scene. Five angry people stood guard over one suspect, daring him to make a false move. Oh, the wheels of justice. Deputy Susan Mondel pulled in right behind him.

"His name is Mick," Elena said.

Deputy Mondel started with questions.

"I'm not sure what happened. I was sleeping soundly and something woke me up. Kinda strange, like someone slapping me and keeping me from speaking. Anyway, when I came to Elliott's room, this guy was punching him in the face." Seth couldn't shake the uncanny feeling that someone unseen woke him. He believed in God, but had never attributed strange happenings to Him.

"You seem unsure," Mondel said.

"No, just perplexed."

"Elliott, what do you remember?"

"Nothing really. I was sleeping but something was tickling my face and my ear. I was barely awake before this guy starts hitting me. I guess I was slow to react, but I tried to fight him off. Then Seth came in and grabbed him. The guy tried to fight off Seth's hold, but couldn't. Then Jeff, Claire and Elena came, and the guy quieted down."

"Anyone have anything to add?" Deputy Mondel took time to study each face.

"Claire and I were across the road. I heard someone banging on the window," Elena said.

"Then it sounded like the bell was trying to ring. More of a pinging noise," Claire added.

"Did any of you bang on their window?" Mondel asked the others.

"I didn't and Seth was already in here holding this guy when I arrived," Jeff answered.

Mondel looked at Mick, read him his rights, handcuffed him and led him out to the car. She turned back to the group, "I'll be in touch. I may have more questions."

* * *

"He's co-operative," Sheriff Joe Briggs answered Hap's question when he called. "He will spill his guts if we reduce his charge. I'm waiting for verification from the district attorney."

"Has he mentioned Dominic?"

"No, but I have. His expression changes when I do, but he isn't talking. He's not a seasoned criminal and I believe he'll talk as soon as a deal is confirmed."

"I stayed with Elliott for a while after Susan left last night. He was talkative. He says he's seen Mick at the casino, but never had any run-ins with him. He confessed his prior gambling that ended in one mess after another. His dad refused to bail him out this last time. Elliott swears that Dominic sent Mick to mete out his punishment."

"I'll get back with you as soon as we hear Mick's story."

An hour later, Joe called back. After the DA accepted Mick's deal, the dam broke. Mick confessed to 'taking care of matters' for Dominic several times. Usually the first visit was a warning, the second more serious."

"Seems like Dominic relishes flexing his muscles, or ordering his minions to do it for him," Briggs said. "Was this Elliott's first or second warning?"

"Mick's not sure. It's the first he's been involved in, but Dominic uses several men to do his dirty work."

"What were his orders this time?"

"To take care of Elliott and teach him a lesson he wouldn't forget. Although Dominic didn't give orders to kill Elliott, he believes that he would like it if he did."

"Sounds like you have enough to go after Dominic."

"Yes, I've contacted the Syracuse police department. I plan to drive over there when they bring him in."

* * *

"I told Mick to rough him up a little, that's it. Frighten him."

"Rough him up or kill him?" Syracuse's Detective Flanagan leaned forward.

Joe Briggs, watching from the next room, took an immediate dislike to Dominic. He was the epitome of the mob-type personality that Hollywood loves. Self-absorbed and narcissistic enough to be a comic strip character.

"You have no grounds to hold me. I admit that I sent Mick out, but I rescinded the order. Check his cell phone. I left a message."

"What was the message?"

"Elliott's mother came by and paid his debt. Mick had already left. I tried to call him and left a message on voicemail. I canceled the order." Dominic straightened the cuff of his shirtsleeve.

"You gave the order. That's intent to do bodily harm, if not worse."

"You'll never make that stick and you know it. Mick's nothing but an ignorant bouncer. He's long on the brawn and short on the brains."

"Sounds like you need better hiring skills."

"He does his job, but sometimes he screws up. This time he did. Check his phone."

"We'll do that. In the meantime, you'll be a guest of the city of Syracuse."

"You can't ..."

"Yes, I can and I will."

"I have a right to speak to my attorney."

"Yes, you do." Flanagan escorted Dominic out of the room and into a cell.

Although they say the wheels of justice turn exceedingly slow, they do turn. Dominic would soon learn this the hard way. Once Mick had confessed his part in Dominic's crimes, two others came forward. In the end he would only serve minimum time in prison, but that would prove to be a costly time to his reputation and his casino.

CHAPTER THIRTY-EIGHT

Bear with each other and forgive one another if any of you have a grievance against someone. Forgive as the Lord forgave you.

Colossians 3:13

I know of justice, of sinners in need of punishment. I've shouldered that knowledge for nearly two centuries now. It is good to see it carried out so swiftly. The man is in custody and I am confident that he will meet the fate he deserves. At the same time, I find humor in everyone's explanation of waking up and helping. I feel good.

I think of all the decades I allowed only anger and the desire for revenge into my thoughts, and yes, my actions too. I regret my revengeful deeds. The land would have flourished even more if I hadn't interfered. I can tell you my actions hurt nothing, but I know that all actions have consequences.

Although I have no idea what became of Eaton, I still find myself hoping that justice was somehow served.

As for me, I did a few good deeds along the way, but mostly I hurt the land and the people who worked it.

Mary Ann watched Horace's expressions change. Funny how a spirit face can be even more expressive than a living one, she thought. Each expression tugged at her heart, though in different ways. The last time she had seen any contentment in him had been long before her Shaker shaming. The despondency, she had seen far too often.

I feel someone watching me and open my eyes to see

Mary Ann standing across the room. I don't turn my head away as I see understanding in her eyes. It's the first sign of acceptance I have felt since the Shakers termed me 'deranged.' I fight back tears, or at least what feels like tears. When I touch my face, I find only dryness, the shriveling of age and decay. I tentatively move toward her and she doesn't back away.

We speak. We converse. I want to tell her everything that is in my heart, but for now I am content. I listen and I understand her pain. We are two wounded souls, damaged by the same careless hand. Although we come as friends, I suspect we may never speak of the one who tore our lives apart.

* * *

Eileen watched as the two spirits talked. It was the first time she had seen them together. She couldn't hear their conversation but she thought it was friendly. It made her happy. She had never talked to another spirit, because she was never quite sure that's what she was. It had taken her years to understand she was no longer like the living, but she had never seen another spirit who walked around as a living person. She suspected she lived somewhere between the two worlds. If she could only find her mother, she could ask her.

EPILOGUE

Time is a great teacher.
Carl Sandburg

"I HATE TELLING YOU GOODBYE," Elena hugged Hap. "You too, Luke." She loved the feel of the soft white fur as she planted a kiss on the top of his head. He shook his head and squirmed away.

"He'll never get over that. He hates anyone messing with his head," Hap laughed.

"I know, but his fur feels like a comfortable old blanket, all warm and cozy."

Hap noticed the man coming out of the horse barn.

"See that man with Sara?" Elena asked.

"Yes."

"His name is Sam Johnson. He told me he was there the day Cheri rescued Diamond. He lives on a farm near where she lived."

"I take it he's keeping tabs on her progress."

Elena nodded as she motioned for Sara and him to join them.

"Sam, I want you to meet my friend, Hap Lynch."

"Nice to meet you," Sam shook Hap's extended hand.

"Elena says you knew Diamond back before her injuries."

"I've known her since she was a foal. She's always had a sweet disposition. Broke my heart to see her abused like that."

"I can imagine. I've enjoyed watching her the few times I've been here. I'll miss this place."

"They do good work. Diamond wouldn't be alive without their help."

"Sam's visited her regularly," Sara said. "It won't be too long before he can give her the treats he brings."

"Yep," Sam nodded. "She just has to accept being around a man again. I wish I'd given her more attention when she was younger.

Didn't care much for her owner, so I had to watch her from my pastures. Care even less for him now." Sam pulled out his pipe. He tamped down the tobacco in it, giving himself time to do the same with his anger. He didn't begrudge a penny he'd sent for Diamond's treatment. His only regret was that he hadn't paid attention to his neighbor's actions before it was too late.

Sam tried to shake his negative thoughts. "Guess I'll be going. Nice to meet you." He headed to the pasture for a last look at Diamond before heading home.

Claire walked out of the barn and waved.

"Come on over. Hap is leaving," Elena called.

"Not without saying goodbye, I hope."

"No, I came to tell everyone goodbye."

"I have so much to thank you for," Claire began.

"No, I did a little nosing around, but Sheriff Briggs could have handled it on his own."

"Could have, but would have? I'm not so sure."

"Well, in any case, I'm glad you're safe. Jake is behind bars, hopefully for several years."

"I dread the day he gets out. I already spend too much time thinking about it. But at least, for the time being, I can stay here and work. I love the farm and the care we give the animals."

"Time changes many things, Claire. Don't dwell on it. Live your life here and if someday, you have to face a decision about moving, you'll have help."

"Thank you for everything." Claire hugged Hap and looked around for Luke. "Where is Luke?"

"Who knows? He has something on his mind or he smelled something new." Hap called for him.

"Bet he's in the house again," Elena said.

They walked toward the house. Seth came around the corner and walked with them.

"You're gonna miss out on some good fishing trips, you know."

"Yeah, but you never know. I'll be back someday and I bet they'll still be biting."

"We'll check it out, for sure. Thanks for all your help. We'll all miss you."

"Thanks. I'll miss this place, too. One can feel the history and the promise here. I enjoy learning about the past, but I'm most impressed by the promise of the future. You all are doing good work here."

They reached the house and called Luke again. No answer.

"I'll go in," Elena stepped onto the porch. A few minutes later, she emerged with Luke in her arms. "You're not going to believe this, but he was sitting near the old chair, which was rocking back and forth. He was intent, but not at all apprehensive. In fact, I saw his tail wag a couple of times. What do you suppose he saw?"

"That girl has an imagination, doesn't she?" Seth reached out to pet Luke. "Think he saw one of our ghosts, Elena?"

"Yes, I think his senses are more highly developed than ours, so it's possible."

They turned as Elliott braked his scooter behind them.

"You're going to miss that thing when you get your cast off." Hap said.

"I doubt that."

"Better keep it around. You've proven to be quite a klutz," Seth poked him in the shoulder.

"Get used to it. I'm sticking around here if Cheri will have me. Hap, thanks for everything."

* * *

'Tis the gift to be simple
'Tis the gift to be free ...

Shaker hymn

The dim light in the old house enveloped me as I sat in the rocker. I pondered how far I'd progressed in the past few months. Time has no meaning except as a reminder that the world moves forward without me. I still live in darkness, but I am not as alone. I find myself more interested in the lives of the current residents of the farm than of the one I've hated for so long.

I contemplate the many ways the Shakers influenced my life, before I rejected their teachings of peace and forgiveness. It has taken nearly two hundred years, but Mary Ann and I have finally reached out to one another, accepting and anticipating. Then there's the young girl, Eileen. Something tugs at me whenever I see her. I believe she is here for a purpose. I will watch her more closely.

The little dog, Luke, walks into the house, sniffs the air and sits by my side. I notice that his fur does not stand on end this time. His intelligent eyes search my face with a hope I cannot understand. Then a beam of sunlight filters through the dirty windows and bathes his white head. His fur glows and I reach out to touch him. He wags his tail and I smile.

BUNKHOUSE

CRACKER BOX PALACE BARN

Author's Notes

THIS BOOK IS A WORK of historical fiction. The United Society of Believers in Christ's Second Appearing (known as Shakers) did purchase and live at the property now known as Alasa Farms from 1826 to 1838. The Shakers believed that to live a perfect Christian life, one had to confess their sins, accept celibacy and live a simple and utilitarian life. They formed a communal society and celebrated their beliefs through dancing, which was a key element of their spirituality. Far ahead of their time, they believed in racial and sexual equality, love of their neighbors, peace and conservation of our natural resources.

About thirty members moved to the farm from New Lebanon, NY, to begin a new community and evangelize their faith. A true communal society, Shakers gave up private ownership of all goods. Even the clothing they wore belonged to the community. Men and women lived separately and practiced celibacy as a way to please God. The church grew by recruiting converts and taking in orphans.

Simplicity, a major tenet in their faith, became the trademark of their building and furniture designs. A hardworking, industrious people, they turned the rich farm land they purchased into a profitable operation before they sold the land to a man who planned to build a canal through the property. The sale took place in 1836 but it took two years to complete the move to their new home in Groveland, NY.

At its height, the Sodus Bay community numbered one-hundred-and-fifty members. They built the farm to thirteen houses and ten barns. Three of the original buildings are still standing today. Some of the Shaker characters in my story, like Eldress Polly Lawrence, are real.

The farm passed through several hands before Alvah G. Strong purchased it in 1924, renaming it Alasa Farms. It remained in his family until his grandson, Griff Mangan, arranged its sale to Cracker Box Palace in 2013.

Legend has it that Mary Ann and Horace have lived in the house since the days of the Shaker community. Mary Ann was kicked out of the society when she became pregnant. Supposedly she was a real person in the community, although I have found no record of her name. I did find a reference to a woman who became pregnant and left the community, taking extra clothing with her. According to Griff Mangan, Mary Ann's baby died.

There was a Horace Holloway who 'got deranged and left' in 1834. He returned in 1836. I found no further reference to him.

During the War of 1812, the British burned every house in Sodus Point except for the Mansion house, which later became a tavern.

The Sodus Bay lighthouse was built in 1825. In the early 1830s, farmers, including Shakers, hauled in rocks to build a pier in the bay.

At the time, the Red Brick Church in Sodus Center was the only church building in the township. The Episcopalians did own property and held services where Christ Church in Sodus Point now stands.

The following people are real and allowed me to write them in the story. I did promise not to kill them. Cheri Roloson and her husband Burt own Cracker Box Palace Farm Animal Rescue. Sara Buys is the current horse barn manager. Jeff Stevens is the farm operations manager. Griff Mangan, Alvah Strong's grandson, sold the farm to Cheri and currently lives with his wife, Joni Montover, and fur babies in South Padre Island, Texas. They own Paragraphs on Padre Blvd, the only bookstore in the area.

Jerry and Claudine Karczewski own and operate the beautiful Carriage House Inn B&B in Sodus Point, New York.

All other characters live in my head, which can be crowded and disorganized, but filled with activity and a sense of adventure.

Acknowledgments

FOR ME, WRITING THE ACKNOWLEDGMENTS is frequently the hardest part of finishing a book. I break out in fear at the thought I may forget someone, remembering only after I hold a physical book in my hand and a missing name pops into my memory.

Spirits of the Sodus Bay Shakers is indeed a product of many tales and many voices. It probably began in Griff Mangan's mind soon after he sold Alasa Farms to Cracker Box Palace Farm Animal Haven. Guessing at his thoughts, I imagine him ruminating on ways to help a much-needed non-profit rescue organization while preserving the history of the land. Now a home to animals in need, it is a land blessed with fertile soil, clean air and proximity to the living waters of Sodus Bay and Lake Ontario.

When Griff suggested I write a book that highlights upper New York state, the Sodus Bay communities and Alasa Farms, I envisioned stories encompassing aspects of American history that are common throughout the country, yet singular to the role played out on 1600-plus acres of rich farm land that is now home to farm animals in need. I soon discovered that one book couldn't do justice to the centuries of history. That knowledge gave birth to The Alasa Farms Chronicles.

Cheryl Roloson, her husband Burt, and the staff at Cracker Box Palace welcomed me, walked me through their mission and the farm, and gave me the freedom to explore. What I had envisioned as a mystery set on the farm evolved into a series exploring the history of various residents of the land, told through the eyes of a spirit soul who has inhabited the farm for nearly two hundred years. His life on the farm is both real and legend; my interpretation of his story is pure fiction.

My husband and I spent a fantastic week at the Carriage House Bed & Breakfast in Sodus Point, NY, enjoying the hospitality of owners Jerry and Claudine Karczewski. Warm smiles, friendly conversations and delicious breakfasts ratcheted the week to "dream vacation" level.

The Sodus Public Library staff, as well as area residents and businesses, willingly shared their stories. I discovered that people who live in upstate New York love their home state, its history and its natural beauty. Sharon Maher shared the history of the Sodus Point Lighthouse. The museum is a fascinating look at the early years of our country.

Mike and Colleen Hedges opened their hearts and their home as they introduced us to their beloved Syracuse. Likewise, my niece and her family (Sarah McGrath, Tim Bauman, Hannah, Daniel and Maggie) showcased the enchantment they find in Rochester.

Thanks to David Hutton for the detailed information you gave me about EMT procedures and the care of horses. Also, thanks to Jennifer Hutton, David's daughter, for patiently explaining the care and grooming procedures.

Thank you to the Wayne County Tourism Bureau for paving the way to learn about their fascinating corner of the world. My husband and I toured the Hotchkiss Peppermint Museum in Lyons. I admit we left with several peppermint goodies. From Rochester to Syracuse we explored the Erie Canal at every opportunity. It's fascinating to visit a waterway that changed New York's history and America's westward movement and now, nearly two hundred years later, enchants locals and visitors with its stories, engineering marvels and recreational opportunities.

Everyone we met on our New York visit willingly and proudly shared their history and love of their home state. If I missed your name, please accept my apology. I appreciated everyone we met.

I always appreciate the time and talents of Joyce Faulkner in the layout of the book and the design of the book cover.

For all of you, who read the manuscript and/or encouraged me along the way, thank you from the bottom of my heart. A special thank you to Joe Campolo, Carolyn Schriber, Janie DeVos, Bob Doerr, Evelyn Staatz and Griff Mangan, who took the time to send comments and some last minute edits.

www.ingramcontent.com/pod-product-compliance
Lightning Source LLC
Chambersburg PA
CBHW060639260626
47161CB00008B/2920